Also by Tom Piccirilli

The Cold Spot

The Midnight Road
The Dead Letters
Headstone City
November Mourns
A Choir of Ill Children

THE
COLDEST
MILE

Tom Piccirilli

BANTAM BOOKS

THE COLDEST MILE
A Bantam Book / March 2009

Published by Bantam Dell
A Division of Random House, Inc.
New York, New York

Bantam Books and the rooster colophon are registered trademarks
of Random House, Inc.

ISBN 978-0-553-59085-2

Printed in the United States of America
Published simultaneously in Canada

www.bantamdell.com

OPM   10 9 8 7 6 5 4 3 2 1

For Michelle

mad reasons
and reasons not at all

ACKNOWLEDGMENTS

Special thanks need to go out to:

Ken Bruen, Peter Abrahams, Ed Gorman, Norman Partridge, Duane Swierczynski, Allan Guthrie, Ray Banks, Victor Gischler, Jason Starr & Megan Abbott.

And a big shout-out of appreciation to my editor, Caitlin Alexander, who really did shoot a man in Reno just to see him die. His name was Cecil. Buy her a drink sometime, she'll tell you (but not tequila, man, she reacts *badly*).

I dream across the altar of my past,
have many enemies.

—DEREK RAYMOND, *How the Dead Live*

PART
I

Chase's first day on the job they took the sobbing chauffeur out back, gutted him, then handed Chase the cap and the little white gloves.

They threw the guy in the open trunk of a Chrysler 300 Super Stretch, where he clutched at his belly and bled out between his fingers. There was a full bar in back of the limo and the others sneaked some booze and talked about horse track results.

In his gradually lessening terror the chauffeur quietly spoke in a trembling but resonant voice of grace. Prayers, passages from the Bible, names of his family. Bobby. Emily. Maria. Maria. His eyes met Chase's only once. A charge danced through the air. The dying man's mouth eased open into a strangely empty grin. Maria. Chase's fists were stones at his sides. The trunk was lined with plastic bags duct taped into place, and when the chauffeur vented, the others smelled it, finished their drinks, then slammed the trunk hood.

Chase thought it must be a test, snuffing the guy

right in front of him like that, twenty minutes after walking in the door. But nobody seemed to give a shit what he thought.

He was told that the chauffeur had been pinched a couple months ago for running whores out the back of the limo during his off-hours. He'd drive around the west side of Manhattan with a couple drunk businessmen and three or four girls lying across the leather seats, giving head. He ran a light on 91st in front of a black-and-white, and that was the end of that setup. The chauffeur had met with the DA on the sly to talk about the Langan family and cut a deal.

Assuming this was an object lesson meant for him, Chase did his best to appear both impressed and intimidated. Someone handed him the keys.

He tossed them back. He explained how this wasn't his area of expertise. He'd been hired to be a driver, not a hitter, and not a shovel man. They told him he'd do what he was goddamn told. They said there was room in the trunk for another body. One of them started to get especially loud and tried to take a poke at Chase. Moe Irvine showed up and told the others to take off, go find a landfill in Newark or some fucking place.

That afternoon Moe brought in a stoop-shouldered Jewish tailor from North Bergen, who got Chase up on a tiny stool, made him put on an oversized suit, then stuck pins in and drew chalk marks all over the black cloth. The tailor noticed the bandages beneath Chase's T-shirt but said nothing about them.

"Single-breasted or double?" the tailor asked.

Moe Irvine answered. "Single."

"High rise or low?"

"Low."

"Full sleeve or narrow?"

"Narrow, of course."

"Four days."

"You have two."

"Three days."

"You heard what I told you, Isaac."

The tailor said nothing more and slipped from the room, giving Chase a slight eye roll as he passed.

Moe, who would've been called a *consigliere* if the family had been Italian instead of blue bloods going back to the Minutemen, told him the suit would look nice, now he needed some ties.

It took Moe a couple minutes to find a few he was satisfied with. He held them up to Chase's collar, let them drape this way and that, then pinched them down in place like there was a tie tack. Finally, Moe nodded to himself and pulled four aside, then plucked a diamond stickpin from his pocket.

"You understand your duties here?" Moe asked.

Chase looked at him for a moment until he realized Moe was serious and actually wanted a response. "I drop people off and I pick them up again?"

"Their well-being is your responsibility. You protect them."

"I'm not a bodyguard."

"You are now."

"That's not what I do. You've got plenty of hired muscle in the crew for that. I'm a driver."

"While you drive, you are the bodyguard. That's the job. If you're not up for it, tell me now."

Having just watched a guy get aced, Chase figured the time to say no had already wafted past.

"All right," Chase said.

"Good. You have a piece?"

"No."

"You don't carry a gun?"

"I told you, I'm a driver," Chase said, sounding stupid even to himself. It was impossible to make some people understand that the best wheelmen never carried hardware.

Reaching into his briefcase, Moe appraised Chase once more, searching deeper this time, his face heavy with thought. Chase did the same thing, studying Moe and seeing a man who was used to running a dangerous but lucrative machine that was suddenly breaking down all around him through no fault of his own.

A carefully hidden, slow-burning anger leaked out at the seams around Moe's mouth and eyes. He was around sixty, well kept and solid, with silver-white hair receding from a prominent widow's peak. He had the kind of maple-syrup tan that you had to spend months working on, slathered in baby oil in the backyard holding a metal reflector up around your neck. A broad spatter of caramel-colored freckles flecked his nose and cheeks. They looked this close to going cancerous. His three-piece suit was formfitting with just a little heft in the shoulders to square him off.

Moe pulled a Browning 9mm and a shoulder holster from his briefcase and handed them to Chase.

There was something almost precocious in how unsubtle these people were. Chase stared at him for an extra second and accepted the Browning. Chase hated guns but now wasn't the time to argue.

They let him bunk in the servants' quarters, a late-nineteenth-century, three-story brick building about a hundred yards away from the main house. It had been converted into a kind of modified duplex. He was told that fourteen people lived there. Most of the muscle, the hitters, the butler, and the landscapers stayed on one side, and the three Polish maids, the lady gardener, and the cook resided on the other. It was like a college dorm. The estate covered sixty acres, about a mile from the Hudson. Chase thought he could smell the water but it was probably his imagination.

He carried his gym bag to a small bedroom and checked the upstairs windows of the main house across the way. The big boss, Lenny Langan, was dying up there, wasting away from prostate cancer. An '07 black Buick Lucerne with medical plates was parked at the side entrance, on a slight angle, like the doc had come screaming up the driveway in a panic to help save Lenny. The guy going through the motions despite the foregone conclusion.

Before Chase could unpack and settle himself, a

torpedo came marching in with the front of his shirt covered with dry smears of blood. The guy stopped just inside the doorway, gave Chase a quick once-over, and said, "Hey, welcome to the action," then proceeded down the corridor to another room.

Jesus Christ, these syndicate people, Chase thought, they're all fucked.

He shut his door and phoned the Deuce, asked him, "What the hell kind of mob outfit is this?"

Deucie sounded like he was talking around his cigar stub. "Thirty years ago, one of the best. Now, they're disorganized and on the run. Look, I told you it was a bad setup, with all the infighting and mob-war bullshit. But you wanted me to make the call, set up the meeting."

"You told me they needed a driver. Instead I'm a chauffeur. And a gun-toting chauffeur at that."

"Jackie Langan said he wanted a driver. Is it my fault the mook doesn't know the difference between a getaway man and some smoke he wants to call Jeeves? Do you have to wear a hat?"

Sometimes you couldn't let out a sigh or it would never end. "Yeah. They gave me white gloves too."

"Jesus, they like to play the role to the hilt, don't they? It's one of the reasons they're off the media's radar, because nobody takes them seriously anymore. All those news anchors storming into the fish markets and the butcher shops with their camera guys, chasing the old mob bosses down the street? They never hassled Lenny and his chauffeurs with the gloves. The feds never wanted to infiltrate them because it was no fun. They couldn't grow mustaches and wear Hawaiian shirts and sunglasses at night, use wiseguy accents. The feebs held classes, teaching their agents to say, 'fegeddaboutit' and 'pasta fasool.' But so who gives a shit? You sit back and drive those rich pricks into the city to do their shopping. Pretty soon Lenny will cough up the ghost and the rest of them will move to Chi or Palm Springs. You won't have to put up with it for long."

"They want me to play bodyguard too, Deuce."

"It's mostly for show. They can't get any of the regular crew to get behind the wheel—those wannabe wiseguys all figure the job is beneath them. No action to it. Sitting on your ass and taking orders is no way to get promoted and get your button. Besides, the family is afraid that some of those muscleheads waiting around behind the wheel might start taking some incentive on how to move up the ranks. So they farm the job out."

"But I'm a total stranger."

"Gives you less reason to pop them than one of their own."

Chase had been going full clip for more than a month now, with almost no rest. It was the way he wanted it. He didn't want to think about being alone in the world now that Lila was gone. But hearing the chauffeur's last words, spoken in that voice. Maria. It was starting to make Chase think again.

"They aced the previous chauffeur right in front of me. Those gloves I mentioned? They were still warm from his hands. Not a clean kill either—they opened him up and left him in the trunk crying for his kids."

"Fuck sake, for what? Not tipping the hat? Driving over too many potholes? You better not make any sharp left turns." Deucie wheezed out a laugh that died abruptly, the way it should've. The Deuce had sharp instincts, and he could hear the wheels spinning inside of Chase, the shifting from first into second. "Wait a second here, you're not looking to boost the house, are you? You nuts? I didn't send you over there to score the joint."

"How could you not?" Chase asked. "I'm a thief."

"You been straight for the last ten years. Now I don't know what you are." Deuce let a few seconds go by, got rid of the cigar butt, spoke clearly into the phone. "Listen, kid, didn't you hear your own fucking story? These people aren't clean. They do things dirty and ugly. So why the hell are you even there? You don't have to be there."

"I've got to do something with myself."

"Go back to teaching auto shop."

"I think those days are all behind me now."

"Only if you want them to be. You should cut out—they probably got nineteen hitters on the payroll."

"Yeah, a couple live right down the hall. One just welcomed me to the family. I think he might be back soon with bundt cake."

"At least they won't have far to walk to ice you. That outfit's got grief up to the neck. Lenny was slick, but Jackie's an apple that fell too far from the

tree. His sister Sherry is sharper and nastier and being primed to take over, so that just makes for more
internal trouble. Already they can't hold off the
Russians and the Chinese and the feebs. RICO cases
are being made. Capos flipping, all kinds of back-
stabbing, taking potshots at one another in restaurants. You don't need that shit."

In the background, the Deuce's chop shop
sounded way too busy for this time of the afternoon.
Deucie was getting a little sloppy too, having his
crew make runs in broad daylight. "Get out of
there," he said to Chase. "Now. Just go. Don't score
them. It doesn't matter if you take ten bucks or a
hundred g's, it makes them look bad. You know
these syndicates. They never stop looking for the
people who rob them, hit them, betray them—it's
their number one rule. It's what they live for. They'll
come after you forever. You don't need that grief. I
know you're still recuperating. Guy takes a beating
like you did, bullet wounds, loss of blood, a couple
cracks to the head, you gotta give yourself time to recover. You're not thinking straight. Depression, it's
genetic, you got the gene. I know you're hurting
about Lila, and what happened with Jonah, I know
you're out there on the edge right now, and part of
you wants to fall over. A lot of bodies are turning up
in the Hudson, or not at all. Don't—"

"Yeah, they've got a landfill someplace," Chase
said, and hung up.

There were fourteen cars and trucks in the estate garages, everything from a three-year-old Mercedes to an F430 Spider and a Ford pickup.

They were all in bad shape—scratched, dinged, rusted, sludge wearing out the engines. They'd been driven hard by amateurs who didn't believe in regular care. Chase was a little worried about just how well the crew had cleaned out the trunk of the Super Stretch.

Since nobody had given him anything to do yet, Chase went to work on the vehicles.

He pulled them out into the huge egg-shaped driveway in front of the main house and eavesdropped on the Langan crew as they milled about. There were supposed to be guards patrolling the grounds but everybody just stood around smoking and bullshitting.

He learned that in the six months since Lenny Langan had more or less cashed out of the game, lying in bed with tubes in his nose and down his throat and in his crank while everybody was on death watch, his son Jackie had really spiffed up the estate. The guy had added a nine-hole golf course out back and vamped the main house by stripping all the cherry paneling and painting the place a *pale chamois*. It was all wasted flash since they'd probably be leaving soon.

Chase picked up on the particulars. The Langans were being run out of Jersey by the Korean, Chinese, and Russian mobs, among others, and they'd soon be moving on to Chicago to start up again as a much smaller outfit. Most of the crew knew they were getting the ax and had started up little side businesses, like the chauffeur had done.

The Mercedes had a fine stereo system, and Chase climbed in and turned on the radio, found an oldies station, and felt the tuned engine hum through his bones. He shut his eyes. The music took him back to when he was a kid and his parents danced around the living room together, his mother staring over his father's shoulder and making funny faces at Chase. It brought him back to the nights when he'd drive down the ocean parkways with Lila, heading out to the point, where they'd find some stretch of beach and she'd say, "Sweetness, you get more than flirty with me down in the dunes and you're gonna scratch us both raw." He'd say he didn't care and she'd go, "Glad to hear it, love, 'cause neither do I."

When he opened his eyes, he snapped off the radio and focused on the house.

Considering how things were going down, security inside the place looked even more lax than it was outside. It was Jackie's fault. He had a habit of sending different people on small errands. Chase watched as members of the crew wandered in and out and around the house, picking up Jackie's briefcase, his gold cigarette case, his .22, checkbook, golf clubs. These were serious guys, hitters and even some made men, running to a stationary to get Jackie some Vicks VapoRub because he thought he was coming down with a cold.

Jackie favored three fingers of scotch on the rocks, but not too many rocks. No more than two cubes. His voice was deep and calm unless something went wrong, and then it became instantly laced with near hysteria. You could hear Jackie's neurotic ranting all over the place when he didn't get exactly what he wanted.

Wrong VapoRub, not Vicks, go get the Vicks. Two cubes, not one, not three, not crushed ice, three fingers, not two, not four, the fuck couldn't anybody listen?

Chase finished up with the Mercedes and started drifting around inside. If Sherry Langan was anywhere around, he didn't see her or hear anything about her. He checked the windows to see what kind of a security system they had. It was bush-league at best. He looked into empty rooms. There were dens and libraries and parlors furnished with antique, fancy furniture. Statues, paintings, ornaments, and books no one had ever read. He watched Jackie and his men come and go. Nobody said squat to him.

He did a quick search of Jackie's office and found a safe hidden behind a hinged oil reproduction of Rembrandt's *Aristotle Contemplating a Bust of Homer*. He only knew it because the high-school auto shop where he'd taught was next door to the art classes, and one of the teachers there had the same print taped to a wall.

He'd been a thief since he was ten years old, pulling scores with his grandfather Jonah, but Chase had never actually seen a safe behind a painting before. It sort of stunned him.

No wiring around the frame, so there was no alarm, but he wasn't a jugger, he didn't know how to crack.

Sometimes they got cute and left the tumbler only one digit off to save time opening it. Chase tried it but the handle still wouldn't pop. Sometimes they scribbled the combination on a slip of paper and kept it close at hand, just in case they forgot. Chase checked the corners of the drawers of Jackie's desk but didn't find anything of value except a switchblade. He pocketed it and skimmed out the door.

*T*he next day it was threatening rain and a cold wind kept blowing through the area. Chase was under a nice SUV but he couldn't do as much on the truck as he wanted to because the fingers on his left hand began singing with pain. He'd fractured three of them a few weeks back and he wondered if this nagging ache would be a new constant he'd have to put up with for the rest of his life.

He thought of Lila again and a distant sweeping sorrow moved through him like a storm on the horizon heading inland. He bit back a groan. He'd made a mistake, he'd relaxed too long here. Two days was already too much. He had to stay in motion. Sweat burst across his forehead. And just like that, his pulse was suddenly thundering. He dove for the cold spot trying to find his cool, but it just wasn't there no matter how deep he went. He wondered if he'd ever reach that place again.

Chase felt as if he should just wait on this barren

shore for the hurricane to hit and take him and everything else along with it.

One of the henchmen bent and peered around the engine block at Chase and said, "Boss wants you."

So here it was.

Smelling of old man's aftershave and wearing a blue ascot—Christ on the cross, seriously, an ascot— Jackie Langan was seated in his office. Chase walked in and decided he didn't mind the pale chamois paint all that much himself.

Hovering nearby were two strongarms—Jackie's personal bodyguards, a couple of the guys who ran for the Juicy Fruit and the Vicks. They carried long-barreled .357s in shoulder holsters under poorly fitted sport jackets. The hunch-shouldered tailor hadn't made their suits for them.

Their biceps were so huge, the clothes so tight, and the gun barrels so long that it would take them two and a half minutes to draw their weapons if trouble ever came down.

Jackie wanted to make Chase wait for a minute so he pretended to be busy with some paperwork on the desk even though he hardly glanced at the pages. Chase figured it was something that Lenny

Langan had done and Jackie was now emulating without quite getting the nuances right.

Chase didn't really mind. He knew how disturbing it was to feel the presence of a powerful father or father figure not even in the room. Perhaps long gone, perhaps even dead, but forever present in your blood. You couldn't get away from it, couldn't really make peace with it. You just had to put up with it.

Eventually Jackie looked up and said, "So far as I can tell, the men of this organization are broken into three main groups. Accountants, capos, and muscle. Which are you?"

Chase thought Jackie was forgetting a few guys, like the butler, the doctor, and the groundskeeper who took care of the golf course. But Jackie was after effect.

"I fall outside those categories," Chase said.

"Yeah, you do, I suppose, so how about if you tell me, what's your purpose?"

"General man-about-town."

That made Jackie's face close up like he'd just sucked a lemon out of somebody's ass. It seemed to pretty much be Jackie Langan's everyday expression. "Are you making a joke?"

"You would think so, wouldn't you," Chase said.

It looked as if nobody had told Jackie about snuffing the other chauffeur or the fact that Chase had come aboard. Probably just an oversight, but Jackie seemed like he wanted to make a big deal out of it.

He was still asserting himself in the organization.

From what Chase had picked up, Jackie had spent years floating through Ivy League universities failing law school. He'd worked with diction coaches to lose his Brooklyn accent, but now that he'd returned to become head of the outfit he had to struggle to reacquire it.

He sounded like he'd been watching old film noir lately, studying up on how Eddie G. used to do it. He tried for a dead-eyed stare and didn't come close. He had no idea how to get anybody to respect him. The ascot didn't help.

"What the hell does that mean?" Jackie asked. "Man-about-town?"

Chase said, "I'm a driver."

"Another chauffeur?"

"The new chauffeur."

"So that's why you've got grease under your nails."

"I've been tuning your cars."

Jackie's mouth went slack. "You didn't touch my Ferrari, did you?" The hysteria was already creeping back into his voice.

"Yeah, I did."

"But nobody touches my Ferrari."

"No, nobody has," Chase said. "The battery was dead, the belts were loose, your brakes were gone, and the intake valve was busted. I fixed it."

"I don't like this."

"You don't like this?"

"I don't like you talking back," Jackie said.

"I thought we were having a conversation."

"You're still talking back."

"I am?"

"You are, goddamn it."

Chase assessed his options here. He thought maybe it wasn't worth any more of his time trying to score these dips, despite the fact that there had to be a lot of loose cash around someplace. But maybe the Deuce was right and Chase just wanted to be out on the edge. He was anxious about becoming bored, and in the boredom where his mind would take him.

Easing from his chair now, Jackie leaned over and planted his fists on the green leather desk mat, firmed his chin and almost snarled like the King. You had to give it to him. He was trying to fall into the role. But he realized he was going too far and pulled it back at the last second.

Chase couldn't help smiling, not the smartest thing to do considering the situation.

Jackie went back to the lemon-out-of-the-asshole face and said, "Boys, break one of his appendages."

Man, Chase thought, this crew *really* doesn't like chauffeurs. And to say appendages instead of arms or legs? The guy had to get his patter down.

The two bruisers lumbered over, shaking their heads because they didn't understand any of this either, but they did as they were told. They frowned and held up their hands in a *Whattya gonna do* gesture.

It was dumb as hell. Nobody wanted to fight. The strongarms looked at Chase with a kind of pleading

twist to their mouths, hoping he'd take a couple
shots to the belly and just shut the fuck up.

For a second Chase figured, What the hell, I can
do that.

But then they each grabbed him by a wrist, making their killer faces. Showing teeth, nostrils flared,
squinting. They thought it made them look slick.
They were dumb. You squint like a spaghetti cowboy
and you cut off your peripheral vision.

Chase allowed them to begin wrenching him forward. He couldn't figure out how they intended to
break his bones holding him like this.

In his head Jonah said, It's time to move.

Chase moved. Pain flared in his collarbone, where
he'd been shot. He'd lost some muscle mass being
laid up and felt the effects immediately, the weakness that had never been there before.

Cheat, you idiot, Jonah said.

Chase stomped the foot of one of the thugs. You
see somebody do that and you think they're trying
to break the guy's toes or something, it looks kind of
sissy. But if you do it right, the way Jonah had taught
him, you smash the instep and you tear tendon away
from bone. It'll take the guy two months in traction
before he can limp out of the hospital.

The bruiser went down screaming. Chase hadn't
expected screams and apparently neither had Jackie,
who jumped away from his desk and huddled against
the wall. The other thug stared at his buddy wondering why a soldier going two-fifty would fall down and
shriek because somebody stepped on his foot.

Despite the bad fingers and the wrenching in his shoulder, Chase unleashed a flurry of jabs and crosses on the guy still standing. He bit the inside of his cheek and took shallow breaths, hoping to keep his damaged ribs from scratching around too much. His punches weren't especially effective, but he still had grease on his hands and he managed to work it into the thug's eyes. That was a pretty good cheat too.

The strongarm raised his fists to his face and tried to thumb his eyes clear. That was enough for Chase to snake his hand inside the guy's jacket and yank out the .357.

He cocked the hammer and jammed the piece under the strongarm's chin.

Cherry paneling—there was a reason why the goombas always did a house in a nice dark red-brown. It hid the bloodstains. Pale chamois wasn't going to cut it.

He was thinking what a fucked mess this was when Moe Irvine and three other men busted into the office, all kinds of heavy hardware flashing. Chase was trying to decide if he'd put himself into this stupid position because, somewhere deep inside, he wanted to suicide like his father.

That sorrow swept through him again, the storm much closer to the beach this time.

Lila said to him, Love, it's time to stop this foolishness.

The torpedo who'd walked into Chase's room with blood on his shirt now stepped in front of the

others and held his hand out, palm up, waiting for
the pistol. When Chase didn't turn over the long-
barrel fast enough, the guy actually snapped his fingers.

What a crew. They might ace him for a lot of
things, but not this.

Chase gave the gun up.

Checking the scene, his bronze chin angled first
in one direction and then another, Moe Irvine took
his time before he spoke. "So . . . somebody explain.
What's going on here?"

Another stupid question. Chase had been in jams
before, but he had to admit this time he was a touch
edgy. He'd always dealt with cops and professional
thieves, guys who followed a code. But somehow
these people, who used to be at the top of the crime
chain, just didn't seem to have one, at least not anymore. He couldn't tell which way things would jump
next.

The torpedo took another step. He stared down
at the bruiser who'd finally quit screaming and was
now mewling like a newborn. The torpedo's eyes
shifted to Chase.

"Don't hurt him, Bishop," Moe Irvine barked.
"He's new."

"Nobody's going to hurt him," Bishop said.

"Why not?" Jackie asked, still hiding out in the
corner, and Chase found himself echoing the question. Yeah, why not?

Stepping over to the collapsed thug, Bishop
lightly toed the guy's damaged foot. The strongarm

started making rubber ducky noises—it was the kind of sound no man liked to hear another guy make, because it meant he might make it himself someday.

Bishop turned and gave Chase a warm, friendly smile. It even reached his eyes, which was a damn hard thing for a stone killer to learn how to do. But Bishop did it.

"You made short work of them," he said.

"They're sloppy," Chase told him. "And they really didn't want to hurt me without a good reason."

"You've done some muscling."

"No, that's not my area."

"What is?"

"I'm not a strongarm," Chase said, "I'm a wheel-man."

"Strongarm?" That got an amiable chuckle from Bishop. He almost sounded like a normal guy instead of somebody who could cut a nun's throat and wash the blood off his hands in a baptismal fount. A nice nun too, not one of the mean ones. "I haven't heard anybody use that term in a while."

It was another holdover from running around with Jonah and his strings when Chase was a kid. A fourteen-year-old getaway man for a crew of middle-aged pros. He had a throwback mentality and sometimes used grift speak that only old men or guys born into the life would know.

Bishop was caressing the .357 in his hand. Unconsciously he plied it, like touching a woman's wrist at dinner while the wine was being served. His thumb circled over the casing, his forefinger easing back and forth across the trigger guard. It made Chase sick to his stomach.

"What do you drive?" Bishop asked. "When you're not driving a limo?"

Everyone put their cannons away and stood around trying to follow Bishop's lead without knowing exactly where it was going. They looked to Moe Irvine, who didn't do anything either. They glanced at Jackie, who glanced back. They couldn't keep their eyes on him too long without pulling a face. That ascot.

Chase said, "You ever met a driver who didn't answer by saying 'anything' when you asked that question?"

"No."

"There it is."

Everybody listened in, wondering what Bishop might do next. Chase was pretty interested in that himself.

The fondling of the pistol was getting creepy now, Bishop unable to help himself, really working over the gunmetal. He kept his smile up the whole time.

In the back of Chase's mind Jonah said, *You were stupid, you should've kept the gun, you should've shot him in the face.*

Bishop asked, "What was the problem here?"

"Jackie got mad because I changed the plugs in his Ferrari," Chase said.

With a gurgle of aggravation Jackie started to step around his desk and then thought better of it. He went to sit in the chair again and thought twice about that too. Finally he decided to lean against the corner of the desk like a doctor in a commercial about to talk about erectile dysfunction.

There was the gurgle again, this time louder, with an edge of protest. Jackie said, "Listen—I have something I want you all to know—"

Everybody ignored him. Moe Irvine finally got a move on and said to Bishop, "All right, get Crowley to the emergency room. Give Elkins back his piece. We've got work to do." He frowned at Chase. "Stay away from the goddamn Ferrari."

"Sure."

These others, Chase didn't have to worry about them. It was Bishop he needed to keep his eyes on.

They helped Crowley to stand and carried him groaning from the room. Bishop turned over the pistol with a quiet laugh. Elkins had some trouble putting his long-barrel back into its holster and the seam in his jacket's shoulder started to give with the loud and distinctive rending of cheap material.

They all filed out, even Jackie, leaving Chase alone in the room. He looked around, mulling over the score, trying to figure out why he was really here, and thinking, My grandfather could come in here with nothing but a nail file and kill every one of us.

In the dream, his dead parents sat at the kitchen table with his dead wife, talking in hushed tones as if they didn't want him to hear. When they noticed he was in the room, they looked at one another with anxious expressions and passed their last whispers. After a moment, they turned their attention to him. They waited, unblinking, for Chase to say something.

His heart began to hammer as he stood there trying to get out the words, but nothing would come. Nothing ever did. In a fourth chair sat his unborn sibling, murdered before its own birth. Their mother had been shot in the kitchen, and that's where he always dreamed of her. The kid might be a boy or a girl, Chase still couldn't tell, no matter how many times he had nightmares like this.

He wanted to ask it, What are you?

A breeze blew in. He smelled floor wax and furniture polish. His father wiped down his glasses with some kind of citrus-scented cleaner. Lila never wore perfume but she bathed with a vegetable bath oil. Cucumbers, avocados, aloe. His memories and dreams were getting tangled. Her hair twisted across her eyes. He expected her to brush her curls back, but she didn't. Just kept sitting there with her hair covering most of her face.

Sometimes the kid spoke in the nightmares and sometimes it didn't. Chase waited. So did the kid. So did the other dead. It had gone on like this for a while now and he wondered if it would ever end, or if he even wanted it to. Lila murmured something from beneath her hair that he didn't catch. He tried to move to her but couldn't get any closer.

The kid hopped out of the chair, crawled across the table to Chase, and said, Listen to me. Find the girl.

Blunt, aching pain drove him up from sleep. It ini-tially centered in his fingers, which were purple and throbbing as he came awake, but a second later he hurt all over. His fight with the thugs had torn open the gunshot wounds again. His ribs sang. His collarbone raged. It was still infected. The fingers were fucked, he must've refractured them.

He carefully climbed off the bed and made it out into the hall bathroom he shared with the rest of the floor. Nobody else was around. Under the sink he found a good supply of bandages, hydrogen peroxide, tape, even catgut. The real stuff—it had probably been in the house for forty years. Chase changed his dressings and set the bad fingers in place. He checked for painkillers in the medicine chest. All they had was aspirin. Family probably made fifty mil a year from opiates, but they shared none of the good stuff with the hired help. He took the bottle and chugged five tablets.

He gathered the old bloody bandages and carried

them with him to his room, where he hid them at the bottom of his gym bag at the back of his closet. He'd dump them sometime in the afternoon. He didn't want to advertise that he was a couple steps slower than usual.

Chase stood in the window and stared out toward Jackie's golf course and caught the scent of water on the wind. His thoughts twisted. His dreams were growing more intense, the details clearer. Lila had grown up in the back hills of Mississippi and always had a wide superstitious streak. She'd once told him the dead would always make their will known, and it had stuck with him.

His own history was prominent in his mind. A tangle of emotions and half-understood compulsions and motivations. The Deuce had been right, Chase shouldn't be here, but what else was he going to do? Go back to stealing cars? He had a chance to lay in a big score here, and he'd need the money for the girl—for Kylie. He stared in the direction of the water.

He tried not to think about what had led him here but something had broken inside of him and he could feel the memories surging forward, wanting out.

Lila had loved the ocean and Chase had eventually grown to enjoy it too. He'd once thought he'd never be able to sit on a beach again because his old man had snuffed himself by taking a sailboat out into the Great South Bay one winter.

His father had suicided because he couldn't handle the grief after Chase's mother had been found shot dead in their kitchen. Fifteen years gone now and no one knew who'd done it, but Chase was finally starting to get a few ideas.

Jonah, his grandfather, a man he'd not only never met before but had never even heard about, plucked him from foster care and convinced him that family was all that mattered, that blood was important. Maybe it was true.

Jonah—carved from rock and just as feeling. Chase started working professional strings and crews immediately. First short cons and small grifts, and then acting as a second-story burglar and a wheelman. He'd been brought in on bigger scores because he was a first-rate driver and kept his nerve. It had gone on like that for years, until the day he'd watched Jonah ice one of his own men.

He severed ties with his grandfather and tooled around the South. That was how he met Lila—a deputy sheriff in a Mississippi county—during a score gone bad. He went straight, they got married, and eventually came back to New York where she joined the Suffolk County cops and he taught high school auto shop.

Chase pressed his forehead to the cold glass, hoping it would cool his heated thoughts, but it wasn't nearly enough. Lila in his head telling him, *It's all right, love, I'll help you through this.*

Six weeks ago she'd been murdered on duty while trying to stop a crew heisting a diamond merchant's

store. The driver, Earl Raymond, parked in the
street and waiting to roll, had shot her three times
with his left arm hanging out the window.

Chase hadn't seen Jonah for ten years, but his
grandfather was the only man hard enough to help
him go after the string. The old man showed up
with Angie, a woman forty years his junior, who was
the mother of his two-year-old daughter, Kylie.

It was a weird setup and Chase had a hard time
picturing what the little girl's life must be like, but he
knew that Jonah would ruin it for her. Angie knew it
too and asked Chase to take a run at his grandfather,
pop him twice in the back of the skull.

Chase had a lot of resentment, but he couldn't do
that.

He tracked the crew to a motel in Newark, and at
the last minute Angie put two in the old man's back.
It didn't slow Jonah or stop him. He killed her while
Chase had an old-fashioned shootout with Earl in
the middle of the parking lot. Earl driving his sweet
Plymouth Superbird with the funky extended front
end, the 440 V8 tuned up right, while Chase just
stood there already shot a couple of times, his ribs
cracked, fingers busted, and tried to lift his gun to
hit a moving target. Though Chase wasted five shots
without even cracking the windshield before he finally put one in Earl's head.

Jonah in his mind saying, You should've taken
him out with the first blast.

He was right.

Now Chase thought of Jonah out there, maybe

with his baby girl and maybe not. Angie had left
the kid in Sarasota with her sister Milly. Chase didn't
know anything else except that she was married to a
professional surfer. He figured there couldn't be
that many professional surfers in Sarasota with wives
named Milly.

He could find the kid one way or another. With the
money he hoped to score from the Langans, he figured he had a better choice he could offer the child.
Some way to protect her from Jonah, from the kind
of life that Chase himself had been drawn into.

There was nothing else for him to do. Jonah had
been right about one thing. Blood was important.

Lila said, Save the baby.

*S*tanding at the window, Chase watched the doctor pull up and park at an angle at the side door again, the guy taking a last couple puffs of a cigarette then carefully putting it out against his heel. How would that make a cancer patient feel, seeing his own doc hacking up yellow phlegm and smelling like a second-floor boys' room.

After all this time, Chase still had a lot of questions. He wanted to know why his father had said that he'd asked to make an appeal to the killer, when the truth was the cops had backed him into doing it. He wanted to know why his mother had cried so much the night before she died.

Talking about Jonah, Angie had said, *Everyone else he destroys. More than you know.*

And Jonah had said someone else had tried to kill him over a kid.

Another foolish woman.

Chase couldn't shake those words. They hummed and buzzed and bit at him.

He thought, Did Jonah murder my pregnant mother?

The kid said to find the girl. Lila told him to save the baby. Blood was important. Chase needed to finish taking this score and get on the move.

Later that morning the suit was delivered to Chase along with a fresh pair of white gloves. He couldn't quite get over it. They really wanted him to wear a chauffeur's uniform.

The suit fit well. He didn't like the ties Moe Irvine picked out so much and threw on the one he found least offensive. The diamond stickpin caught light like a laser.

The phone in his room rang. He answered and a curt voice he didn't recognize told him, "Mister Langan and Miss Sherry are to be driven to the First National Bank at 232 Madison Avenue, in Manhattan. Then they shall lunch at Pietro's on West 51st Street."

Chase thought, They couldn't tell me that themselves once they got in the back of the limo?

He walked out to the garage and backed the limo down the drive to where Jackie and his sister stood at the front door looking like they'd been sitting in a funeral director's parlor for hours. The soldiers were milling around, glancing out at the golf course like they wanted to play a couple rounds while Jackie was off in New York. A few more were on the sundeck, their collars open, relaxing in chaise lounges.

So their well-being was now his responsibility. He wondered how much of all that internal-war shit was true, and if it was, how long it would take for someone to make a real move. Jackie bulldozing his sister, or she popping him? Or Moe Irvine taking out both of them, then going upstairs to whisper in Lenny Langan's ear, "You treated me like shit for thirty years, you prick, now I'm in charge." Then pulling the dying guy's plug.

Jackie eyed him up and down, noticed right off that Chase didn't have the hat and gloves on. He said, "Hey, one second here . . ."

Chase ignored him and opened the back door of the limo for Sherry Langan. It was a cloudy day but she wore big dark sunglasses. He offered his hand but she didn't take it, climbing in on her own and swinging her legs clear of the door. She stretched them out, her toes pointed, muscles perfectly defined, the skin pale but exquisite. She wasn't showing off for him. She hadn't even looked at him and probably thought he was the dead chauffeur.

It annoyed him and he didn't know why.

He continued holding the door open, his shadow thrown across her knees, until she slowly turned her chin and shifted in her seat, those shades finally focused on him. He could feel her innate strength and knew right then that the Deuce was right, she was sharp and primed to take over.

He pretended to tip the hat that wasn't there and said, "Hello, Miss Langan." Then closed her in.

Moe walked out of the house and started giving

orders to one of the capos but stopped talking when he noticed Chase wasn't wearing the hat and gloves.

These people, Jesus Christ.

Jackie Langan stood back and waited for Chase to open the door of the limo for him. Chase walked past him, slid behind the wheel, and tapped the door lock. The security gates were already open. He left Jackie, Moe Irvine, and the rest of the stumble-fuck crew standing there while he kidnapped the woman.

In the back of his head, Lila whispered, Sweetness, why're you doing this?

It was a good question.

Maybe the answer was blood, maybe it wasn't, you just couldn't tell anymore. Chase hadn't intended to play things out this way, but he went with his instincts. Jackie didn't matter. Jackie would only have chump change around, even in the safe. Sherry Langan was the real head of the family and would probably be whacking her stupid-ass brother any day now. Chase had to get on her radar somehow, so why not be bold about it? His grandfather always told him never to follow someone else's rules.

Jonah in his skull said, You're doing this because you want to die.

Chase gunned the limo toward the Holland Tunnel. He'd overhauled the engine and was able to squeeze some real speed out of it, the front end perfectly aligned, tires balanced, the extra length of the vehicle cutting a nice channel as he cruised.

The satellite radio had been set to sophisticated talk shows and classical music. He found an oldies station and kept the volume low, the sweet harmonies of Motown reaching out and filling his belly with a nice thrum.

The partition window was down. Sherry Langan said, "So, you're a showoff."

"Not really," Chase told her. "I'm just a driver, not a chauffeur."

"What's the difference?"

"Among other things, I don't wear the hat and gloves."

"Then I daresay this wasn't the job for you. Perhaps we should have weeded you out during the interview."

The backs of her hands were covered with thin wisps of veins. She made herself a drink at the bar and sat back, sipping it, sighing a little as she swallowed.

She crossed her legs. They were her best feature and she knew it. He suspected that she was always hoping for a reaction—had probably heard the old wiseguys whispering about her stems since she was a kid.

"Are you the one who's been raiding my Glenlivet?"

"No."

"Your friends then."

"I don't have any friends," he said, and the truth of it rang inside him, echoing through the emptiness.

She watched him taking the smooth turns, weaving through traffic, in no real hurry but still making good time. "Are you trying to play out a flash move here?"

"What do you mean?"

"Earn your bones by creating a stir? Garner respect and rise through the ranks by pissing off your employers?"

"People really give that a whirl?"

"They have in the past, yes."

"Were any of them still breathing the next day?"

A demure laugh rippled up her throat. "I suspect not many, at least not in the old days. So tell me, what's your game?"

"I don't have one," Chase said. "I'm just taking you to the bank on Madison and then to Pietro's for lunch."

Nails clinking the rim of the glass elicited a sharp tone. "But you abandoned my brother."

Chase tried to force his features into a shocked expression, knowing it probably wasn't going to work. But how well could she see him anyhow? Way back there through those big black shades?

"What?"

"Yes, he was supposed to join us."

"Nobody told me he was coming."

"He was standing there in the driveway next to the limo."

"Really?" Chase said. "So why didn't he get in?"

"He was waiting for you to open the door for him."

"Oh, right, I'm supposed to do that. I thought he was just seeing you off."

Her top leg began to bounce slightly and she held the glass against her bottom lip, rolling it, the ice clicking in time with the shoop-shoops on the radio. He could feel the depth of her concentration, the way she pored over him now. It ignited him somehow, made him perk up in the seat.

She took off the Jacqueline O's.

He met her eyes in the rearview. They were hot and calculating and full of education and traces of the dead. That was her strength. Crippled and crushed boys scattered down the years in her wake, starting when she was about thirteen. A few maimed but alive enough to limp along in the world, deformed but still thinking about her, maybe even loving her. She'd never been struck with a pinprick of conscience. That was the tragedy she'd never feel. He'd seen a few like her before.

The road rolled in and out. He could feel her trying to assess the situation, wondering if he was working with one of the other outfits and making a grab. Or if he might be a feeb fucking around with her. Or just another dumb member of the crew overstepping his bounds, perhaps looking to nail the boss's daughter. She kept her purse close. He knew she must be packing. Probably a little lady's snub .25, something that would do real damage if she got close enough to put it to a guy's head. The bullet whipping around in there turning everything to cream.

But she had her cell phone and Chase hadn't made any overt moves, and they were still on their way to the bank. Not like he was hijacking her to Atlantic City or the Poconos. He liked the way she showed no alarm, sure of herself, on top of the action.

After a moment she said, "No. You're not one of us." She finished her drink, grabbed her purse, slid up directly behind him, and spoke through the partition. He heard her digging around past her lipstick and hairbrush. "There's something not right about you."

A mob princess putting him in his place. Chase felt oddly insulted. He said, "Hey now, is that a nice thing to say?"

"Let's keep focused, shall we? All right, driver, so are you actually such a moron that you left my brother behind by accident, or is this some kind of a shakedown? Are you abducting me? And please be quick in answering, I do have a .38 pointed at the back of your head. The partition glass isn't bullet-proof though the windshield is."

He glanced in the mirror again. It wasn't a small, lady's snub, but a nice pearl-handled revolver. No chance of jamming, she went in for practicality.

Sherry Langan was like nearly every other woman he'd met in the bent life. Hard, calm, and a lot smarter, tougher, and more on the ball than most guys. You could never call her beautiful, or even pretty really, but there was something about her that made you look twice. And not just at the legs.

Maybe it was self-assurance or icy composure, the way she held herself above and out of reach. Or maybe it was the inherent understanding that some guys liked that sort of woman. Chase was a little afraid he might be one of them.

He'd been right. Jackie wasn't in the boss's chair. And the real power behind the family since Lenny had taken to living under a plastic tent wasn't Moe Irvine either, it was Sherry. Moe really did care about ties.

Chase thought it was pretty ballsy, her just coming out and asking, Are you abducting me? Like you'd have an honest enough abductor to tell you flat out, Yeah, I am.

"I didn't abduct you, and you know it. If you really thought so, you'd stick that thing in my ear."

She stuck the revolver in his ear and said, "I planned on doing that anyway."

"If you ace me, you'll have a long walk to Pietro's."

They entered the tunnel and crossed over toward Manhattan. In the dark now with the interim lights flashing overhead, and that sense of pressure growing over them as they got deeper under the Hudson he focused on the cool gunmetal against his neck. Freezing actually, which made him think of his mother's grave, standing there in the snow with his father drunk and sobbing on the ground, his hair growing thick with ice.

"What's your name?" she asked, sitting back, placing the .38 on the seat beside her. She poured herself another drink and turned so that she was casually facing the partition, her hair wafting in the breeze from the air-conditioner vents.

He gave her the name of the fake ID he'd gotten the job under. It would hold up, at least for a while, depending on how hard she pushed it.

"You've got nerve but that's not enough, you know."

"For what?"

"For being one of my employees."

He caught her eyes again, astute as hell, but she wasn't onto him as a heister. She thought he was trying to show off to her, trying to impress her so he could get in her pants, marry her, share in her millions. "I'm just doing my job."

"But without the gloves and hat."

"I am wearing a tie," Chase said.

"I don't like it."

"Me neither. You can blame Moe."

A crisp smile twisted across her lips. "It's an old man's style."

"Yeah, like Jackie's aftershave."

"Yes. Our home is draped in ancient history. My father's, the men who've worked there who are dead or in prison now. The families that came before us. My father bought the estate from Jimmy 'Toots' Defazo, who was machine-gunned in the living room by his own consigliere. There are still some paintings in the halls of him. My father liked taking the man's home. And his belongings. And his heritage, and then adding it to his own. My brother is trying to do the same thing. Like this incident, for instance. Jackie can get one of the other men to drive him into the city, but he won't allow that. It is, after all, why we have a chauffeur."

"Why doesn't he just take the Ferrari?" Chase asked.

"It doesn't run."

"It does now. I gave it a tune-up."

"The car doesn't actually matter. He's afraid of it, I think. It's too much style for him to live up to. Did he get angry with you for touching it?"

"Yeah, he tried to have two of his bodyguards break my appendages."

"But they failed," she said.

"Mostly."

She gave a slow *tsk tsk tsk* with a pursed bottom lip, making it sexy. "Be careful fooling with someone's conceit, even if it is broken. It's what people fear most. Being forced to face up to their own charade, having their weakness exposed. They'll die with their teeth in your throat before they allow that to happen."

Telling him this after cleaning his ear out with a gun barrel.

"When I was a girl my father once took us to Asbury Park, before the renovations began, when it was nothing but a dead boardwalk in a mostly lifeless city. Autumn. But without the colors, or the leaves, or anything else, really, just the empty sand. It was very cold, a dark day, overcast, but with no wind. More than that it was bleak. You couldn't touch anything without getting covered with splinters. All the buildings creaked and complained. Broken glass everywhere. You could feel how motionless and lonely and *corrupted* the pier was, the ocean barely rippling. The birds already gone."

She took a sip, rattled the ice in tune to her own memory. "Jackie started crying as we looked out over the park, our backs to the water. He thought the corpses of drowned sailors were going to grab hold of his ankles between the slats of lumber. I believed our father was angry with us for some reason, even though he seemed in a happy mood. He'd invested in some property there as a tax write-off, and knew that in the years to come the city would rebuild itself and his interests would pay off in a big way. It was something for him to be proud of on every level. Outfoxing the IRS, contributing to the community, investing in the future. It's one of the few things he'd ever done with his money that he felt was truly clean, but he had to do it in a murdered place."

She stopped then and Chase waited for the rest of the story. But she stalled there, adrift in her memories. "And what weakness did you expose of Dad's on that day?"

"Not a weakness, just a hidden aspect. I asked him if he was going to be sad when they rebuilt the park. I could see that he enjoyed the place exactly as

it was. Decrepit and desolate. It was probably because he'd been chopping up snitches and feeding
them to the fish."

She let out a hum that was part laughter. "But
Daddy didn't like me knowing that about him, seeing through his talk and knowing in my heart he was
lying, perhaps even to himself."

These Langans, they liked to do things fast and
out in the open. No wonder they were losing to the
other syndicates.

"And that's when Lenny threw you into the water
and told you to swim," Chase said. "Said that you
had to be strong, that you had to prove yourself wor-
thy of the Langan name."

"Of course not. My father doted on us. We went
out for ice cream."

They found each other's gaze in the mirror again.
Chase didn't know if it was a tell or not, but the
thickest vein in her throat pulsed and shivered.

"You're lying."

Smiling without any humanity now, her hot eyes
completely iced over. It was a very slick maneuver,
throwing spooky truths out there that were meant to
unnerve, but pulling back on everything else. She
walked every inch of the walk.

"Attempting to expose my secrets too?" she asked.
"Didn't I just tell you it was dangerous to try that?"

"That's the thing about secrets," he said, "they
have a way of exposing themselves."

They entered the city. Traffic was heavy crosstown,

but the Super Stretch really sliced up the lanes. It ma-
neuvered easily and had an intimidation factor that
even the taxi drivers picked up on.

Sherry Langan said nothing more and he wondered if she was deciding to leave him with a king-
size exit wound in his temporal lobe.

He drew up to the bank on Madison Avenue,
double-parked in the street, and undid his safety
belt. He got out, opened the limo door for her, offered his hand again, and helped her out of the
back. Sherry moved to the bank door and he followed.

"Where are you going?" she asked.

"Your well-being is my responsibility. I'll walk you
inside."

Chase escorted her in and watched the manager
and the other employees kowtow while Sherry took
it all in. She shook hands like Marie Antoinette,
holding it out there palm down, high in the air, forcing the other person to reach up to take it.

Chase stood behind her trying to act like a bodyguard. He scanned the tellers and thought about the
one bank job he'd been involved in as a kid.

He was only supposed to drive the getaway car
but at the last minute one of Jonah's string had gotten pulled in by the cops and Chase had been forced
to cover. The boost had gone off perfectly, Jonah
grabbing the drawer counts, careful of all the secret
alarms. Chase wasn't armed, he just ran around the
place grabbing people's wallets. The next day Jonah

bought Chase a thirty-five-dollar hooker in celebration. If he thought too long about that moment, seeing what a thirty-five-dollar hooker looked like and what was expected of him, Chase could still get red-faced over it.

When Sherry Langan was done, he accompanied her out again, opened the limo door, all that. He slid back into traffic and headed toward Pietro's.

"Forget the restaurant," she said. "I don't dine alone. Just take me back home."

An oppressive stillness filled the car. He swung back toward the tunnel, turned the oldies station up.

"It's proper to ask your passengers what music they wish to listen to rather than putting on your own," she told him.

"I'll remember that," he said and started humming along.

Jonah said, You're an idiot to keep pushing her.

When they drew up to the estate, Sherry moved to the partition window, leaned in close, got right up to his ear again, this time without the pistol. But her voice was just as chilly and inflexible as metal.

"You won't always be so strong and gritty," she said. "So durable. There'll come a time when your guts are gone, when you'll end up like my father, dying and feeling every inch of it. I hope I'm there to see it."

"It's already happened," Chase told her.

*M*oe *Irvine was waiting for him. Chase expected* some heat but didn't know how much might come down. He helped Sherry Langan out of the limo, did the fake hat tip thing again, then hovered near the driver's door in case he had to blow now. He kept one hand on the stolen switchblade in his pocket, keeping an eye out for Bishop. It wouldn't be much, but if he was fast, it might be enough for him to live into the next minute.

He watched her walk into the house, the gams striking in the afternoon light.

Moe glared, trying to cut Chase's legs out from under him. Chase turned to him and said, "What? You don't like the tie? You're the one who picked it out, Moe. You want I should get some others?"

Smoothing back the point of his widow's peak, Moe kept his composure, making the effort to smile, the teeth shining in that maple-brown face.

"You drove off without Jackie this morning."

"I didn't know he was coming."

"You were specifically told that he and his sister were going into the city."

"I don't remember that."

"Regardless, you failed in your duties."

"My duties are to protect the well-being of my passengers. Words from your own lips. Miss Sherry was my passenger, and her being continues to do well."

Moe just stared. "I think I may have made a mistake with you. Until I decide whether I should terminate your services here, I want you to restrict yourself to your room and the garages. Stay out of the main house."

"Sure."

"You'll also apologize to Jackie as soon as you see him."

"Okay."

With a nice flourish, Moe turned his back, started to walk into the mansion but stopped short. He spun back and said, "You've done a good job with the cars," then marched inside.

Chase waited, expecting Jackie to come running out ranting, but no, that was it. No one else said anything to him so he walked back to his room, sat on the bed, and gave himself a time limit.

Two weeks. He could deal with these people that long. Then he'd split with or without a score. He pictured a two-year-old girl standing at Jonah's knee, and he nearly doubled over.

*   *   *

He worked on the other vehicles and kept his eyes open. The older capos kicked up their payments in cash, sometimes in paper bags or manila envelopes, sometimes in nice leather briefcases. These were the guys still out there hijacking trucks and materials from construction sites, not the whiz kids who'd turned identity theft and e-mail scams into a four-billion-dollar-a-year franchise, hacking into bank accounts and snatching direct-deposit social-security checks. Paper money was still coming in.

Chase watched but couldn't pick up on any system. Sometimes the thugs were all around acting like security while somebody brought a package in, like he was handing off diamonds. Sometimes a white-haired little wiseguy might bring his payoff rolled up in a newspaper and just hand it to Moe Irvine without a word.

Sherry Langan was hardly ever around, but Chase figured she knew where every dollar was, when it was coming in, and where it was going. He could walk over and maybe nab a briefcase full of cash but he had no idea how much might be in it. A grand? Five? Twenty? He had no way to tell. A smash and grab had to be worth the risk.

Jackie gave Chase some shit in the limo while they drove into Manhattan. Jackie bitched him out for leaving him behind, not wearing the cap and gloves, not calling Jackie "sir." The litany continued for ten minutes, with Jackie's voice getting higher and higher, and even cracking a couple times. The Ivy League accent came and went. Chase apologized. He worked it hard and called Jackie "sir." He'd also filled one of the glasses in the back with two cubes of ice. It seemed to steady Jackie some.

The threat of rain filled the sky. A few drops spattered across the windshield every minute or two but it never opened up and poured down. The water added a throbbing sheen to the world. It reminded him of his wedding day, when the crazy preacher had started speaking in tongues and jumped into the river. Chase had dived in after him and dragged him up on the shore, and stood there looking at Lila's family and all his guests with the sweet water dripping into his eyes.

"Hey—" Jackie said.

Chase said, "Yes, sir?"

"You're good, you know how to work the roads."

"Yes, sir."

Jackie was visiting a high-class Japanese massage parlor in Soho to get stepped on by a lilliputian woman in teak sandals before making it in a boiling hot tub. Chase didn't need to know about it, but Jackie liked to talk about his action.

"You ever had a chink girl?" Jackie asked.

For a second Chase was confused, unsure if Jackie was talking about this Japanese parlor or not, but then realized it was all the same to Jackie. "No."

"They're very subservient."

"I think I've heard that."

"They're trained damned near from birth in the

art of pleasing a man. It's part of their culture. For them it's not about the money, it's about finesse and expertise."

"Yeah?"

"Mastering technique. That's what satisfies them. They live for their man. It takes all the pressure off. It's very liberating."

"I see," Chase said.

His years on the road with Jonah had been educational ones, and Chase had met a lot of Asian girls on the job. He suspected their lives had little to do with finesse and mastering technique, or about satisfying any of their johns either. They were about as subservient as any other woman in the life, and they'd slash your face up with a straight razor if you tried to rip them off.

Easing through SoHo, Chase slowed and found the place. He pulled up out front, but Jackie wouldn't let Chase drive off, and the sumo-sized doorman wouldn't let Chase double-park out front and wait in the limo. The big guy badgered him with offers of exotic geisha who would crack his spine for him and dip his crank in warm sake.

"You like sake?" the big dude asked.

"I like drinking it, anyway," Chase said.

You had to say the cultural differences were at least very interesting.

He wound up sitting in the corner of the lobby. He watched the johns walk in looking eager and breezy and watched them walk out looking like they needed a chiropractor. The madam came over and offered him a free massage, meaning she'd tack the price onto Jackie's bill and let Chase explain it later. She seemed to take it personally that he was just sitting there minding his own business, as if she was failing at her job. He sent out a vibe that she should leave him the fuck alone and she eventually picked up on it and let him be.

She and the sumo wrestler forgot about him and soon Chase got up and went to look for Jackie so he could lift the boss's wallet.

The parlor was split up between the legal trade and the actual trade. Rooms to the front offered real massages, oil baths, hot tubs, maybe a little handjob action, but in the back was where the little bedrooms were and where all that sake was being put to use the wrong way.

Opening doors at random in a place like this wasn't a good idea, but Chase could feel the hours drifting through his hands. The girl Kylie was becoming more and more present in his mind.

He put an ear to the thin wooden doors to see if he could hear Jackie whining about too much ice in his glass, the wrong kind of edible lotions. The cinnamon, not the vanilla, not the cranberry.

He picked up on lots of grunting, but it didn't sound like happy sex. More like physical therapy, guys straining their muscles and bones back into shape after a car accident. Daring to take a peek, he caught sight of a fat businessman on his belly, lots of vanilla pudge wobbling around while one of the girls laid into him with her elbows, sort of body slam-

ming him like they were in the ring. Working on the
joints, really digging into his soft tender spots. Chase
grimaced and drew his chin back. The guy was
damn near barking. The girl kept chopping away.
Chase was curious but not curious enough to keep
watching.

Next room had Jackie in it, really grooving along.
He was in the saddle on top of a very young Japanese
girl who moaned in pidgin English, trying to sound
enthusiastic. She immediately spotted Chase but didn't
even stutter as she spoke. "Tha's eet, fasta, fasta, you so
strong, you so big, you lay it into leetle me . . ." Chase
nodded to her, one working person to another.

He grabbed Jackie's pants from the floor, found
the wallet and riffled through it, hunting for the safe
combination. The safe might not be where the real
big money was, but you grabbed what you could
when you could.

Jackie liked to carry cash. He had over two grand
in fifties and hundreds. A couple black credit cards.
No photos, no safe combo, no tiny keys, nothing
in the little hidden plastic compartments. The girl
watched Chase impassively while Jackie kept working it. Chase pulled a wedge of bills out and left
them under a lamp so she'd keep quiet about this.
She gave him the okay sign behind Jackie's back.

As usual, the voice in Chase's head was not his
own. Jonah was saying, You wouldn't even need a
pistol, just break the prick's nose and he'll spill the
number. But the way he screams, you'll have to kill
him afterward.

Slipping back to his seat in the lobby, Chase observed the madam greeting tourists, Wall Street execs, a couple drunk construction workers. He liked the way she never broke form or discriminated.

Fifteen minutes later Jackie walked out with his skin a deep but mottled crimson. His shirt was buttoned up wrong and he wasn't wearing any socks. Behind him came the pudgy businessman, straggling along, in his suit but wearing a completely baffled expression like he didn't know where he was or even who he was anymore.

In a display of generosity, or maybe feeling a need for everyone to suffer equally so they could then commiserate together, Jackie offered to pay for Chase to go get his rocks stomped. Chase declined but tried to look grateful. It wasn't easy.

Jackie curled up on the backseat of the limo and was out cold but wheezing painfully by the time Chase got to the first red light.

*C*essy the cook looked like she'd stepped right off a maple-syrup bottle. She wore a yellow do-rag with white polka dots and even talked with a Southern accent despite the fact that she grew up in the South Bronx. That evening Chase pulled the pickup out of the garage and drove her to the local grocery and helped her shop. She noticed him giving her sidelong glances and stood waiting for him to tell her what was on his mind.

"You gonna talk about it or just keep drinking up all my beauty?" she asked. "You welcome to come close and stare."

He cracked a grin. "Why the hell are you in that getup?"

Looking at him like he was a special child, she told him, "They gotta get what they pay for or I'm out on my fat ass. There's fifty million bitches want my spot, including my three sisters and nineteen cousins and my mama too. I don't give these Langans what they want, I'm gone. When they get you, they get all of

you, they get the very idea of you. You'd be wise to remember that, sugar. They talk about you some now
and again."

"Yeah? What do they say?"

"That Jackie boy, he's loud, he lets everybody
within earshot know his business. Not smart, but sure
does love to shout. You're the best and the worst
driver they ever had. They like you fixing the cars,
and the way you handle yourself behind the wheel,
but you don't wear the hat and you don't belly down
enough. You ain't long for the job, honey."

He was squeezing honeydews making sure they
were ripe. He felt sort of pervy, groping the melons.
"From what I hear nobody's going to be around for
long. The Langans are packing up and moving on,
right? You going with them?"

"There's niggers everywhere. They can find 'em
in Chicago, they don't need to bring their own."

"So what are your plans?"

"Oh, don't you worry about me. There's enough
rich motherfuckers around who can always use another Polish maid or Mexican gardener or black
cook to match the little nigger jockey they got on
their lawns."

"They still got them?"

"Fuck sake, yes! And stop holding them cataloupes
like they your mama's titties, you gonna bring the vice
squad down on us. Anyway, I'll get by better than you
will."

Sometimes you couldn't do anything but nod.

"What are you really doing here?" she asked.

"What do you mean?"

"Oh, baby. I've been married four times. All four are in prison. The same prison. I think they started their own gang in there, they're a big brotherhood. I know trouble whether it's tattooed and carrying a semiautomatic or whether it's got cute brown eyes and a ten-year-old boy's smile."

He put the melons in the cart and there was a hint of a sugary, fresh scent that reminded him of the wind sweeping down from the hills where the moonshiners hid their stills out beyond the cane fields. He'd sometimes tool around with Lila on the back dirt roads and drive her police car after the runners hauling moon through the county. Listening to her voice as she spoke the code numbers into the radio and he'd turn his nose slightly to the open window and breathe in the sweetness.

"What are you doing here, sugar?" Cessy asked again.

"Hoping to save my family."

"That's all any of us is trying to do," she said, then let out a brief but knowing, almost hateful laugh. "If I didn't have five kids to feed, you think I'd be doing this shit, with this rag on my head, dressed in these clothes? But you humble yourself for the cash so you can take care of the ones you love."

He thought, If that's all it took.

He could be humble. He'd learned humility during his straight life. Some, anyway. Working in a garage fixing trucks with three hundred and twenty thousand miles on them. Later in the auto shop teaching eleventh-grade girls how to change their oil, showing them the proper way to change a tire. No action, and not needing it, not wanting it, because he had Lila.

And now with her gone, with no kids, with no home, with no gamble, with no sign of the next exit down the road, his tires spinning on the shoulder in the mud, he was maybe going a little crazy, the dreams getting worse.

His highway led only to one place. He knew he would have to face Jonah, probably for the last time.

He wondered how far he would have to go, how far he would be able to go, in order to save the girl.

One of the three Polish maids, Ivanka, wasn't Polish at all but Romanian. Nobody at the house could tell the difference, and since the Langans were also at war with a local Romanian outfit, she decided to play Polish.

Ivanka had a booming sideline business and wasn't very discreet about it. She was the contact for an illegal Eastern European immigrant ring and seemed to be in charge of setting women up with rich spouses. They paid her well to do so. Sometimes, if they didn't have all the cash up front, Ivanka took payment in the form of children under the age of two and worked the black-market adoption racket.

Chase drove her out to Newark in the stretch and picked up the women. Ivanka offered Chase a big tip as the ladies climbed in. It was a fair wedge of cash in fresh bills. She offered to throw in some sex on top of it. He figured the previous chauffeur had forced her to kick back some of the skim.

He was given his choice of her or any of the new

incoming ladies. There were five of them in the back
of the limo. Four of them looked scared but willing
to do whatever needed to be done. Their expressions were hard but a little hopeful, trying to turn on
the wattage after Christ knows how many hours in
flight and then the tie-up at Customs.

They knew you couldn't take a nap your first
hour in the land of opportunity. They were going to
do just fine here.

The fifth had a sleeping toddler in her arms. Her
thumb wagged across the child's chin in some kind
of a demonstration of love or just an oblivious man-
nerism. The child grinned, had a couple nubby
teeth coming in. The mother was glassy-eyed and
listless.

Chase tried to get her in focus. He wondered if
she was drugged or if she was just getting her feet
under her. Or if they didn't tell the mothers that
they were taking their children from them until after they got off the plane.

"You know," Ivanka said, doing her best to flatten
the heavy accent, "you get some girls back here and
you could make a lot of money. Drive around the
way you do. When the boss is busy. You get your
friends, you find businessmen, a lot of money found
there. And you do nothing but drive, buddy. Easy."

So she did know what had happened to the other
chauffeur. Sounded like she was the one who put the
bug in the guy's ear, urged him to be a pimp, and got
him waxed.

Ivanka wanted to know why they weren't moving

yet. She still had the cash in her hand and was trying
to get Chase to take it through the partition. He
grabbed it. The impatient cabbie fucks who were
lined up behind him started blaring their horns and
screaming at him in unknown languages.

He and Lila could never have a baby. They went
to different specialists for years, but nothing ever
worked. Despite the cold facts and the charts pointing out all the problems in their plumbing, the
promise of a baby was a spark that never died out.

He looked at the girl in back and imagined some
other couple who'd also been given a tour of their
malfunctioning reproductive systems, waiting for
the baby—this very baby—so they could run around
to their friends and family and finally throw off
some of the shame of not being like every other person out there.

Chase stared at the girl and finally she raised her
chin, her eyes dark and lifeless as shale. The kid hiccuped and finally the woman's face registered something. It was pure and almost beautiful in its own
way. The planes of her face folded into pure terror,
and he knew why. The sound the kid made reminded her that she'd never hear her own child's
breathing, or crying, or laughter, or cries of mama
again after today.

Every child had a threefold hook in Chase, re-
minding him of others. The first was his unborn
sibling, the one his mother had lost. The next was
the one he and Lila could never have. The last was

Kylie, waiting for him to take up the burden of raising her with a human warmth Jonah was incapable of.

He threw the limo into drive and gunned it.

Ivanka wanted to be taken to some place on Staten Island first, where three of the women and the baby would be dropped off. He followed her directions, that accent of hers beginning to grate more and more as the others occasionally pointed out the windows and spoke among themselves in Romanian.

He pulled up in front of a high-class one-family home out on Stepleton Hill, where a spectacular view of the Verrazano swelled before them. Chase got out and opened the back door for the ladies fresh from Romania. Their excitement brimmed and they began to giggle and chatter together as they climbed out. The girl with the kid didn't move and Ivanka began to push and shout at the girl and clutch at the child.

Hardly aware of what he was doing Chase reached in back and snapped Ivanka's hold on the toddler, took her easily by the arm, and gently drew her closer.

"You too, Ivy," he said. "Out."

She misread him and thought he wanted to take her up on the sex. Her face hardened. "What is this? You missed your chance, buddy. I make one offer. You do not take me up on it, you lose, buddy."

"I suppose I'll eventually get over my heartbreak," he said. "Out."

"What is this?"

"The Langan family doesn't like sideline businesses being run out of their house," he said. "Or their limo. You're leaving your job. Don't come back to the house. If you do, I'll blow your deal."

Ivanka said, "They know of this business. It is their business!"

"What?"

"It is their business! I am here for them! I only manage. You think I do this on my own? What kind of stupid are you?"

That took him back. He'd been foolish to think the Langans didn't know. Of course they knew. Of course it was their action. Why the hell wouldn't it be? It was probably one of the reasons why the Russians were muscling in on them so much. They wanted to keep a lid on the slave trade of their own people.

Shooting in the dark, he said, "Yeah, but you skim a lot. I tell them how much and you're buried behind Kennedy Airport. Now get out."

"I skim nothing!"

"Bullshit! You skim, baby!"

"You crazy! You crazy man!"

"That's right, I'm crazy man!"

"But the money! I paid!"

"Oh that," he said. "Yeah, I'm keeping it."

"That is two thousand dollars! It is your cut for helping. You do your job. If you do not do your job . . . the Langans . . . Mr. Bishop . . . he will . . ."

"Fuck him."

She tried to scratch at his face, but he caught her wrists and shoved her away. "You rob them? You really are crazy man."

"I rob them. Get out."

"You want to screw me? You want me to go down on you, yes?"

"No."

"You want more money."

"No."

"I give you five hundred more."

"I knew you were skimming, baby!"

"I give you."

"Let me see it."

She dug around and came up with another five bills. He held his hand out and she forked it over.

He pocketed the cash. "I just told you I was a thief, lady. Get out."

Stunned, Ivanka's eyes widened as she realized what had happened. An animal noise started low in her chest and made her lips flap. She turned to the girl, who hadn't reacted at all yet, but her eyes seemed to be filling up again, returning to life. The kid cooed.

"You want Mara, yes? I see the way you watch her, buddy. She make you a good wife, for as long as you like. When you tire of her, there will be another."

"Get out."

"Ah, the child. You want the baby."

"Lady, shut up and get the fuck out now."

When Ivanka made a brusk gesture to the girl, Chase said, "She's staying."

"Ah, you do like her, yes? So we can do business. I will give her to you, no charge."

"We can't do business. If I see you again, I'll blow the whistle. I'll tell them ten women and three babies came in."

"It is lie!"

"Yeah, it is lie, but they've got a lot on their minds and I bet they're not checking up on you the way they should. If they did, they'd find you were taking off the top. Get out. Go work for the Romanians."

She gave him the death glare. She was pretty good at it, but not nearly as good as some guys on the strings he'd worked.

Chase looked at her and she finally climbed out. "You are dead. You are dead man. I have brothers, cousins. I have many boyfriends. I do not forget this."

"You shouldn't. It will make you a better citizen."

"You are not long for life," she told him and started to grin.

"Who is?"

Chase had no idea what to do with Mara or the baby. He asked her if she spoke English but she only stared at him blankly. She must've thought he was the next broker in line, ready to steal her kid and sell her to a fatcat. Or take her home and make her do his laundry and clean his bathroom before raping her.

He called the Deuce. "Did you know the Langans traded in Eastern European women and babies?"

"They're a syndicate. What, you think they're building children's hospitals and going into AIDS research? There's only so many scams in the world, and the top ones are still drugs and flesh peddling. The family's got their fingers in those pies, same as every other outfit."

"You know anybody who's Romanian?"

"You working with them now?" Deuce asked. "They're goddamn rough. They've been through genocide, those people, the real thing with death camps, you know. Secret police, assassination-squad shit. There's not much that fuckin' spooks them any-more."

"I'm seeing that. So you know anyone?"

"Mobbed up?"

"No. Just somebody who can speak the language. Help an immigrant girl and her baby get settled in the States and out of the life."

"Most of them do porn," the Deuce said. "It's a hot item, guys banging these chicks who can barely speak English but got that nice pale look to them. They're so goddamn happy to be out of a freezing country and in Southern California, they do double anals, the whole gonzo shebang. Or they do the Web site thing. You go in a chat room and tell them what you want and they do it right there, live on the webcams. You say, 'Lift your legs wider, I want to see beaver' and they do it. Mooks ordering them around from a safe distance, their wives in the other room bitching about the broken dishwasher. Guys like that." It took him a couple seconds to add, "So they tell me."

"Uh huh. So anybody who can help?"

"These Romanian people I know, they live down the block from my mother. Good folks, been here in Jersey a long time, but they still got ties. I used to cut their lawn when I was a kid. In '79 they got a Pontiac LeMans that I nabbed for a night. Took my girl-friend to the drive-in. She gave me a blowjob while Kirk and Spock and some bald chick tracked down the Voyager module."

Chase said, "I'm hoping these people never

caught wise to the stains on their leather interior and they'd still be willing to help you."

"Yeah, sure, they'll do what they can, they've set up relatives before. But the old man's retired and they live on his pension. They're not going to be able to pay her freight."

"I've got twenty-five hundred to give them to get a head start until she finds a job and a place to live."

"That'll help a little. You're giving money away now?"

"Give me the address then call them."

Deucie gave him the address and said, "Who is this girl?"

"I don't know. Just somebody in trouble."

"Since when is that your problem? Aren't you supposed to be robbing the family instead?"

"I've got time to do both," Chase said.

"Anything else?"

"Yeah, see if you can find Jonah."

"I thought you'd split with him after what happened."

"Just see if you can track him down."

"Scoring the Langans, dealing with your grandfather again, it's not good business, kid. Listen to me, you don't have to do any of this. Come on in, I can give you a nice safe job, something that won't be so rough for you. I can use another good man with your skills."

"I think I want to see this thing through."

"It's all about being on the edge, right? You think your wife would want this for you? You think—"

Chase hung up.

Mara had started to nod off. She'd snap her chin up and murmur in Romanian and tremble as she became aware of her surroundings. Her body jerked as if being pricked with needles. She caught Chase's gaze in the rearview and gave him a true death glare. There it was, the real thing. No anger, no wanting, just bottomless human emptiness.

The baby hiccuped. The woman unbuttoned her blouse and began to breast-feed her child, who sucked greedily. She looked out the window with stagnant eyes, and every so often she'd run her hand over the sleeping baby's hair, plucking at it, curling it around her fingers the way Lila used to do with Chase's after they'd made love.

The dead owned him.

The dead would always find a way to make him listen. The threefold hook twisted deep. Blood mattered, even if it wasn't his own.

Lila said to him, Never let your heart dim, love.

Sometime after the moon had risen, with the severe gray light rolling in across the bed like foam drifting by the Asbury Park pier, Chase came awake to find a .44 pressed to his forehead, Bishop standing there giving the friendly smile.

"So what's this for?" Chase asked.

"You're not even worried?"

"Not much." Chase tried to sit up but Bishop exerted pressure, holding his head down to the pillow. Chase very slowly reached out and pressed the gun aside, liking the way Bishop's eyes went wide like he couldn't believe Chase wasn't just going to lie there. He must've had nothing but easy kills lately. "If you were going to ace me, you'd do it on the ground floor so you wouldn't have to carry my body two flights."

Raising the pistol, Bishop rubbed the side of the barrel across his chin, lulling himself like a child with a blanket, loving the feel of contained murder.

You couldn't do much with guys like this. Money

was only a part of their action. They didn't get thrills the way everybody else did. Their juice was hard-wired in the God complex.

Studying Chase, Bishop pursed his lips, really trying to see who was in front of him. Chase didn't like the look.

Bishop said, "No, that's not it at all. You're hoping someone will do it. You're a snuff case."

"You're trying to slur me? You nearly creamed your pants touching that Magnum the other day." Chase swung his legs over the edge of the bed. "You pop people for pay. I think I'd hold my own against you at Sunday morning mass."

That got an earnest laugh out of Bishop. "What happened to the last load?"

"The last load?"

"The women. You came back empty-handed. Where's Ivanka? Where's the women? The kid?"

"I dropped them off in Staten Island, like she said."

"They checked in but didn't stay. Where'd they go?"

"How's that my problem?"

"If I say it's your problem, it is."

"Then don't say it."

Dust in the moonlight looked like swirling snow drifting around them. The room a little cold now because Chase had left the window open and Bishop had left the door open when he sneaked in. Chase wondered how long he'd been in the room, watching him sleep, savoring his urge toward murder.

"Where are the women?"

That smile was really getting to Chase. He thought he might have to needle Bishop some, see if he could draw blood. "I sent them back."

"What?"

"I sent them back home. I hate these loose immigration laws. The Mexicans and Norwegians and the Irish and all those Biafrans. They all come over and steal American jobs, put the workingman on welfare, and like that. So in the name of American values, I sent them back."

"You want it, don't you? You want it right in the head."

Stone killer eyes and flashing teeth in the silver moonshine. Chase hadn't met many hitters, but those he'd come across were just like Bishop. They liked to have a little fun before pulling the trigger. Liked to talk. These guys who were paid to kill, sometimes they'd buy their marks a beer first, pretend to meet them in a bar, get to know them a little. Spend a night talking about wives and kids and almost become friends with the patsy before putting two in the back of his head. Maybe it was instinct, a cat playing with a dying pigeon. Chase didn't know what it was all about, but he wasn't about to accept a beer from Bishop.

"Who are you working for?" Bishop asked.

"You people."

"Did you deal yourself in? Did you score the merchandise?"

"Black-market babies aren't a score," he said. "And they're not merchandise."

"You don't think so? It's a hundred-million-dollar-a-year industry."

The two of them now in the dark, the wind rising outside in the frigid predawn, draft floating by, the house creaking and settling. Somewhere a television was playing, the electrical hum of it working through the walls. Chase heard gruff asshole comments and low canned laughter beaming in.

"How old are you?" Bishop asked. "Twenty-five, six? But you've been in the life for a while, it's written right into you. That might mean your parents were on the grift, except you toss around terms like 'strongarm.' So maybe not your parents, more likely a grandfather. Took you on the bend early. You've been at this for a long time. But what are you doing here? If you're a driver, you ought to be crewed up with bank heisters, stickup men."

Chase was impressed as hell that Bishop had been able to glean all that and hit so close to home. A killer with acumen. The guy only had Chase's fake ID but maybe he'd cracked it, had asked around and found out Chase's real name, his story. That would be bad news. It would back Chase into a corner. He liked the idea that he could always fade back into his own life if he ever needed to. Not that it seemed likely to happen.

"You don't get charming conversation like this with stickup men," Chase said. "You've got to go all the way up to the big hitters if you want to chat about stealing babies from their mothers."

"Jackie said you liked to talk back."

Bishop brought the barrel of the .44 down hard on Chase's bad shoulder.

Red, pulsating agony swarmed Chase's brain, but he somehow managed to swallow down a scream. The torn muscle hadn't healed yet and the hole, poorly stitched in the first place, had remained constantly infected. He felt hot fluid pulse down his back.

Thrashing across the bed, Chase swept his hand out as if to prop himself in place, but he was actually going for the switchblade under the pillow. He'd felt a little stupid putting it there, the weight of it pressing against the side of his face while he tried to sleep, but he was glad for it now. Of course, if he'd really been smart, he would've slept with the 9mm under the pillow, instead of leaving it in the gym bag at the back of the closet. He thought he'd have to somehow get over his hatred of guns.

Bishop was still talking. "I saw that someone was using the bandages in the bathroom up here. So, you do like to tussle, huh? That a bullet wound? You got some mean friends someplace?"

"Don't we all?" Chase said through gritted teeth.

He popped the blade thinking, I have to be fast.

In a short, direct arc he slammed the point of the knife into Bishop's wrist, turned it hard, and slashed up the arm.

Blood lunged in a short fountain. Bishop let out a

laugh, the prick. You really had to worry about the
guys who had fun when you hurt them. The knife
hit the floor. The .44 fell on the mattress and gave a
short bounce. Chase made a grab for it but Bishop
elbowed him aside, leaving a swathe of blood down
Chase's T-shirt. Before the pistol could hit the bed
again, Bishop made a snatch for it with his left
hand. He wasn't as good with that one, Chase noticed, but he was still damn fine. He caught the gun
and started to turn and point.

Chase chopped him with a left hook under the
heart. Bishop coughed up another laugh while Chase
swallowed a shout, his damaged fingers flaring. The
blow should've slowed Bishop down but it didn't, and
the .44 continued to come around. The blood swept
with it, a black pumping spray that splashed Chase's
chin and made him think of the parking-lot show-
down with Earl Raymond, seeing Earl's head exploding in the Roadrunner, all the weeping red on the
inside of the windshield.

Focus, Jonah said, or you're dead.

Going in tight, Chase snapped his forearm up
against Bishop's elbow, shoving the gun away again.
He clamped his hand down on Bishop's wounded
wrist and squeezed, digging his fingernails into the
gash and listening to the slup of running blood
washing over his own knuckles. Bishop didn't laugh
this time. Good. Chase kicked out with his right leg
trying to catch the hitter in the groin, but Bishop
had started to back away, dragging Chase along. He
tried to stomp Chase's left foot, doing it the right

way close to the instep, just like Chase had done to the thug the other day, but in the dark Bishop missed and caught Chase on the big toe. It hurt like fuck-all, but the only thing that mattered now was trying to get the gun.

All of this but Bishop wasn't calling to anybody else in the house. He wanted to take care of it himself.

Chase hooked too wide with his right and Bishop stepped inside and head-butted him. He'd been going for Chase's nose but instead caught his chin. Chase's teeth snapped together painfully and he felt a small sliver of his tongue come off as his mouth filled with blood. He turned and spit and the .44 was in his face again, the moonshine glinting off the highly polished metal.

Lila said, Love, and Jonah said, You idiot, you never should've stabbed him in the hand, you should've gone for his throat.

When the old man was right he was right, and there was nothing you could do.

Blood oozed across his lips.

Backing toward the door, Bishop reholstered the pistol and said, "Don't worry about anything. I like you, I really do. Maybe you didn't have anything to do with the merchandise, maybe you did. I'll find out. We'll settle up then. I'll even save you some bandages in the bathroom up the hall, okay?" He grabbed his leaking wrist with his good hand, the smile glowing. "Hey, how about if we go out for a beer sometime?"

At eleven in the morning, the phone rang and the same voice that Chase didn't recognize told him he was to drive Miss Sherry to her theater group, which would be meeting at the Winter Garden Theatre on Broadway in Manhattan. Like Chase might get it confused with another Winter Garden Theater on another Broadway in a different town.

He was stiff as hell and the right arm was mostly useless. So was the left hand. The retaped fingers had turned a nasty purple. The piece of tongue he'd nipped off had been from the side and didn't seem to bother him much. He could talk fine and still managed to eat a late breakfast.

Cessy saw his pain and said, "I got aspirin."

"I think I need something a little stronger."

"I got that too," she told him, and left the kitchen to return with an unlabeled bottle of huge white pills. "Take two or three of these now. Don't take any more for at least four, maybe six hours, then you can have another two. No more than that tonight.

They'll mellow you out and take away the hurt, but you'll still be able to think clearly and drive as fine as ever."

"Thanks."

She never mentioned what they were and he didn't ask. She looked at his fingers and said, "You wrapped them too tight. They must really hurt if you couldn't tell. They'll go numb and fall off." He popped the pills and swallowed them down with a glass of milk while she cut the tape off. "You don't even have on any splints. What's the matter with you? You need a doctor, but I'll do what I can."

"I appreciate it. And while you're fixing me up I'll be able to drink in more of your beauty."

She got out more tape and bound his fingers together much better than he'd been able to do. It made him feel odd, being mothered by her, with the goofy getup on, the polka-dotted do-rag.

"Can you get me something else?"

"What?"

"Antibiotics."

"For what?"

"A wound that doesn't close."

"Let me see."

Chase took off his suit jacket, shirt, tie, and T-shirt. Cessy carefully peeled away the bandages and pulled a face when she got a look at the seeping gunshot wound. She probed it, and he grimaced and hissed through his teeth. She looked at the other recent damage, the pink scars and the purplish marks where the drains had been put in and taken out again. Another bullet had taken him in the right side beneath the ribs and deflated his lung. The spiderweb of mottled tissue was courtesy of Earl Raymond's sister, Ellie, who hadn't gone down easy. Raymond's whole crew had been hard.

Washing her hands in the sink, Cessy said, "I didn't know it was that bad. Take another two pills. I've got some speed, it'll counteract the effects. Asking for antibiotics is like asking for medicine. There's all different kinds for different troubles. I've seen plenty of gunshot wounds before, but nobody's going to be able to help you if you keep tearing it open. Man who sewed you up the first time did a shitty job."

"He was a safe doctor up near the Harlem River, a cokehead burnout. I saw catgut in the bathroom down the hall from me. Can you use it?"

"I can use it."

He opened his wallet and laid a couple hundred dollars on the table. She snatched it up and tucked it away in her apron.

"See what you can do about those antibiotics too."

"I'll make some calls."

He had a large cup of coffee and drank it slowly. It reminded him of getting into the auto shop early before the kids arrived for their first class. He'd sit there staring at a couple of cars with their engines in pieces, a chalkboard full of notes behind him, and a Styrofoam cup of coffee in front of him steaming in the frigid room. The same as garages, high-school auto shops were always cold, the metal shutters never sealing properly, the cinder-block walls holding in the chill. He'd sip his coffee and wait for the first bell. The kids walking in chattering about trivial matters that weren't trivial at all. He'd never been to school and still had a romanticized notion of what it must be like, the rich complexities of such rituals. Learning about life side by side with hundreds of your peers instead of being on the grift at ten, climbing into people's bedroom windows and boosting their watches and silverware.

Cessy returned with the catgut and another bottle of pills. The amphetamines were black, which surprised him. He'd always thought they were red. He took two more painkillers and popped two uppers. He was worried about what it might do to his system.

Swabbing his shoulder and sewing him up, Cessy muttered to herself. "Only met a few like you in my time. Quiet but carrying thick scars. Mostly I know gangbangers, drug dealers, and pimps. They're up front with their action. Same as the hoods around here. But you, you live a different kind of life, don't you."

Not asking a question.

"Where's your family at?" she asked.

"I don't know. After this I need to go find them."

"You wear a wedding band on those broken fingers. Where's your wife?"

"Dead."

Cessy let out a slow, lengthy breath. "Sugar, don't you think that—"

Chase said, "What do you know about Bishop?"

She took a second to answer. "He likes to walk around with blood on his clothes."

Before hitting the estate garages, Chase scoped Jackie's office and some of the other rooms again. He tried to find out where Sherry Langan was really running the show from, but it had to be the third floor, where Lenny was dying and his wife and some other old ladies were always coming and going.

There had to be loose cash around. People like this, they might just as soon hide it in a closet as in a safe. Thugs passed him in the corridors. Chase realized he probably should've gone about this another way. Get a string together. Two or three other second-floor men. Walk in right under everyone's noses, climb through the house checking every drawer and shelf and cupboard, just stick a gun to Jackie's temple and make him cough up the combo. Walk out while the rest of the mooks were out putting on the ninth hole.

But Chase was still on the edge, trapped between two lives. He didn't want to call anybody in. He didn't want to have to draw down on the boss. He didn't know what he was going to do next. The three-prong hook was holding him in place as much as it was tugging him out of his shoes.

Chase was sweating and his hands trembled. The drugs in his system hadn't found a balance yet. He felt light-headed and antsy, but at least all the pain was gone for the first time in weeks. He fought for focus. He checked his watch. He had to get ready to drive Sherry to her theater group, and who the hell knew what that was really all about.

On his way to the limo, Moe Irvine stopped him. "You're late. Miss Sherry is waiting."

"Sorry about that."

"You're not wearing the hat and gloves. I've been giving you some leeway because you're new here, but your attitude hasn't improved any."

"I saw what happened to your last chauffeur. Let's say I'm not feeling all that comfortable here yet."

That slow-burning anger leaking around Moe's eyes wasn't so slow today. Moe had problems on his hands. He knew the business was skittering out of his grasp. The number two man was going to have to hand over too much to Lenny's kids and Lenny still wouldn't drop off the cliff.

"I was informed about some trouble last night in the servants' quarters," Moe said.

Actually calling them that, the servants' quarters.

Chase said, "I didn't hear anything."

"And you weren't involved?"

"I do what I can to steer clear of trouble."

"It doesn't appear that way to me."

"But you're just getting to know me, Moe."

Moe stared at the stickpin he'd given Chase, like he wanted it back, didn't want it to go to waste in the landfill. "Miss Sherry is waiting."

"Yeah, you said that."

Chase got the limo backed out and turned around in the driveway, then smoothly sailed up to Sherry, who was waiting out front in the Jacqueline O's. A few strongarms paced around, acting tougher than usual, sort of squabbling with each other. They were trying to get a little more territorial now—show their stuff and hopefully get picked to go to Chicago.

Chase opened the back door for Sherry, and when she took his hand she held on to it for an extra second, full of intent.

The painkillers were starting to override the bennies. He felt a flat, heavy mellowness work through him. The heat at the back of his head began to cool. He thought he should take another upper to get back some of his step, but for the first time in weeks he was relaxed. Maybe it wasn't so bad. Maybe he should go with it for a couple hours.

Traffic was heavier than normal but he used the limo's intimidation factor to carve access into loaded lanes. He slid the stretch toward the Holland Tunnel again, waiting for her to say something. She didn't. She appeared as calm as ever, but he kept picking up some extra vibe. He didn't know what it was. It drew his eyes to the rearview time and again, but he couldn't see anything different.

Except maybe the vein in her throat. It throbbed. She was in a state, but didn't show it in her expression.

So much for the mellow. He popped another bennie dry. The serene veil that had draped over him immediately shredded and fell away. His heart bucked in his chest.

Jonah said, She's going to kill you.

* * *

Sherry made herself a drink and sipped it, crossed her legs and balanced the glass on her knee. Her skirt hiked back a little farther than it should, showing off the elegant and elaborate network of muscles leading to her thigh.

"Why are you here?" she said.

Maybe the truth—some of the truth—would be best. "I got a call that the Langan family needed a driver. A wheelman. Turns out that's not who you needed at all."

"Why didn't you just quit when you found that out?"

"It was too late by then."

She clicked her nails against the glass. It wasn't much of a tell, but he could see she needed to do something while she worked through her thoughts. The Jacqueline O's stymied him. He wasn't going to get much more from her measured gaze, but even that was better than plastic.

"Take off your shades," he said.

She turned her head to stare out the tinted window for a moment, considering. Then she took them off.

"Maybe we can use you in some other capacity," she said.

"You've got too big a crew as it is."

"What makes you say that?" she asked.

"Wiseguys playing golf on the job, for starters. Everyone knows the Chicago setup will be smaller.

Most of the strongarms will be skipping out on you
soon. They're afraid of looking weak to the other
outfits. So they'll be badmouthing you when they
jump. It'll cause you trouble when you get to Chi, so
many of your own people disparaging you."

"We're working on avoiding all of that."

"I'm sure. But you should tell Bishop to quit ad-
vertising his messes. Brains on your tie doesn't earn
you points, it just shows you're careless about foren-
sic evidence."

That got to her. Sherry Langan's eyes flared for
an instant. Chase got a primeval kind of joy out of it.

They entered the darkness of the Holland Tunnel
and Chase came back to himself, aware that he was
driving a little slow for the pace of the place. Funny
it should be like that. The amphetamines raging, his
blood slamming through his body, the taxis crowding him, cops and Army everywhere as they crossed
over toward Manhattan, and he didn't even have the
hammer down. The last time they'd done this she'd
pressed the cold gunmetal against his neck. He
headed north to the theater district.

Sherry made eye contact in the mirror and said,
"I want you."

"You want me to what," Chase said.

"I want *you*," she repeated, and Chase got it as she
slipped off her panties over her high heels and
tossed them onto the bar.

He thought, Oh shit.

It wasn't a display of lust so much as a demonstration of power. She owned a lot, and she thought she

owned him. "Come on," she said, "park it and get in back with me. Let me pour you a drink."

He looked around at the foot traffic. Little old ladies dragging ass and pulling carts with their stockings rolled down to their ankles. Quick-stepping tourists trying to look worldly. Long Island housewives in for a day of shopping.

These Langans, they really did like to do things fast and out in the open. "What about your theater group?"

"They're a bunch of fatcat tristate politicians' wives. My father always said you had to put in your time pursuing irrelevant activities with those you needed. It gives them a sense of honest bonding."

"Like golf."

"Exactly."

"Maybe they hate it just as much as you do."

"Of course they do. Those wives despise each other, and me, as much as I do them. It's all very foolish, despite its self-serving mainstay."

"I suppose you don't find it culturally stimulating."

"Why are you still talking?"

Lila had loved the theater. They'd tried to hit the city every couple months to take in a show—not just the musicals, but the classic plays. Chase had a fondness for Ibsen and Brecht, but you could never catch one of his pieces anywhere on Broadway. You had to go way off off and sit in a small theater of ninety seats and watch how it used to be done a hundred years ago. Up close and without an orchestra. No dancing cats, no movie stars slumming until their agents set up the next major deal. Lila would hold his hand in the dark and he'd press her palm to the side of his face.

"I said to park it," Sherry told him.

"You can afford the penthouse at the Ritz and you want to make it in the back of a Chrysler on 38th Street?"

"Yes," Sherry said. "I like the limo. I like it dirty and I like it on the streets. It's where the action and gamble is. I want you to shove my face against the window, so I can watch them go by out there while you fuck me from behind."

So that was her juice. This lady, Chase thought, she had a lot of demands. "You must get interrupted by a lot of meter maids."

"Why are we still talking? Get back here with me."

He wondered if Bishop had told her about the missing women. He wondered if Sherry was only turned on because she was planning to send Bishop after him and was sniffing the death scent.

"Sorry," he said. "I'm married."

"Who gives a damn about that?"

"She would."

"She's not here."

He wanted to tell her, Sure, she is, she's always here, but Lila was talking, saying to him, Sweetness, you need to get a move on here, no more of this lollygagging, there's a little girl waiting for you to pluck her out of an evil man's hands.

"You're not going to fuck me?" Sherry Langan

asked. Color bloomed in her cheeks. She didn't look shocked or surprised or even angry, just a touch puzzled and maybe a little bruised in that spoiled rich girl not getting everything she wanted way. He knew that what he was seeing in her face wasn't the truth. He knew she would harbor a deep resentment now that only blood could clear away.

"I'm not going to fuck you. You want to talk about Ibsen I can prep you a little. You'll wow the fatcat politicians' wives."

He'd made another mistake. He couldn't blame the pills. She'd even warned him. Don't screw with someone's conceit.

Now he knew one of her secrets—that's the thing, they have a way of exposing themselves. She didn't get off on good old hot sex. She wanted it dirty and with the rest of the world going by, staring into a crowd who didn't know she was there.

Now she wouldn't be satisfied until he was dead with her teeth in his throat.

It was going to come down fast now. His self-imposed time limit of two weeks was nearly gone, and the score was no closer to being in his hand. He'd made enemies of the head of the family and her right-hand hitter. He might just have to rob Sherry's jewelry box in the middle of the night and be done with it.

Ten o'clock the next morning, Cessy brought him the antibiotics and more painkillers. He paid her another c-note and she said, "I labeled the bottle myself, with instructions. Follow them. If that shoulder doesn't close up in the next few days, you need to get to a real doctor, not some crackhead."

"Thanks for your help."

"You don't look good. You're pale." She went down the hall to the bathroom and came back with a wet hand towel. She washed his face and ran it over his sweaty hair. "You've got a fever."

"I'll be okay."

"You take care of yourself. And when you do

whatever it is you're planning to do, just don't blow up the kitchen. Not while I'm in it, anyways." She smiled, going for the big mama loves her chillun act, but it ended abruptly. "Don't get lazy. These people seem ludicrous to street hustlers like us, but they hold on to their hatred and they never let up. They got nothing to do in life but cause others pain."

An hour later, while Chase finished fine-tuning the Ferrari and stood there deciding whether he wanted to escape with the suit or not, a convoy of town cars and SUVs came roaring onto the estate.

The doctors had told the family to make any last calls because Lenny wasn't going to make it through the day. Wiseguys from all over the place showed up to Judas kiss each other on the cheeks—goombahs and blue bloods hugging it out, just waiting to clip each other and take the Langans' East Coast pie.

A big catered lunch was served while Lenny sucked in his last breaths. People wailed all over the house. The family wasn't Italian but these people sure knew how to act out their grief the way the Sicilians did. Every so often a few of them came outside to have a smoke and hand each other envelopes. The ME rolled Lenny away by one o'clock and the fleet vanished out the gates following the body.

That very afternoon the Langans began to liquidate Lenny's possessions. Neither Jackie nor Sherry put much of a premium on antiques, and they considered anything over ten years old a relic. All day long appraisers came in and checked out the furniture, the crystal, the artwork.

Then the wiseguys all went out back and played a few holes of golf. All the crying was out of their system. Lenny's demise got them two under par. Chase watched the Langan crew start packing up the necessities for their eventual move.

Smoothing a blue ascot, Jackie strolled out to the garage and said to Chase, "I need you to take me to the city this afternoon."

"Sorry to hear about your father."

"Thanks. Not like we didn't have time to get ready. Better this than watching him lie there goddamn brain-dead, turning yellow as his kidneys shut down, tubes up his nose and down his throat and in his ass."

Chase had nothing to say to that.

"Anyway, I need to get out of here and straighten my head out for a while," Jackie said.

"Back to the massage parlor?" Chase asked.

Jackie bristled at the words but there wasn't much else you could call the place. "Yeah, I need to get my ashes hauled. My old man, he told me that when his father died he went to Vegas for a weekend, lost eighty g's, snorted a pound of coke, and fucked nine chink hookers, including a couple sisters."

"The heart wants what it wants," Chase said.

Jackie glanced over and saw that the Spyder had its hood open. "Are you still fucking with my Ferrari?"

"Yes."

"You don't learn, do you? Why are you still messing with my car?"

"To get it to do what it was meant to do. Get in."

"What?"

"It's finished. Let's take it out and I'll show you what it can do."

"My father's dead."

"Yeah, I know. Get in. We'll take a cruise, in his memory."

"What?" Jackie didn't know what to do or say. "But—"

"All the antiques will still be here when we get back."

"But—"

Chase wasn't sure Jackie was going to go for it, but without his thugs around, he seemed more pliable, eager for acceptance. He was also probably a little more broken up about his father's death than he'd ever understand himself. Chase reached out and pulled the ascot off Jackie's neck and said, "Come on, it'll help you unwind." Before they left, Chase smeared mud across the plates.

He wanted to feel the miles whip by. It had been too long since he'd been in charge of some real horsepower. Chase knew he was making another mistake, but the heart wants what it wants.

He decided to open it up a little on the way to Newark, down to Avenue P, where the cops had been fighting a losing battle against street racing for years. It was still early evening but there was muscle all over. GTOs, souped Mustangs, Vettes with some reinforced bodywork. The air was already thick with nitrous. Chase knew Jackie had never opened her up. He eased on the gas and let his guts lead him through the machine, inch by inch into the engine, feeling the vibrations deep within.

Forget the skinny Jap chicks kicking the fuck out of your vertebrae, this was the way to get loose and get laid. His nuts were heating up. Jackie stuck his arms out against the dashboard like he expected to hit a wall any second. He was keeping up a steady line of chatter but Chase tuned him out and kicked it higher, up to seventy, eighty, ninety, the road wide and endless ahead of him.

Drivers had been wiping out here for years, kids a lot younger than him, old men looking to get back their hipness, their sweet spots. Chase hit triple digits and Jackie let out a whine like a hurt dog. He flinched and writhed in the passenger seat. Maybe Chase had been thrown off his game by driving the goddamn limo. If he hadn't been so out of it he would've realized he needed muscle to really get better.

Two cop cruisers picked them up just as Chase made a screaming left turn. Other cars flashed their lights and honked in support. The cops flipped a bitch and came roaring up behind him. Jackie looked hypnotized and started to hyperventilate.

Lenny had probably owned DAs, judges, and congressmen, but Jackie was afraid of a speeding ticket. No wonder his sister was taking over the empire.

Chase played tag with the cruisers all around Newark. Two staties joined in as he headed north up US 1 & 9, angling for Palisades Park and ripping toward Fort Lee. The Jersey Turnpike flattened out ahead and dumped traffic right into the heart of the city. Chase punched it and zagged among street-crawling suburbia. No matter how fast your car is or how big a head start you have on the cops, you can't lose them on straightaways. You need to turn off and creep around some burg, get lost among your neighbors.

Jackie kept leaving himself and then coming back. His eyes rolled in terror and then focused, and then immediately unfocused again. Sherry had called it— *It's what they fear most. Being forced to face up to their own charade, their weakness exposed*. Jackie was scared of his own car, of what it represented on the road.

"Stop!" Jackie screamed. "Jesus Christ, stop it! Pull over!"

"You want to give yourself over to the cops?" Chase asked.

"You're going to crack us up!"

"You haven't been paying attention. Aren't you impressed with how the car handles?"

"Who the fuck cares about that now!"

"You should."

"They'll get the plates!"

"No, they won't. Jackie, didn't you ever get into any trouble when you were a kid?"

"Christ, not like this!"

"That's why you're a mark."

Jackie wasn't listening anymore. There were more Jersey cruisers around now, sirens and lights giving a nice background bloom of noise and color, trying to box Chase in. He headed to the Bridge Plaza, sped onto the Palisades, and weaved in and out of the traffic coming off 9W. One hot-dog statie hung with him for longer than the others, but Chase shook him by slicing across a shopping-center parking lot, slowing down enough so that soccer moms in SUVs could pull out around him, clogging the aisles so the trooper got gridlocked even with his siren and lights on. You could always count on the ladies not to look in their rearviews when they wanted to get home to start dinner.

When Jackie next came out of his stupor he looked around expecting cops everywhere and saw none. He let out a chuckle and relaxed in his seat as Chase dropped to forty-five, swung back on the Palisades, then leisurely took the next exit and drove back roads toward the Langan home.

"Holy shit," Jackie said, reaching around like he wanted his two ice cubes, his Vicks Vapo-Rub, teakwood sandals, anything to fill his hand and his neediness. "You got away."

"It's what I do, Jackie."

"I can see that. You're good, you're really fucking good. But you're crazy, you rotten prick. You're supposed to be taking care of me. I finally got my inheritance, you think I want to join my old man in the ground?"

But when they drew up to the gates of the estate, Jackie was smiling so wide he looked deranged. It wasn't a whole lot better than the lemon out of somebody's asshole look. "That was really something else. What you did with my car. Jesus."

"When you said you needed a driver, this is what I thought you wanted."

Confusion set in, Jackie's eyes wide, still smiling like he was punch-drunk. "But why would I want anybody to do that?"

The phone call came in half an hour later on Chase's phone, the butler's voice—or whoever it was—telling him in haughty tones that Mr. Langan would be driving into the city for a chiropractic appointment.

Uh huh. By the time Jackie was ready to start off for the Japanese massage parlor, he'd gotten into a nice, cool funky groove. He came out of the house grinning and clapped one of his thugs on the arm, even tried making a bit of small talk. His cheeks were still a little flushed and he kept running one hand through his hair, tugging at tufts like he could still feel his scalp crawling.

In the limo he asked a lot of questions about driving. He wanted to know specifically what Chase had done to the Ferrari. He came close to apologizing for ordering the brawl on the first day but didn't

quite do it. Jackie had a compadre now. Chase wondered if he'd be bumped up to strongarm or whatever the hell these people called their main crew.
There might be time to hang around and figure out
what happened to the cash that came in and somehow jug the safe.

Turning off of Houston, double-parking in front
of the massage parlor so Jackie could get his spine
snapped and de-stress from his father's death,
Chase's cell rang. Jackie returned to form and said,
"Hey, no private calls while you're—"

Chase answered. It was the Deuce. "I might have
a line on your grandfather."

A homeless guy with a spritz bottle moved out
from behind a couple trash cans across the street
and started staggering over.

"Can't talk any more right now, Deuce," Chase
said. "There's a hit going down."

The Langan shooters had been having so much luck the last couple months that they'd gotten a touch sophisticated and more than a little sloppy. You always came out fast and blasting, it was the only way to do it. But they were taking time to have a little fun now, getting slick. Maybe because they were making a move on the head of the family.

Chase watched the squeegee man shuffle across the street with a spritz bottle. There hadn't been a squeegee guy in New York since before 9-11, when Rudy Giuliani promised to get the homeless off the streets. Who knows what the hell he did with them, but the squeegee guys had been gone for years.

Chase recognized the hitters from around the house. Young turks trying to make their bones, thinking too much and making a game of it. They should've just walked up with converted automatics and sprayed the car.

Better yet, Bishop should've taken care of it himself. He must've been worried about the politics of

the hit, even though it had to be obvious to everybody that Jackie was a dead man. Sherry stepping
up was the right thing to do, but still, the wiseguys
had a thing about openly whacking one of their own
family members. Just because Pacino did it didn't
mean everybody else could. If you did it, you had to
do it quietly. You had to act like it was breaking your
heart. Had to hire out, bring people in from another
country who didn't speak English. Otherwise it
looked bad to the other outfits.

But dressing in costume? Chase could just imagine this guy with a pad and pencil writing notes
to himself on the perfect way to ambush a limo.
Drawing pictures of himself wearing different dis-
guises, fake noses, beards, yarmulkes.

Chase watched him shuffle step by step toward
the windshield of the Super Stretch. In the movies, it
was always the shoes that gave the bad guy away.
Walking through a hospital wearing the lab coat and
a stethoscope plugging his ears, and he's got muddy
black boots on.

But the squeegee guy wore scuffed shoes, had a
black plastic trash bag with holes cut out for his head
and arms. He was playing the part too well. Only the
schizophrenics on antipsychotics wear trash bags,
and then only when it was raining. This one, he had
his spritz bottle out, and Chase noticed a flash off his
finger.

The hitter had a pinkie ring on. Chase had
shaken his hand once and felt the bulge of that
thing. Probably worn it for so many years that he

couldn't get it off anymore no matter how much butter or cold cream he slathered around it. It was a diamond setting, he'd just twisted it around to face the diamond the other way, pointing toward his palm. But the sun still picked it up.

Acting on Sherry's orders, Bishop would have told the guy the windshield was bulletproof. But the windows all rolled down, which meant they were regular safety glass. He tried to figure out who would bother to take half measures like that? What was the point? Like a torpedo was only going to stand right in front of your headlights and try to—

Chase shut his eyes for a moment, not the smartest thing to do under the circumstances, but he was seeing Earl Raymond's head exploding inside the Roadrunner again.

One of the ugliest images Chase had stuck in his skull, but the one that he got the most pleasure from prodding.

His stomach tightened. The 9mm was still at the back of his closet. Okay, he could deal. Chase clicked the lock button just as Jackie tried to get out of the back.

"Hey," Jackie said, the whine already in his voice. "What are you doing?"

"Buckle up."

"What?"

"Hold tight."

"What?"

From what Chase knew, and admittedly it wasn't a lot, these dips worked in teams. He waited for another squeegee guy to appear—attack of the fucking windshield-washer panhandlers—but he didn't spot anyone else nearby who might be in on the hit.

The torpedo reached under his plastic bag into his waistband and Chase punched the gas, wrenched the wheel away from the curb, and knocked the guy down. The gun went off before it flew from the shooter's hand, sounded like a .32.

Jackie instantly panicked. "What? What's going on!"

"Somebody's trying to ice you."

"Well, Christ . . . don't let them!"

While the shooter was down in the street, Chase stomped the pedal and ran over the guy's leg. The limo jerked and jostled. The crunch didn't sound bad unless you knew what was being crushed.

He climbed out of the seat and pulled the torpedo out from under the limo. Chase got to one knee beside him and said, "You have a friend with you?"

The shooter did his best not to scream but he wasn't having an easy time of it. The tire marks went over his knee and the lower half of his leg swung out too far to the right by maybe six inches, a pool of blood easing down the sloping asphalt toward a sewer grate. The trash bag was tented with busted bone.

Jackie rolled the back window down, stuck his head out, looked down in the street, and threw up.

Chase grabbed the .32 and said to the squeegee guy, "Seriously, how long were you out here wearing a plastic bag? Don't you feel stupid? If Sherry ever uses you again, make sure she offers medical benefits." Chase kicked the guy in the face and put him out. Taxis veered around him, hardly slowing.

He stood in time to see the massage parlor door open, someone a little more hard-core stepping out. There was the second man. He must've been distracted waiting inside, looking at all the girls, the madam giving him a hard time and offering free massages, the sumo wrestler telling him about having his dick stuck in hot sake, listening to all the businessmen being boiled in their hot tubs and clopped on in teakwood.

He was one of the young guys who just wandered around the estate too, looking tough but doing nothing much. So here he was supposedly stepping up. He looked in the back window of the limo trying to get a line on Jackie and make sure he was sighting the right guy. The windows were tinted. It threw him off for another second.

Chase clutched the .32, swung his arm up onto the trunk of the limo and drew down on the kid. "Heya, drop it."

He didn't wait to see if the hitter did it or not, he just shot the mook twice in the left leg.

It reminded him of the day he met Lila, while he was working with a string in northern Mississippi boosting antique and jewelry shops. Chase waiting out front in the getaway car while Lila almost got the drop on the crew. Chase held her while the others decided whether they should rape her before they killed her. He shot all three of them in the leg, and his courtship with Lila began with blood and the hint of a smile.

Jonah said, Finish it, put another one in his head.

Chase walked around the back of the limo to the second shooter and grabbed his gun too, an S&W .38. Number two was in shock, white-faced, sweating, and panting heavily, but still cognizant. Chase asked, "So who paid you?"

He didn't expect an answer and was surprised when the guy said, "Elkins."

It took Chase a second to remember. The strongarm with the .357 that Bishop had practically been sucking on that day of the rumble in Jackie's pale chamois office. Jackie's personal bodyguard, who hadn't been around all that much anyway.

"He pay you half up front?"

"No, nothing up front. All back end."

"You're another idiot. Don't go back to the Langans looking to get paid for pain and suffering. If you see Bishop step out of a doorway in front of you, shoot first."

Jackie cracked the nearest window a couple inches and peered out. He raised his lips to the space and said, "Are they dead?"

"Did you hear what he said, Jackie?"

"What?"

Chase toed number two and said, "Repeat."

But the guy didn't. He was out cold.

There were sirens coming, but there were always sirens coming. Chase pocketed both pistols, got back in the limo, got out again and pulled the squeegee guy away far enough so he wouldn't get run over one more time, climbed in and took off. The cops would never catch on. The madam would plead ignorance, never give a straight answer, speak in pidgin. The description of the stretch wouldn't help at all in Manhattan, and the two hitters would be questioned, released, and the next time they got sent up they'd get laughed right out of Rikers. Or Bishop would bury them.

Y*ou need to leave town," Chase told Jackie, thinking,* Here's my chance.

Jackie was out in left field. For a guy who'd grown up in a mob house his mother must've kept him completely insulated, always sending him off for milk and cookies whenever the heavy action went down.

Jackie might've heard him, Chase couldn't tell.

"You need to snap to it and get on the ball," Chase said.

"What?"

"Wake up, come on."

Jackie made himself a drink, disturbed enough to add four ice cubes this time, that's how fucked he was. He filled the glass with JD, four fingers. "Who did this? Whose men were they?"

"Who do you think? Who knew you were coming to get walked on today?"

"Nobody," Jackie said, his eyes receding into his head.

"Think about that answer."

"Nobody, I tell you, there's nobody. There's never anybody."

"The butler knew."

"Porteroy?"

"The butler's name is Porteroy?"

"Yes."

"Holy shit."

Wagging his head in disbelief, Chase figured Porteroy was playing the game just like Cessy. His name was probably Harvey Glupman from Passaic. Chase said, "If he knew, then everybody could know. You need to get out."

"What?"

Chase didn't really give a shit about Jackie, but he also didn't want to be personally responsible for killing the mook, especially not after saving his life already today. Plus, if he could get Jackie to jump, then a little cash might fall out of his pockets.

"You need to run for it."

"Run? Run where? I can't go anyplace. Where am I supposed to go? My father hasn't even been buried yet."

"You told me you didn't want to go into the ground with him." Chase figured Jackie, like most wiseguys, would never believe that his own blood would come gunning for him. "That was Elkins. This was an inside job, don't you see that?"

"See that it was an inside job? Elkins? You think it was one of my own troops? That's impossible."

"Why?"

"I trust them implicitly."

Chase tried not to sigh. Some people didn't want to be saved. They wanted to go over the side of a sailboat into the icy water and merge with the depths of their heartache and absurdity.

"You trust everyone? Even me? You even know all the names of your crew? Jackie, those two guys we just left out there work for you."

"That's impossible."

"The estate is no longer safe for you. You need to pack it in, hide out, until you clean house. You got a place you can hole up for a couple of weeks until you've found your rats?"

"They might hurt my sister. Or my mother. I have to stay and take care of things."

Chase knew that he could explain it to Jackie for ten hours and the guy would never get it. He would never believe his sister was behind it, that she was already running the crew, and had been since Lenny got sick. Jackie could never imagine that Sherry might ace him, not even when she came up to him with that .38 and put it between his eyes.

"Your sister isn't the one they want, Jackie. Neither is your mother. It's you. You're the head of the family. They'll be fine."

"I can't leave. My father's funeral is tomorrow."

"If you stay, they'll toss you in the box with him."

"Stop saying shit like that!"

It wasn't going to work, the way Chase was playing it. Jackie couldn't face facts and was just going deeper into denial. But Chase knew the way to get a man to do the things he didn't want to do, he'd been taught by the best.

"What would your father do, Jackie? Think it through the way Lenny might've. How would your old man handle a situation like this? Where would he go?"

"Vegas," Jackie said. "I have a little place in Vegas too. I can stay there for a couple of days."

"I'll take you to the airport. Don't pack anything except cash. You have to be autonomous, Jackie, self-reliant. Didn't your father teach you anything when he threw you off the pier at Asbury Park?"

"How the fuck did you know about that?" Jackie asked.

They pulled up to the estate, everything the same as usual, except Jackie was in the back climbing around like a wet cat. He poured himself another drink and Chase reached back through the partition and put his hand on Jackie's shoulder.

"Just be cool."

"Will you—?"

"Yeah, I'll come in with you."

"Thanks."

The thugs lolled about. For the first time Jackie seemed to notice just how many guys there were standing around doing nothing, everybody trying to figure out what they could grab for themselves before they left. Moe Irvine was out on the sundeck, his face dappled with baby oil.

The house was already emptying fast. Furniture was being moved out the side door, lots of boxes and bundles all about on the lawn.

Chase walked Jackie inside, followed him to his office, and watched as Jackie stepped directly to

Aristotle Contemplating a Bust of Homer. It was a five-tumbler combo. Jackie had wads of cash in there and pulled a briefcase out from somewhere under his desk, filled it with the money. The stacks were thick but there weren't all that many—it would be enough to go after Jonah and Kylie, though.

Chase had been right, the safe wasn't where the big money was kept. He'd never cracked the pattern and now he wouldn't score the serious cash. He looked up at the ceiling thinking about Sherry up there, waiting for the call that would tell her that her brother had been capped.

He said, "You should take more, Jackie."

"That's all I have access to."

"What about all the cash flow? You must have it squirreled away all over the place."

"It all goes into accounts to keep the business solvent. We've taken hard hits the past year. Attorneys' fees cost us more than two million the past six months, trying to keep our men out of prison and the right people paid off."

Briefcase in hand, Jackie led Chase upstairs. Jackie's mother was sitting in a rocking chair, her bedroom mostly packed, a couple photos and paintings still on the walls. Lenny Langan as a young man. Jackie and Sherry as kids. Chase shut his eyes and tried to resist the pull of history around him, swirling him backward into an ocean of his own life, full of the dead.

Jackie kissed his mother and she said, "You're leaving." The lady was smart, and she knew Jackie would be wrecked in the fallout. "Good, it's time. I wasn't sure if I could protect you. Go find a safe place to stay for a month or two. Let me know where you are when you get settled. On my private line. Don't talk to anyone else."

"I'll be home soon, Mother."

"There's no home left, Jackson. This is the way it happens sometimes. I'm sorry."

"You forgive me for missing the funeral?"

"Your father wouldn't give a shit, why should I?"

"I need to talk to Sherry first."

"No, Jackson, you don't. She's busy."

"I'm taking money from the safe, Mother. I should tell her."

"Leave her be. Go now. Go."

She kissed her boy and Jackie turned away, Chase following, wondering if Jackie's mom would've warned him if he hadn't shown some initiative.

Nobody noticed them leaving the house. Chase backed the limo up to the servants' quarters and got out. Jackie squawked, "You're leaving me?"

"For a minute."

"That's all it might take."

Chase ignored him and ran inside. His gym bag was in the closet stuffed with his fake ID, meds, some clothes, the Browning, and extra cash. He moved fast.

He ran back out and got behind the wheel of the stretch, the two pistols he'd pulled off the hitters in front of the massage parlor heavy in his pockets, and tried to imagine what it was going to be like when

Sherry and Bishop caught up with him in a couple weeks or a couple months or a couple years down the line. Sherry stepping up with the Jacqueline O's, Bishop smiling amiably. They weren't going to let him go. Sherry already hated his guts for turning her down, and now he had helped Jackie get away, and he was about to score the family too.

Jackie was on his cell calling the airlines.

"You coming with me?" he asked. "I could use you."

"No, I have something I need to do."

"What?"

"Clear up my own family troubles."

"I only have a few guys out there. You could be top man."

"What's the setup?"

"I'm partial owner of a casino. A small one. I get a nice cut and I have a couple books and parlors. My father brought me in when I was a kid. They generate cash, but—"

"But they're legal, so you never gave a shit about them before?" Chase asked. "You never should have come back from Brown to take over the business."

"I didn't want to. My sister made me. She convinced me it was the right thing to do for my father."

Jesus, Chase thought, that bitch is hard. She didn't want to ace Jackie because he might get in the way of her power play. She just wanted him dead because it was easier than having him on the loose, living his own life.

They drove the limit to the airport. When they

got close, Chase saw a shuttle stop, pulled over, climbed out, opened the back door, and plucked the briefcase off the seat. Jackie just sat there and stared at him while Chase counted the cash. A hundred and fifty grand. Enough to make the whole foolishness at the Langan household worthwhile, but not enough for the heat he was going to bring down on himself. There were easier ways to snuff yourself if that's what he was trying to do. He'd have to think about it soon.

"Now get out, Jackie."

"What?"

"Go sit on the bench and wait for the shuttle."

"What?"

"I'm robbing you."

In some men the light of understanding would've dawned in their eyes, but Jackie was still confused, his face twitching. "What?"

"I'm scoring you. Go sit over there."

"You. You did this. Those were your friends back there!"

"If they were my friends, Jackie, I wouldn't have run one over and shot the other. I didn't set up the hit. You've got enemies under your own roof. Your own mother said so."

"I don't—"

"You should've brought more than one-fifty."

"I told you, that's all I had access to. That's all Sherry had in the downstairs safe."

"Okay. Go."

"You're leaving me here? We're not even at the terminal!"

"A shuttle will be along."

"You can't do this!"

"I am doing it."

"But you work for me!"

"I quit. Get the fuck out."

"But my money!"

"You own a casino."

The hysteria was back in Jackie's voice, worse than Chase had ever heard it. "Partial owner! I'll need something to help me set up, to be secure!"

Chase left Jackie ten grand. It would be enough to keep him alive for a couple weeks in Vegas until he figured out how to protect himself. If he ever figured it out.

He grabbed Jackie by the arm and pulled him out of the stretch. Jackie came along like a mental patient zoned on lithium.

Chase said, "Lay low. Don't contact the house. Hide. Don't come up for air for a while. Stick with your own friends. Your friends, you understand, not the family's."

"You . . . I trusted you."

"Jackie, that's just more proof that you don't know what you're doing."

"Goddamn you."

Chase looked back once more and, in another odd moment of even deeper pity, said, "Jackie, wake up and watch your sister. She's going to ace you before you hit Chi." He threw the briefcase in the front seat, climbed in, and drove off, his thoughts focused entirely on his grandfather now.

Knowing Jonah was out there telling him not to come after the family secrets, to keep clear of his mother's ghost, to stay away from the girl.

It was only a half hour's drive to the Deuce's chop shop. On the way over Chase threw his cell phone out the window. Five minutes later he spotted a GTO in the middle lane and jockeyed in behind it. He eased the window down and listened to the engine, letting its heritage fill him. It sounded a touch flat but powerful, righteous. It ran with new plugs but a couple hadn't been gapped properly. The pipes were a little loose and rattled, but the muscle was there, hard, waiting.

The tires were too wide for real speed. Chase could feel the thrum of action and legacy in the car even from a lane away. That clinched it. Chase memorized the license plate and pulled alongside. The driver was maybe forty-five, bald, anxious, and sneering. Another pissed-off almost-was trying to find a little cool as he slid backward and mewling into middle-age. Angry with his wife, his college-dropout son, the pregnant teen daughter, fuck no he wasn't going to stop for milk, dairy products were out, fish oil would keep him young. He was getting Viagra cheap online from overseas.

Besides Jonah, all the meanest guys Chase had ever met were in that same state of disappointment and trying for reinvention.

It wasn't smart to stay out in the open with a stolen mob Super Stretch, but it was even more dangerous to carry a hundred and forty g's in cash around. Chase stopped at two banks down the block from each other, took out safety-deposit boxes with two different fake IDs he'd held in reserve, and cached forty-five large in each.

He pulled into the Deuce's shop, but the limo was too long for any of the stalls. He parked at an angle and several new faces poked up beneath open car hoods and glared at him, no calm, no composure.

Deucie showed up before anybody got too hot, a new unlit cigar looking too huge for his mouth. He checked the stretch, nodded. "Anybody in the trunk?"

"Not today."

Giving him the deep look, wanting to know more than he should, Deuce decided to ask, "How big did you score them?"

"They won't miss it," Chase said.

"Not the money, maybe, but they'll never let you go for heisting them. You know that. When you go on the run now, it's for good."

Of course it was the truth, but there was no reason to go into all of that with Deuce or anybody else. "It's a dead outfit."

"Almost dead anyway, now that Lenny's gone. Heard about that. They're free to move on, but I wonder if they'll hold over for a while longer now, despite the Koreans and the Russians and the Yugoslavians and whoever the fuck else wants a piece of them. You better hope they don't get a shot of adrenaline from this boost of yours. You mentioned a hit was going down?" Deuce held his hand up, turned his face away. "Don't tell me about it, I don't want to know. Listen, like I said, I'm sorry I ever sent you there. I realize that family was a mess. I feel a little responsible you ever got involved."

"It's not your—"

The Deuce, on a roll. "Hey, you ever get out on their golf course? I hear it's pretty nice, especially the putting greens. Mikey Rhino played there a couple times with Jackie and Moe. Moe shaves strokes the way he shaved points back when he ran book. I ain't hit the links in I don't know how long. I never liked it much when I'm there doing it, but when I'm not I want to get back. It's all right, so long as some prick isn't trying to play through. No, forget all that. I'm distracted, got troubles of my own. My wife, she's on her third hysterectomy."

"Listen—"

"I thought the whole point of the damn thing was to go in there, take it all out, but she must have more than most women, whatever the hell's in there, who knows. Fuckin' doctors, she's in the hospital for nine days and I owe six figures. My brother-in-law works a medical-insurance fraud scam, and even he says they're raping me. He went up for four years to Sing Sing, and these doctors, Jesus Christ, you talk about golf, that's all they do. Walk in with tans darker than braised pork bellies, half a bottle of mousse in their hair, these little sticky curls all over their foreheads."

Deuce pulled back, his expression a little stunned, knowing he'd talked too much. He lit his cigar, took a few deep puffs trying to get it down to a manageable size.

It made Chase think for a second that he'd been wrong counting on the Deuce now. Deucie still had strong ties to the syndicates, would give cut rates to the capos so the wiseguys could buy Maseratis for their daughters' sixteenth birthdays. And now, hearing he had home troubles, something Deuce never let on about before. Chase couldn't see the Deuce turning him in, but he thought maybe he'd outworn his welcome in this part of town for a while. He had to cut fast, take the pressure off, get Deuce back on his side somewhere down the line.

"I need wheels," Chase said.

Pointing around at the cars up on the lifts, engine blocks lying around mostly in pieces, Deuce said, "Take your pick, I can give you a deal."

"I need muscle."

"I know you do. All you wheelmen do, even if you're just driving up the block to get a quart of milk. I ain't got anything like that here right now."

Chase ran off the license plate number of the GTO he'd spotted. "Get it for me by tomorrow."

Grinning around the cigar butt, smoke trailing

from his lips. "Okay, I'll get my girl at the DMV on it, put a couple of the boys out to grab it. They'll go in tonight, burn off the VIN. You sticking around for a few days?"

"No. I'm splitting in the morning."

"You gonna meet my price?"

"You can take the Stretch."

"It's not a fair trade," Deuce said, trying to sound hurt and not making it.

"You're right, but I don't mind losing out here." Chase drew the .32 and the S&W .38 he'd taken off the pair of dip hitters and tossed them on the front seat. He opened his gym bag and tossed in the 9mm Browning as well. "Here, you can take these too."

"Smith & Wesson? A pissant .32? Browning? Who uses these nowadays? It's all Glocks and Desert Eagles. They got nine-year-olds in north Jersey with semiauto mags." Deucie threw up his hands, shook his head, tried to purse his lips, which didn't work too well around the cigar. "You should keep them. You need to carry something. I know it was never your thing before, but you're different now, into a new kind of score, on your own. If you're back in the life, which I'm still not too sure about. Are you?"

No calm, no composure. Funny how it was a question Chase kept avoiding, even while he was still carrying a briefcase filled with a stolen fifty grand. He hadn't been thinking about getting back into the bent life. Hadn't been thinking about life at all. What had mattered was driving down Earl Raymond and his crew. Now all he needed to do was to see as far as the next exit down the road and find a way to get to Kylie.

"I don't know, Deuce."

"Your wife, the way you two were. Close like that. I know you're—"

Chase's jaw tightened. He reached for the cold spot, the place where he was frozen and hard, where nothing could reach him, but it didn't seem to be there anymore. He went for it again, trying to hide from Lila in his mind. Her laugh in his ear, her voice there, even now, telling him not to trust Deuce. He closed his eyes but said nothing, trying to draw himself backward from the moment, and when he opened them again to see Deuce just staring at him, worried but maybe not worried enough, he was pleased that the Deuce had at least shut up. Chase was glad he couldn't see his own face.

"How's Mara?" he asked.

"The Romanian girl? The folks I told you about, they love her, got her set up working in some Romanian restaurant in Princeton. I never heard of such a thing, who the fuck says, 'Hey, you want Italian, French, or Romanian tonight?' What do they eat over there anyway, and are you gonna call it cuisine? She's a waitress, they said. They sent me a photo of the kid on my cell. Cute."

"Thanks for helping."

"Sure. What else do you need?" Deuce asked.

"Another cell phone. And another set of IDs."

"The paperwork will take a week. And it'll cost."

"I know. An extra grand if you rush it."

Shrugging, like the Deuce had to put a lot of consideration into it. "I'll see what I can do. You must've scored big to toss money like that around."

Chase thought, What, I need to worry about this now? If he's going to rat me out or try to rip me off before I can bolt? Chase looked into Deucie's face, trying to see just how bad the guy's money troubles were, or if he was acting out of sorts because his wife was sick. He decided that Deucie was just as worried about Chase as Chase was about him. Chase was acting like a pro doing unprofessional things, and it was throwing Deuce, leaving him with a definite lack of faith.

"You said you had a line on Jonah," Chase said.

"He was trying to put together a deal in Sarasota a couple of weeks ago."

Chase hissed between his teeth. The man, closing in on seventy, had taken two bullets in the back, and yet he was still coming up stronger and faster than Chase. Already down South in Florida, in the town where his two-year-old daughter was living with Angie's sister.

Deuce had his cigar down to the size he liked, where he could chew around it pretty good. "It didn't work out too well."

"What do you mean?"

"I'm not sure. It's just a lot of noise right now. He was putting together a string but somebody wound up dead."

"You mean he killed someone."

"Yeah, I think so, but I don't know that circuit, it's

a new bunch of people. They're young and fresh. What I hear is just buzz. So I can't say if he was in the wrong or not, or what the fallout will be like. I think he's still there though. He hasn't come up anywhere else, so he's probably still working on some kind of heist."

"You have any names for the new string?"

"Just one. Duster. No wait, I'm wrong. Dexie. No, I'm wrong again. It's Dex, that's it. He's a little older, been around for a while, but only pulls big jobs once every few years. They're sometimes messy. Not somebody you want to deal with."

Chase nodded. He didn't want to deal with anybody, just wanted to find Jonah. He almost reached through the window of the limo to pull back the .38. He could feel the twisting frustration inside him trying to work itself up into his head and overwhelm his thoughts, but he pressed it back down to where it frothed his blood.

PART
II

Blood, fuel, and cash. It's what ran inside him and what made him run.

Chase cruised to an oldies station until it faded in Delaware, kept tuning in to others for almost six hundred miles before his cool started to loosen. He hadn't been down South since he and Lila had lived in Mississippi over four years ago, up the road from her father, the sheriff. When he crossed the North Carolina border Chase knew he should pull over, get a motel room, get steady again, but he didn't want to get out of the Goat. That was a bad sign, but it didn't change anything. Lila grew louder in his thoughts, and so did Jonah. The two had never met while she was alive, but now they seemed to be arguing all the time.

Lila saying, I fell in love with an outlaw, you do what you need to do for now. So long as you remember to take hold of that child.

Jonah telling him, If you brace me, you're dead.

It went on like that mile after mile. Chase thought

some action might clear his head, which proved he was too tired to keep going.

He pulled into a motel outside of Winston-Salem, walked in, and a whore in the lobby sighted him. It was his own fault. He knew the stink of cash was on him.

She rose and approached him while he bit back a sigh, knowing there was no way to avoid this.

Fair-skinned, freckled, redheaded, with a blatant smile that no one would find attractive but a lot of men would still appreciate, he thought she must've been quite pretty when she was sixteen, and had probably skipped right to worn-out at eighteen.

She wore a summer dress and high heels she had trouble walking in. Dangling costume-jewelry earrings caught the harsh light and emphasized pits in her cheeks. Her arms were scabbed. Meth did it, made them feel extrasensitive, their flesh crawling.

She said, "Hey there, sweetie," and a knot immediately formed between his shoulders.

"Hello," he answered.

"How you doin' this evening? You look like you've been drivin' a thousand hard miles."

"They were easy," he admitted. "The rest will be rough."

He should've just shut the fuck up, but he'd gone too far without hearing another living voice, and he wanted to shake the others out of his skull.

There was no right way to play it now. Her pimp would be nearby. Chase figured it couldn't be the kid.

Act rude and tell her you're not interested, and

she plays the hurt damsel and the pimp turns up looking for trouble. Show the slightest sign of interest and she's on your back until you manhandle her away, and the pimp still shows up. Chase should've stopped an hour sooner, when he was fresher and smarter. He would've been alert enough to keep away from this kind of place and stayed somewhere the hookers only went after businessmen.

The kid behind the desk was unnaturally perky. "Hi, welcome to the Winston-Salem Motor Court! I'm Durrell. What can I do you for?"

His eyes were dilated and Chase got a whiff of weed, but that wasn't what was spiking the guy. A nerve in Durrell's cheek twitched and Chase could clearly see the vein in his throat throbbing, scabbed from scratching. Yep, meth.

Chase got his room key, and Durrell spun around behind the counter, then excused himself to the back room, leaving the girl to do her thing. Chase kept an eye out for the pimp, wondering if he should make a run, try to get a few more miles in tonight, but he was starting to ache.

"It's going to be a cold night, darling," she told Chase, leaving the "g" hanging nice and thick, trying to talk northern so he might relate to her better. She put a hand to the back of his neck and softly rubbed him there, the way Lila used to do. "You might need a touch of warmth."

He shut his eyes and almost allowed himself to go with it for a moment, just a few seconds, because everyone needed a soft hand on occasion.

Except it wasn't his wife's. He snapped his head aside and said, "It's ninety-five in the moonlight."

"A man can still get chilly."

"Maybe if he's got malaria."

It took her back a step and she pulled a face. If you didn't show enough interest right off, they went for your balls, started cracking about whether you were gay. He still wore his wedding ring on his fractured ring finger, now covered over with tape.

"Most lonely men still like a little company when they come this far across the Mason-Dixon."

"Who says I'm lonely?"

"Your eyes do."

"Don't listen to them, they're my worst feature."

"I like them," she said, drawing back, inspecting him. "Sad but just a little tough, a bit mean."

She could've been a Southern belle, Miss Pumpkin Patch or the Radish Princess, waving from a float during the big Radish Day Parade, wearing a plastic tiara. But there was a hard tilt to her mouth that was part bitter humor and part affront. She grinned, knowing her teeth were crud and trying to hide the fact. They called it meth mouth. She and Durrell were definitely into that shit, already so far down the road they'd never get back again, headed for dead at twenty-five.

"Thanks, anyway," Chase said.

"I'm Betty Lynn."

"Thanks anyway, Betty Lynn."

"What's your name?"

"I don't have one anymore."

"Whatever you say, sweetness," she said, and Chase turned his eyes on her and stared, suddenly full of hate, in pain at her use of Lila's word of affection, until Betty Lynn's bitter mouth softened and widened as she sipped air, gasping before his unveiled rage, and she hurried behind the counter and hid in the back room.

Chase got undressed and tossed his pants over the chair closest to the door. His wallet was in the front right pocket, a little thin with only two hundred bucks in twenties. It should be enough. Along with the money, he'd left the false ID he'd used at the Langans, the credit card in the fake name. He double-checked the five grand in his gym bag, reassured that the other forty g's he had left after paying Deuce were secreted in the driver's door panel of the Goat. Then he slid the bag under the bed.

He took a shower and checked himself in the mirror. The shoulder wound was finally healing up, thanks to Cessy's stitch work and the meds he'd bought from her. His fingers hurt like hell, but it wasn't the same gnawing, throbbing discomfort as before, and he thought he might be able to take the tape off in another couple days.

Still, he felt slightly feverish, the heat clambering up his back and settling deep where Betty Lynn had been rubbing his neck. He popped two more antibiotics and climbed into bed.

*In the dream, his dead parents stood in their bed-*room, facing away from him, talking and laughing a little under their breath. The noise of a television murmured distantly, the wild screams and roars of cartoon characters pounding against the walls. Someone called his name and Chase moved toward it through the house he'd lived in as a child.

The halls were longer than he remembered. Distorted by memory or nightmare, it didn't much matter. It took him a long time to reach the living room where the TV rampaged with color and sound. He turned it off.

His unborn sibling, looking a little older now, with a shag of golden hair, sat on a love-seat, side by side with Chase himself as a boy.

He thought, Finally, I get to see myself. I get to ask myself, What the hell really happened toward the end there? Help me piece it together. Maybe you saw something and don't even realize what it was. Tell me. We can figure it out together.

He opened his mouth to speak but again nothing would come. Nothing ever did. But he kept trying.

He moved toward himself and saw that he was dead. It came as a slight shock, a part of himself knowing this was a dream and in dreams when you saw yourself dead—well, it wasn't a good thing. A psychiatrist would have a fucking ball taking these nightmares apart, scribbling notes, writing articles that would put him on the map. Chase in a white room, guys with Viennese accents asking him if he wanted to kill his father, sleep with his mother.

This wasn't helping him much so Chase tried to back out of the room, but before he could make a move his sibling gripped him by the wrist. The human contact made Chase freeze where he was.

The curtains drifted open. The backyard needed raking. Looked like autumn. His mother would be dead soon, a bullet in her head. His father would snuff himself right after the record for the second-coldest winter in New York history was broken.

Angie, Jonah's much younger woman, who'd tried to take him out and had failed like a lot of other people and wound up as dead as the others, crouched behind the television with her eyes red from eight-ball hemorrhaging.

Chase actually jumped back a tad, spooked to see her there. She was staring at him and whispering.

He wanted to say, Go on, out with it.

But she drew away, her voice rising but the words still unclear. She covered her face with her hands and hissed.

Someone walked up behind Chase. His sibling tried to warn him, held its hands up and hopped off the love-seat. Chase as a corpse boy flopped over on his blue face. It was a spooky sight but somehow comforting as well, thinking that here he was, murdered along with the rest of his family.

Powerful arms grabbed him from behind. An angel on the left forearm and a devil on the right, both in midflight with drawn flaming swords.

Under the angel, the names *Sandra, Mary,* and *Michael.*

Jonah's mother, his wife and his son, Chase's father.

Under the devil, peering through a pitchfork: *Joshua.* Jonah's father.

And beneath that, not a tattoo but a scar that had gotten infected and was still mottled white and pink.

Chase's name.

He was surprised to hear his own voice now, asking the old man behind him, "Did you kill my mother?"

Jesus, the Viennese docs would straitjacket his ass and toss him in a dark cell, throw one of those masks on him so he couldn't bite anybody.

Jonah's grip tightened, and then tightened further, the immense strength of his grandfather encircling him, crushing him, but somehow protecting him.

His sibling rushed at him, got right in his face, as Jonah's breath ignited the back of Chase's skull, and the kid said, You're sicker than you think.

Chase tried to respond but he'd bitten off his tongue.

* * *

The door to the motel room eased open. Someone kept the hinges nice and oiled. Betty Lynn slipped in and started rooting through his pockets. A thin shaft of light from the corridor glinted off something in her hand. Looked like a straight razor. It was a shitty weapon but the white trash loved it for some reason. Either she was coming in on the sly or she really had no pimp, was teamed with Durrell, the two of them playing games like this every so often to keep them in the meth. They should've just learned to make the shit, for fifty bucks in household products and gasoline they could stay high until their hearts gave out in a year, eighteen months.

She found Chase's wallet and couldn't contain herself from letting out a small grunt of dissatisfaction as she lifted the cash. Good. It prompted her to take the credit card as well.

She took another step forward and considered crossing the room. If she got any closer, things might get disagreeable. She wavered another moment and finally left, not even caring enough to relock the door with the spare key the kid at the desk had provided her.

Her pimp or Durrell would use the credit card. It might throw off Sherry Langan and Bishop for a couple days when they turned their attention from syndicate-related troubles and came after him.

Chase slugged his pillow and slept.

In the morning Chase called Georgie Murphy in Fort Wayne, Indiana. It was time to get a tighter line on Jonah. Chase would be in Florida by evening

Georgie ran a car dealership, fenced merchandise, and ran messages back and forth for career criminals all over the country. He'd inherited the business from his now deceased father, who'd been a drop for decades.

"I need to get in touch with Jonah," Chase told him.

"He had some trouble with his back," Georgie said. "Needed to find a chiropractor in New York to help straighten him out. You know how tricky that can be. Sciatica."

Georgie used code whenever he could, thinking the feebs might have him tapped. The code wasn't especially difficult to crack, so who gave a shit? If the feds were working a case, this kind of info would be the least of Georgie's troubles.

"I know. That was almost two months ago. I need a line on him now."

"It's the last I heard."

"Someone said he was in Sarasota."

"I can check with a couple of guys."

"Do it. See if maybe he met another, ah, chiro-practor"—Chase had to pull away from the phone and shake his head—"to help him with his therapy. Named Dex."

"I'll check his references."

"Yeah."

"And, there's something else. Your granddad . . . listen, I have to tell you—" Georgie was having trou-ble figuring out a way to say whatever he wanted to say with his stupid-ass code.

"Just fucking say it."

"Not too many people like him."

"No," Chase said, "neither do I."

"You heard he left a certain person behind when things went sour in Aspen on a job a couple months ago?"

That would be Lorelli. Jonah had left him behind dead when they'd tried to score a gated community, and the whole thing had gotten botched. "I heard."

"Some of that person's friends might be looking to—"

"Tell them from me that they shouldn't try. I knew Lorelli. He was all right, but he's not worth dy-ing for."

"You still stand up for him, huh? The old man."

"Is that what you're hearing?"

"No, no, I suppose not," Georgie said. "But with his sciatica problems—"

"Get back to me soon as you can. And, Georgie, seriously, one more thing. Drop the bullshit code, you sound like a stammering asshole."

Chase headed for the back exit but Durrell was standing there, smoking. Chase couldn't tell whether it was a cigarette, a joint, or a meth pipe, but Durrell was suddenly extremely antsy, trying to play it friendly but acting a little too crazed. "Hey, checking out?"

"Not checking out, Durrell, just going for some breakfast. Be back in half an hour."

"I think you ought to pay your bill first, and settle up."

"I've stayed in a thousand shit motels like this one, Durrell, I know how to come and go, all right?"

Chase almost booked past him, but it felt too much like running, and he wanted to avoid a confrontation. Besides, he was parked out front and would have to walk all the way around the damn place to get there. Since he'd been trying to slip out unnoticed, there was no point in playing coy anymore. Chase turned and headed up the corridor in the opposite direction, toward the front counter.

Durrell bopped up behind him, no longer smiling, hovering too close like he wanted to put his hands on Chase but was afraid to do so. Trying to escort him along, keep him from leaving. It was weird and Chase just didn't get it.

"Look, Durrell," Chase said, "I've already had a bad night, okay? You and—and—"

For a second he couldn't remember the girl's name and almost said Sherry Lynn.

Sherry Langan was weighing on his mind, he had to focus.

"—Betty Lynn boosted me for two c's, that should make you happy. Don't push it."

"I have no idea what you're talking about, sir."

Chase liked the afterthought "sir," like that made everything better. This kid was going to scam the wrong person one of these days and this motel would become a slaughterhouse. "You need to re-hab, that shit is making you way too sloppy."

They hit the front counter together, Durrell still doing the dancing no-touch body-block thing, his awful breath wafting into Chase's face. The stink of rotting teeth was so powerful that it made Chase cough.

"Sir, I really do think you should settle."

Chase nearly smacked Durrell just to get the punk off him. "Settle, huh? Is that what you call it?"

Betty Lynn and her pimp walked in from the back room. Chase rubbed his forehead. It was clammy to the touch and his front curls were damp with sweat. He thought of the dream where his unborn sibling had told him that he was sicker than he thought. Chase wondered if it might be true.

Now this setup made sense, all that bopping and weaving Durrell had been doing. The pimp had probably told him not to let Chase leave yet. Why? Betty Lynn had gone through his wallet, they could see he had no other cash or credit cards on him. Was it the car? Chase looked out the front window to see if they'd fucked with the Goat at all, but from here he couldn't tell. Maybe they'd gone through the glove box and seen there weren't any papers. Figured he was on the run and they could squeeze him for something more.

On second glance Chase decided, no, the guy wasn't a pimp, just her twentysomething boyfriend pretending to be worldly and tough. He had some meat on him, big through the chest and shoulders but with sagging jowls. Looked like a fallen football hero from the same high school, got hooked on the same shit, and was degrading at about the same rate. His face was also scarred and pitted from the meth sores and scratching. Why anybody fucked with this drug was beyond Chase's understanding.

"That's him," Betty Lynn said.

Chase looked around. Weren't there any other guests in this place? Or was he really the only one taking advantage of all this innate charm and Southern hospitality at the Winston-Salem Motor Court?

The boyfriend stomped up. Chase took the initiative and said, "What's your name?"

It took the mutt off guard. "Huh?"

"Your name. What's your name?"

The guy didn't know what to say. He blinked at Chase.

"You don't know your name?"

"Of course I know my damn name. Augie."

"Okay, now we're getting somewhere. What do you want, Augie? What do you want from me?"

Augie didn't respond. He was too busy trying to resettle himself, get dug back in, play the hard-ass. Chase thought, It must be me. I do something to lure them to me.

Betty Lynn moved around the counter and said, "We want money. What else would you think we'd want, sweetie?"

"You stole all my money."

"I was right. You were awake. You were watching me. I knew it. But you didn't say anythin'. Now why is that?"

"You planted the cash," Augie said. "You're so loaded you don't even care that she took a hundred dollars off you."

"She took two hundred," Chase told him. "She's holding out on you. But hey, she lies to everybody. She told me she liked my lonely eyes. And I do care, I just don't care enough. I have other troubles on my mind."

Augie squared his shoulders and tightened his fists, trying to get the veins pumped on his forearms. It wasn't working. "I'm going to give you even more."

"You've got a lot of problems yourself, man. You want to add to them?"

Chase thought, I can pull the switchblade. I can stomp his foot and drop him. Or I can work out some of the kinks and get ready for the upcoming show.

He swung the gym bag around his good shoulder and said, "You any good?"

"What?"

"Augie, listen. Focus here, son." Snapping his fingers under Augie's nose. "You any good? You had any training? I don't want to waste my time, I've got miles to make today. You know how to fight or are you just big and rude?"

Durrell felt the need to cover for his buddy. "He can fight. I seen him once knock a man down with one punch."

"And I was only half-trying," Augie added.

Chase said, "Yeah, but did the guy get back up and kick your ass?"

As he often did, he figured that the real trouble would lie with the woman, who seemed a little sharper than these mooks and probably still had the rusty straight razor on her.

"You've only got one good hand," Augie said. "How you gonna fight with—"

Chase fired two sharp jabs into Augie's nose and dodged left so the spurting blood wouldn't splash him. He right hooked the mutt to the temple and then elbowed Durrell in the chest as the kid came running forward, his hands up in the wrong position, not even protecting himself. Durrell's breath blasted out of him as he went down and Chase almost broke into a coughing fit, from the stench back in the air. He spun and right hooked Augie to the temple again, enjoying the solid thunk of his knuckles smacking bone. Augie let out a sound like a dying camel and collapsed to his knees.

With his back to Sherry Lynn—goddamn it, with his back to Betty Lynn—Chase hoped she'd draw the razor and try to use it. He presented the target and waited for her to take the chance.

But she didn't. He wheeled and she was standing there, trembling but with a weird, knowing grin. She was hugging herself and he saw the fresh finger-nail scratches bleeding down her arms.

She said, "Take me with you."

"Christ no."

"Please, I'll be good to you, I'll make you feel good, I promise. I can do things that—"

The cold sweat poured off him as he made it out the door. He almost smiled for a moment until he thought, This was just stupid. This wasn't getting ready for Jonah. This didn't prove anything except you're scared.

He'd taken down the crew that had killed his wife. He'd been shot to shreds and managed to come through. He'd watched a man get gutted a couple weeks ago. He'd brawled with an ace shooter. And now he was going to let a fucking *Augie* get under his skin?

No cool, no calm.

Once in the Goat he peeled out of the parking lot, trying to let the machine steady his nerves and work its power into his guts, waiting for the thrum of the engine to quiet his mind, but after a hundred miles he was still thinking of Betty Lynn's grin, wondering what it was she knew about him that he still hadn't realized himself.

*T*he world darkened to that blinding Southern ruby red by noon, and the temperature topped a hundred and two. One thing Chase hadn't checked in the Goat before hitting the road in Jersey was whether the air-conditioning worked. It was a stupid mistake and he suffered for it the entire morning and into afternoon.

He decided not to push himself and found a higher-class hotel in north Florida. Untaped the fingers and flexed them, thinking it might be all right to leave them free now, at least for a while. Ordered room service, used the pool and the workout room, did some easy weights. The left hand held out. Stayed in the steam bath until exhaustion set in and it felt like he'd burned some of the poison out. He didn't want to dream tonight.

Settled into bed and started watching a bang-'em-up action flick on cable while he waited for sleep. He was out cold before the opening credits finished rolling.

The next morning Chase popped the plates off a nearby vehicle and switched them with the Jersey tags. He entered the city of Sarasota and was a little surprised that it was so quaint while still edging toward serious money.

He'd figured it would be a surfer area, shoddy, a lot of punk kids on the street. But everywhere he looked he saw clean, gorgeous beaches, parks, and private clubs. Lots of families out together picnicking, plenty of laughter and music in the air. People were swimming, jogging, sitting at rec benches before barbecues. Huge mirrored condos lined the face of the bay. Piers leading out into private lagoons. Botanical gardens. Moored boats rocked in the marina. Palm trees lined the old downtown Main Street heavy with foot traffic moving in and out of the shops.

He stopped off at Bayfront Square and watched children climbing across jungle gyms, everybody wearing sandals or flip-flops. In some ways it reminded him of Central Park, but with more intense colors. Action anywhere you looked—you had to keep on your toes or be mowed down by a runaway rollerblader.

Lila had never seen the ocean until the day they moved to New York. She loved going to Robert Moses and Fire Island, even though she was a little afraid to swim out more than twenty feet past the first breakers. The two of them spent a lot of time sitting in the surf, the tide dragging the sand around their feet.

It was time to find the girl, Kylie.

All he knew about Angie's sister Milly was that she was married to a professional surfer. Chase had thought that was sort of a dumb thing to do professionally, but as he gazed over toward the Gulf of Mexico and watched the white sands stretching before him, the waters a wildly dazzling green and the sunlight more vivid somehow than he'd ever seen before, he had a change of heart.

He asked around for where the best surfing in the area might be and was told North Jetty, at the south point of Casey Key. He got out his maps and drove over.

The ocean brimmed with muscular, golden-haired kids on boards. He sidled up to groups drying in the sun, lazily draped across blankets and drinking bottles of beer hidden inside Styrofoam holders. He hoped there weren't that many pro surfers from the area. They told him there were. They were wary and looked at him like he was a cop. Chase wondered exactly what the trouble was. A heavy drug undercurrent in the surfer world, smuggling shit in up from Miami in their board wax? He got a couple names and thought he should've brought a pencil and pad.

Nothing to do except keep talking to anybody with a board. He moved from group to group, most of the kids ignoring him and hitting the waves the second he showed up. He pulled out his cell and called information. He reached a few of the surfers and asked questions, trying not to sound too invasive. Hey, you married to a girl named Milly? You got a kid named Kylie? He got yelled at and hung up on a lot.

It took about another hour to connect with the right person on the beach. He was relaxing in the shade of some boulders, watching surfers do their thing and thinking he might want to try it one of these days when a couple girls in bikinis with yellow lycra rash guards tied around their waists walked past. He asked the question and one girl said, "You don't mean Aaron Dash, do you? The guy who got murdered?"

"Yes," he said, everything snapping into place at once, "that's who I mean."

No wonder the kids didn't want to talk to him. The cops and reporters must've already rousted them plenty.

Chase imagined how it went down. Jonah showing up at the surfer's door, saying he wanted Kylie back. Milly asking about her sister. Jonah maybe even telling her the truth, explaining how Angie had shot him twice in the back because she wanted to get clear of him and keep him away from his own daughter forever. Looking into his dead eyes, Milly would know it was real, that her sister was gone and she'd never even be able to bury her. She'd scoop the kid up and make a run for it. The surfer standing there in his flip-flops, threatening to call the cops. Jonah slugging him two or three times in the gut, turning abruptly and driving his elbow backward into Dash's face. The surfer in good shape, making the effort even though his nose was broken, clambering to his feet. Jonah thinking enough was enough and popping Dash once in the forehead with whatever he was carrying, probably a .32. Then making his way to the back bedroom where Milly and Kylie hid even before the surfer's corpse hit the floor. Chase grew frustrated with Milly, thinking, Why the fuck didn't you go out the back door? But people hated to leave their houses, their places of protection, even when they were invaded, he'd seen it a dozen times when he used to burgle for crews. Jesus, there'd be so much screaming, Kylie terrified because Milly was, and Jonah, steel and stone, marching down the hall, kicking the door in, maybe taking the time to get the girl clear but probably not, raising the gun and icing Milly while Kylie was still in her arms. The little girl falling onto the chest of her dead aunt, watching the blood flow free from Milly's mouth. Turning to look at her father and Jonah, incapable of feeling what other men felt, no love inside him, grabbing the kid and taking her into the bent life, spatters of blood already on the side of her face.

"Any idea where this Dash used to live?" Chase asked.

*T*he teenager didn't know, but now that Chase had a name he called information and got out his maps. It took only ten minutes to get over to the Dash house, which was right on the water with a couple hundred feet of beachfront property.

There was crime-scene tape over the front door. Chase was surprised at how similar the place looked to homes down by the Great South Bay on the south shore of Long Island, in the high-end townships. Lots of windows, glass doors, and a couple screened-in sunrooms. Surfing wasn't a stupid profession after all.

He went to the front door, looked around. He noticed that the tape had been very carefully cut and then stuck back into place. The lock had no scratches on it. Either a pro had gone in or an amateur had been kept out. Chase had to wonder about that. Who else was coming by to check things over?

He faded back across the yard and moved to the side of the house, searching for the smartest point of entry. Children's toys were scattered about. Little plastic cars you pedaled. A couple tiny tricycles lying on their sides.

When Chase saw them a knifing pain took him low in the guts and he nearly went down. Jesus Christ, they'd had their own kids. He hadn't even thought of that before. Showed how he'd been obsessing but not thinking.

He bent and righted the trikes. One green and one pink. A boy's and a girl's. So look at that, they'd had a little boy. What would Jonah have done to the kid? Chase knew his grandfather didn't feel things like regular people, but could he have snuffed a child? Chase caught a flash of his own eyes in the chrome of a trike. They seemed to think the old man could.

A huge jungle gym designed of steel and block wood rose from the sand. He could imagine Dash doing chin-ups there, holding on to the metal rings sunk into the crossbeam while beside him Kylie and his boy clambered around on the little ladders. Chase figured she was young enough and had been away from Jonah long enough to call Dash her daddy. Why not. Would she even know Jonah? Chase couldn't see it.

A wooden privacy fence separated the yards on both sides of the house, and farther back down the sand snow fencing marked vague property trails. It was called snow fencing on Long Island. Here, maybe cyclone fencing. The murmur of distant waves began to filter into his head above the sound of his own heavy breathing. He looked at the eyes in the chrome again and they were telling him something.

A sharp call echoed up from the shore with a harsh snap. "Hey . . . you!"

Chase stood and turned slowly toward the voice. You always moved slow when somebody spooked you, it showed you weren't edgy and you had a right to be wherever you were.

Marching up the sand came a squat, overweight woman wearing a one-piece bathing suit. Blue nylon with little frills around it that flapped when she walked. You had to give some credit to folks who wore what they wanted to wear and didn't give a shit about what anybody might say.

Frowning, she plodded forward, mounds moving one way or another or in two directions at once. She really knew how to put it out there, chin held high. Chase knew a lot of guys who would appreciate that and would've been wowed by her.

She'd been in the water for a while. Her fingers were all pruney. Hair drying in the breeze into a wild horsetail. Her cheeks and forehead were so sunburned that he almost winced just looking at her.

He waved and said, "Howdy."

She didn't respond until she got up close. Real close, jutting a forefinger into his sternum. "Who are you?"

"Is this the Dash place?"

"I asked you a question."

She wasn't offering anything. Lady was on the

ball, wasn't about to be dissuaded and let him take
the lead. She leaned slightly to the right, toward the
fence, like she belonged on the other side of it, and
he figured this was the next-door neighbor, keeping
an eye out.

"I'm a relative." It was the truth, but the wrong
answer. He should've just said he was a friend.

"Of Dash's?"

"Of Milly's."

"Yeah, then what's her maiden name?"

When you're cornered you might as well smile,
hit 'em with the charm. He grinned, trying to look
abashed. "I have no idea."

She let her teeth slide out from beneath her lips
in an affectation that was pure Spanish Inquisition.
Chase didn't know how someone who lived right on
a beach in a mansion could ever look so pissy. "You
expect me to believe you're related to Milly, but you
don't know her maiden name?"

"I'm a distant relative."

"Get out of here before I call the cops."

"Who are you, lady?"

"I'm Esther Williams. What, you don't recognize
me?"

Chase let out a chuckle. It was a stretch of a refer-
ence for modern filmgoers, but some of Jonah's pals
had liked Busby Berkeley films. When Chase was
a kid he'd watched a few during a marathon on
Channel 9 while they'd put together a plan to score
an antique-gun shop.

"What happened here? Someone told me he was murdered."

"I said to take off."

"What about the girl? Kylie. And they had a boy?"

"Who the hell are you, mister?"

"I told you—"

"Yeah, but I'm not buying that bullshit. You a reporter?"

What the hell. "Yes."

"No, you're not that either or you would've said so right off. You're a liar twice over now. Get your ass out of here."

She wasn't about to play it any other way. He liked her even more for that. No cajoling, no buying her off. She was raw and rude, and she must've had her reasons. He couldn't push too hard or she might actually follow through. Everyone who was in the know liked to rub it in the faces of those who weren't, and he got the feeling he could work this pruney fat lady if he could just figure out the right opening move.

She was tough but real. Maybe he should respond in kind.

"You know Kylie wasn't their kid, right? She's the child of Milly's sister, Angie." He tried to remember everything Angie had told him about her life. He hadn't known her long and they hadn't talked much, but she had tried to win him over so that he'd make a play against Jonah, and she'd spoken some about her childhood and her sister. "Their mother died of uterine cancer when Angie was nine. Their father was a Cuban boozer who loved the Miami club scene and was a part-time gigolo. She hated him because he'd spend eight hundred bucks on a pair of shoes but wouldn't have money to feed the kids. He hit on a drug dealer's girlfriend and got snuffed in a men's room. Their aunt took them in after that. Any chance Milly ever mentioned any of that?"

"Only the part about her mother dying of uterine cancer," the lady said. A breeze drifted in off the water and flapped the little frills on her suit. "She had a scare herself a couple of years ago and we talked about it some. The rest at least sounds like you're finally talking the truth."

"I need to know what happened here," Chase said. He let the truth rise up from the depths of his chest and soak his words. "I have to find the girl."

Her name was Francie Goodwin and she had a very large dog she called Assassin. Chase saw how it could fit.

Chase sat at Francie's kitchen table drinking some herbal shit he couldn't stand and tried to ignore the fact that Assassin was staring with an unhealthy amount of interest at Chase's groin. Assassin was a white German shepherd and more than large enough to turn Chase into a eunuch with one bite. It was hard to keep his mind on what Francie was saying but he was doing his best.

He'd given her the latest fake name and she

hadn't believed him but didn't push it. She said, "You're trouble but you're not serious trouble. You really do care about Kylie."

"Yes."

"I've been married six times, and yes, you heard that right, me, six times, and they all thought they were the best charlatans, cheats, operators, swindlers, scam artists, bullshit artists, and rip-off artists in the state. The first three broke my heart. The next three, well, I wound up taking them for everything they had. Why they wanted me was their problem, and why I wanted them is my problem. But I learned from my experiences. You can't run a game or a racket on me."

"So I've learned."

She nodded. "Okay then, who are you really?"

"I knew Milly's sister Angie," Chase told her. "And I actually am related, in a way too weird to go into right now. I heard Aaron Dash was dead. Murdered."

Her face tightened with displaced anger. "Ten days ago. Somebody shot him in the heart and left him to bleed out in his own living room."

Ten days. Right as Jonah was trying to set up his new string with somebody named Dex. Chase had been too slow, too late, he'd known what was going to happen and he'd stopped off to pick up cash he could've done without.

But no, that wasn't what it had really been about at all. Chase had been sick and needed to decide for himself whether he wanted to live or die.

Francie said, "He was strong. It took him three days to die. Milly and Kylie and Walt are missing. Possibly kidnapped, the police said."

Chase looked her in the eye and said, "But you're smart enough not to believe them. Nobody would take them and leave a body behind. You don't kill the person who would pay the ransom. They haven't been kidnapped."

Francie shook her head. "And her car was gone. Kidnap victims don't drive off on their own."

"That common knowledge?"

"No, but she always parked her SUV in the drive and it's gone."

"You see anything? Hear anything?"

"No," Francie said. "No one did."

"Not even the gunshot?"

"No."

"What time did it happen?"

"Around three in the afternoon."

Made sense. In the middle of the night, slamming doors and shouts and screaming engines might stir the neighbors, but in the afternoon with the waves roaring, who notices anything?

"Who called the cops?"

"Aaron managed to crawl to a phone before he passed out. He never woke up again."

Sipping the tea, hating the taste and glad for that, Chase tried for the cold spot again and was shocked when he felt the spreading chill that quieted his mind and shut down his emotions, allowing for clarity.

He reached out and patted Assassin's head, the dog licking his hand, sensing the change.

"You know who did this, don't you?" she said.

Chase tried to work it out. It started the same way as before. Jonah showing up at the door, saying he wanted Kylie back. Milly asking about her sister. Jonah maybe telling her the truth, explaining how Angie had shot him twice in the back. Looking into his dead eyes, Milly would know her sister was gone. She'd scoop the kid up and make a run for it. Both the children. Angie had told her about Jonah, she knew what to do. The surfer standing there in his flip-flops and threatening to call the cops. Jonah slugging him two or three times in the gut, turning abruptly and driving his elbow backward into Dash's face. The surfer in good shape, stronger than Jonah expected. Giving him a much tougher fight while Milly and the kids made it to the front door, got outside, clambered into a truck and booked. Jonah thinking enough was enough and popping Dash once in the chest, probably with a .32 because the sound hadn't even carried to next door. Then making his way outside and heading after the woman and the two kids. Chase had grown frustrated thinking that Milly hadn't left the house, but now he saw that she'd been smart and sharp and had immediately run. But where? Miami? It's where she and her sister had been raised.

Or had Jonah caught up with them a few miles down the road and dumped her car and the bodies of Milly and little Walt in the ocean?

Francie repeated herself with more force. "You know who did this."

"I think I do," Chase said.

"Who is it?"

"Kylie's father. Milly ever say anything about him?"

"No. Just that she was watching the girl while her sister worked things out. It sounded like drugs were involved, rehab, that sort of thing. I didn't push it and she never said anything more."

"If she did run, do you have any idea of where she went?"

"No. But she was strong too. Both of them were always swimming, jogging. She was a semipro surfer herself."

Tough, smart, on the run with two children. Or dead in the water.

Francie, her sunburned face going even redder, that righteous anger rising, fists on the table, turning her head toward the home next door where nothing walked, allowed the opening note of a sob to break from her.

Assassin moved to her, put his enormous chin on her enormous lap as the single note rang throughout the tremendous house of ex-husbands. Then it was done, buried beneath the silence, and she turned back to stare at Chase, still not trusting him, but trusting him enough.

"You're going after him."

From inside the place where he was cool and smooth, iced down and feeling right, he said, "Yes."

He got a hotel room on the water and called Deuce and Georgie, checking in and putting pressure on. He needed to find Jonah. Any news at all, rumors, gossip, mutters or bitching, he needed to hear it. Put the word out, turn his cell-phone number over to everybody, whatever it took.

In the meantime, Chase tried to stay active. He swam and ran on the beach. Shadowboxed and used the hotel gym. He ate well in Sarasota's restaurants and enjoyed the food.

After a week he'd put on some weight and re-gained muscle mass and speed. Cessy's stitches were ready to come out and he carefully clipped the threads and tugged them free. The bullet-wound scar was red and ugly but didn't bother him.

Georgie called from his car lot in Fort Wayne, Indiana. There was a huckster in the background shouting something into a bullhorn about low inter-est rates and no money down. "I got some word on your gramps. He's down South. Florida."

"Where?"

"I just told you. Florida."

Chase had to remember that even though Georgie was a second-generation, he'd mostly centered in on the car salesmanship and that seemed to still be where his heart was. "It's a big state. I was hoping for something a little more specific."

"Oh. I think he's vacationing in Sarasota."

"Yeah, that's what I told you, Georgie."

"Oh yeah, but I heard it again this morning. The info I got was a few days old."

So the old man was still nearby. Killing Dash hadn't made him move on, the way he normally would have. What did that mean? Was he still hunting for Milly and Kylie? Or was it because of the score he had set up with this cat Dex?

"What's Jonah doing down here?"

"I'm not sure. There are these new circuits popping up. They don't do things the way we were taught. They're more . . . independent. He got in touch with Lamberson and Sloane about opening his own car lot."

Still with the outdated code words. "What did they tell him?"

"Not certain what the business proposition was," Georgie said while the bullhorn blared, "but they turned him down. Lamberson's been struggling with prostate cancer, they got him in for radiation treatments once a week, so he figures he's got to be selective."

"He told you this himself?"

"Yes."

"Anything about Dex?"

"No. I checked into that. He's got good references. Been around a while, does good work, a lot of happy clients, for the most part. But he can be expensive and he, well, you know how those chiropractors are. One wrong touch and they can break your back. His name turns up every so often, but he doesn't usually work with the guys we do."

"Was anyone with Jonah?"

"What?"

"Was anyone with him? A woman. A kid. Anybody. Was he alone?"

"I don't know. Why would he be with a kid?"

Chase was fed up with the double-talk bullshit. "Keep checking. Jonah's trying to put together a crew for a job. He'll be reaching out. Just give Lamberson and Sloane my number and tell them to get in touch with me. I need more details than this."

Georgie said, "Most guys don't like giving out details about their merchandise and their chiropractors and their plans to open their own car lots, you know."

Chase hung up, thinking, If the feds were listening in on this, then they must think we're truly a bunch of morons.

Chase had worked with Sloane once, part of a string Jonah had set up to score a supermarket in Parma, Ohio.

Chase remembered him as being a little hyper and talkative, drinking too much in the motel room where they'd gathered to go over the plan. Sloane went on about his college-age girlfriend who was studying criminal justice when she wasn't cheerleading or making it with Sloane. Sloane discussed what it was like to visit her dorm room and take showers with her while coeds skimped around in towels. Chase, who was fourteen and intensely lonely, listened attentively and let his daydreams take him away, thinking what it would be like to attend college and live on campus surrounded by thousands of girls.

The score had gone off smoothly while Chase sat outside behind the wheel of a stolen Chevy. Everybody clambered in and Chase eased away, never breaking the speed limit even while Sloane slapped the back of the driver's seat trying to get Chase to move it.

Jonah had turned around in the passenger seat and said, "The kid's the driver, he knows what he's doing."

Remembering that, Chase had a moment of mixed feelings. The pride he felt when his grandfather had shown such faith and respect for him, the love and hero worship he'd felt for Jonah back then.

Lamberson was a pretty solid hood with a good rep for second-story work and tricking out alarms. Chase had never met him but had heard the name a lot when he was a kid.

Lamberson phoned the next morning while Chase was running on the beach, finishing his fifth mile surrounded by bikinis. "I don't know if I should be talk-ing to you. This isn't how we do things."

"I know," Chase said, "but these are special cir-cumstances."

"That doesn't matter to me."

"It must. You called."

Lamberson let out a deep grunt, turning some-thing over in his mind. Chase could feel the guy's annoyance and wondered if it was coming from his health problems or something else. "Yeah."

"Jonah is putting together a score down here in Sarasota," Chase said. "Him and somebody named Dex. I don't care about that. I'm not trying to deal myself in. I just need to get in touch with my grand-father. I heard there were problems with the setup and somebody got killed. What happened?"

"I don't know, I wasn't a part of that. It would've been disrespectful not to meet with Jonah, but once I did, I felt no obligation to listen. I got enough problems without working with that guy. His last few jobs have left way too much heat behind him, bodies all over the fuckin' place. I liked Lorelli."

"I only met him a couple of times when I was a kid, but I liked him too. That what happened? One of Lorelli's friends went after Jonah?"

"Like I said, I have no idea. But it happens, some-times, among us, our type. Not often, but there are guys out there with crews who'll try to settle a score. Anyway, it's all shit I don't need right now. My old man's prostate sent him to the grave twenty years ago, and now it looks like mine might bury me too.

They got me coming in to fry my 'nads once a fuckin' week. I can't go off and hole up for a month the way we used to in the old days."

"I can understand that," Chase said. "You probably did the right thing." There was no point in asking where the meet had been held because it would've been in a room rented by the hour under a fake name. If Jonah had a score brewing, he'd taken an apartment for a couple of months or moved in with a prostitute living on the fringes of Dex's crew. "How do I get in touch with Dex?"

"You don't. He's a cagey prick, that one. As bad as Jonah in some ways. He calls you and sets up a time. You're not there, you won't ever see him again."

"Did you run into Sloane while you were down here?"

"No, haven't talked to him in about a year," Lamberson said. "Listen, it's nothing to me, but you should stay away from the old bastard. You used to be pretty well-known, being so young, working with Jonah, a family team. There was always noise about you. Then I heard you'd cut ties and gone straight, had a house and wife. So what the fuck are you messing around with this life again? You should go back to her."

Chase said, "Thanks for your help," and hung up.

The next afternoon, Sloane called while Chase was in the hotel gym, pushing himself a little harder. The lung was holding up. So were the fingers.

Sloane was as edgy and talkative as Chase remembered him. "We don't talk directly for a reason, kid, and now you're making me make a phone call with roaming charges and it's not even the weekend. You going to reimburse me or what? Jesus Christ, I'm hemorrhaging cash out my asshole and you people keep taking more from me, you're like the fucking IRS, I can feel them crawling around in my colon. What do you want?"

"Heard you were asked in on a score that Jonah is putting together here in Sarasota. Him and somebody named Dex."

"And you want a piece of it?"

"No. I just need to talk to my grandfather."

"And he's ducking you?"

"Let's just say we need to get into a room together and clear the air between us."

"Well, I turned them down," Sloane said, and suddenly grew tight-lipped.

Chase let a few seconds go by. "I heard there were problems with the setup and somebody got killed. You know anything about that?"

"Everybody's a gossipmonger, they all want to know where the bodies are buried. I don't really know anything about that, just that somebody got iced."

"Who was it?"

"How the fuck do any of us know? Some guy sniffing around the motel, I guess he was trailing Jonah. As if that crazy old bastard wouldn't know about it. We were just sitting down to talk business and he leaves the room saying he's going to get ice from the ice machine. He walks down the hall, shoots this guy standing at the candy machine, then comes back and says we have to move the meeting. I up and split right then. For all I know it was a cop or a fed. Who needs to be on the feebs' most wanted list? Your face showing up on television, reenactments being played out on prime time? Not me. Sometimes things go smooth with Jonah, but hardly ever the past ten years. You were his rudder, kid. When he lost you, he lost his way."

Chase thought Jonah had always been off track, but now that he thought about it a bit, he remembered how just a few months after Chase had split and gone out on his own, Jonah's first real botched score occurred. The old man had nearly run over a teenage tourist while escaping from a museum heist gone bad. Maybe Chase really had been his grandfather's rudder.

"He never said who it was or why the guy was tailing him?"

"Didn't tell me and I didn't ask," Sloane said. "Why would I? Like I need to know his business? I said good-bye and got the hell out of there."

"Any idea how I can get in touch with this Dex?"

"No. I had nothing to do with him. Hardly even got a look at him. I walked in, he handed me a beer, and then Jonah snuffed the guy at the candy machine, and I was gone. Besides, it was Jonah got in touch with me through Murphy's kid."

"Was Jonah alone?"

"Who the hell would he have with him?"

*A*ll this heat and sun and Chase couldn't stop dreaming of ice. His father handed Chase a pickax and the two of them worked side by side for over an hour to free the sailboat from the frozen slip. Low under his breath, his old man was saying something, whispering against the wind.

Ghosts were always talking but never quite loud enough to be heard. You'd think they might learn from it and speak up clearly. Either that or just shut up.

A dream, but also a memory. He recognized it for what it was and tried to impress himself upon the nightmare.

This time, Chase threw down the pickax and stared out over the bay, the hacked chunks of ice bobbing off down the channel. Lila, his mother, and the unborn sibling were already on deck of the boat, preparing to cast off. He kept wondering why the rest of the dead didn't join them. Angie, Dash, Milly, and others before them.

The kid leaned over the bow rail and gestured to Chase with its tiny hands. Chase was a little sick of the kid always taking point, the kid being the only one who ever said anything. Chase turned his back and tried to get his father to talk with him. Snow spiraled around them and his father stopped working for a moment to take a pull from a bottle of Jack. Chase thought, quite clearly, What a waste of a dream. This isn't helping me any.

He was close enough to the rail that the kid could reach down and brush its fingers lightly through Chase's hair, thick with crystals. He looked up at Lila but she'd drifted away and started to move belowdecks with his mother, the two of them shoulder to shoulder exchanging the secrets of the dead. He wondered if he got on board with all of them, and sailed off, if that would be the end of him.

He said to the kid, What do you want now?

The next evening, after Chase got back from his beach run, exhausted but feeling much stronger, he showered, lay on the bed, and caught the news.

They'd pulled two bodies out of a lagoon less than five miles from the Dash house. A woman and a young boy, no older than four.

The cops had no identification yet, but Chase sat there knowing Jonah had crossed yet another line.

So either the SUV was in the water too or Jonah had called a local car thief to come pick it up and give him his cut.

The old man had his daughter again and was on to a new score. He'd never look back, never think of Angie, Milly, or Walt again.

Chase sat in the empty room willing himself to be his grandfather's conscience, accepting a guilt and pain that wasn't his own. He played with the switch-blade for a while. His hands were fast, fast enough to take on Bishop, maybe fast enough to stop Jonah too.

He stared at the eyes in the blade and they told him, You need a gun, you stupid fuck.

Chase checked out of the ritzy hotel and found a dive in the shitty part of town. He needed to track down Dex. To do that, he had to connect with somebody on this circuit. He'd start at the bottom and work his way up.

He flashed cash and scanned the place for Durrells and Augies and Betty Lynns. There were a couple in sight, hookers bringing in their clients on an hourly basis, but nobody took the bait.

Two days passed before somebody came after him. She was young, no more than sixteen or seventeen but with a real sharpness about her, dressed to distract. Short red hair tied back in a ponytail so you could see the childishly chubby cheeks in all their sexiness, the angle of her jawline and the clear lovely skin and sloping angle of her throat.

Tight clothes but not too tight, just right to give her natural curves a little extra heft. Braless so she'd bounce a tad more, wearing shorts that clung the way they should, so your concentration would be split and you'd keep an eye on the jiggle.

She pretended to have the room next door to him and stood there fumbling with her key as Chase stepped into the hall. She tried balancing a paper sack on one hip, still fighting with the door lock. The ponytail bobbed and weaved, and her tongue jutted from the corner of her mouth, a nice affectation that could start a man simmering.

He moved as he was expected to move, toward her in an effort to help. Just as he got there, the bag went over and a dozen small grocery items scattered.

"Here," he said, bending to retrieve them. "Let me help."

"Oh, thank you so much," she told him, wetting her lips, stretching out a leg so he'd be sure to notice, "that's so kind of you."

It was a solid ploy. As he was bent over, glancing at her knee, gathering her things—mostly cheap cans of soup and oranges, stuff that would roll and keep him in position—she plucked out his wallet.

She had deft fingers but wasn't quite a pro. Any guy would've felt it without the distraction, but that was part of the con. Get the mark's attention off the swindle, keep him busy. She kept talking, maybe just a touch too much baby doll in her voice. "It's so sweet of you to help a stranger out."

"My pleasure," he said, grabbing the oranges and stuffing them back in the bag. The fruit was old, already going bad. She'd either bought it real cheap off the street or she'd kept it lying around to keep playing this con. He stood and held on to the groceries. "Can I carry this inside for you?"

"That won't be necessary, I've troubled you enough."

"Really, it was no trouble at all."

She wet her lips again, and he thought it might be a tell, a subconscious signal. If she was part of a crew, nobody had ever told her to quit it, because it worked for her anyway. "I think I'll bring this bruised fruit back to the store right now. I didn't notice before but it's not as fresh as I was hoping for." She waited for Chase to move off and said, "Thanks again."

"Sure," he told her, and walked out to the parking lot and slid into the GTO. She'd gotten about fifty bucks off him and nothing else. His ID was safe inside the driver's door with the rest of his cash. He'd dismantle the door and get it later when he needed it.

Chase put on the radio and listened to salsa and reggae music while he watched the front door of the motel. He was surprised he liked the songs so much and actually turned up the volume a little.

She came out about a half hour later, without the groceries. She got into an old, dinged-up Mercury coupe, pulled out, and turned onto the street heading north. He started up the Goat and followed.

She drove to the local mall, parked outside one of the big chain stores, locked up, and walked inside. He climbed out, popped the door to her Merc, and riffled the interior. No registration in the glove box. No weapons stashed under the dash.

Beneath the passenger seat he found a box of fresh checks and two reorder forms, each in a different woman's name. Neither would be her own.

It was another old con. You didn't steal somebody's checkbook. They'd get wise too fast to that. All you needed was the reorder paperwork, then you changed the address and paid for a box of extra checks that the rube didn't know about. You could hang paper for a couple weeks before anybody found out about the excess draws on the account. Then you moved on to the next batch.

It was a little sloppy leaving the forms here in the car where anybody digging around could spot them, but she was still pretty new to the game. At least he knew she was part of a crew now. Small grifts like reorder forms were usually an afterthought during a burglary. While somebody was scoring the silverware and jewelry, someone else was going through the paperwork. If the crew was big enough, it might have contacts to Dex.

Chase popped the trunk and checked the spare tire, found a fairly large stash of marijuana, a few hundred tabs of X, and what looked like about a thousand bucks' worth of coke. No weapons.

He got the hood open and saw that the VIN hadn't been etched away with acid. If the car was stolen, it hadn't been done by a pro. He relocked the Merc and relaxed in the GTO, waiting for her to return.

But there was no breeze, and the stifling heat got to him fast. He should've taken the Goat in to get the air conditioner fixed, but you never wanted to leave a stolen car with stolen plates, forty-five grand and fake ID hidden inside the door in some hick garage.

There was no use frying. Chase popped the Mercury's hood, pulled the distributor cap, and went inside the mall. He got himself a soda and a slice of pizza that could hardly be recognized as pizza, and took up a spot in the food court where he could look out the glass mall doors and down the parking row in case she walked out another exit.

She didn't. She traipsed right past him carrying several shopping bags.

He tailed her outside and watched her dump the packages in the trunk of the Merc. Then she carefully folded up all the separate bags, making sure she had all the receipts.

Chase knew the scam. It wasn't even a con, really, but it could be pretty effective if you didn't get too greedy and go for high-end items. You kept the receipts and the bags, went back to the same stores, refilled the bags with the same merchandise you'd just paid for, then took it to returns and got your money back. Most stores still didn't have a line purchase yet in their computers, and you could get away with the gag.

She returned to the mall and Chase replaced the Merc's distributor cap. He checked the items in the trunk. Mostly cheap jewelry, DVDs, CDs, some women's clothing. Everything would be from a different store. All told, maybe twelve or thirteen hundred bucks' worth of shit. Add to that the fifty she'd nabbed off him and whatever else she'd managed to snatch out of the back pockets of the motel patrons, and she was doing okay for herself. Small-time, but keeping busy. A hustler, an operator, but if she got caught for any one score she wouldn't draw more than probation.

Maybe he'd been wrong. Maybe she was too small-time to be connected with anybody who had a line on Dex. He called Georgie and the Deuce again, hoping somebody had something for him, but there was still no word. Chase would have to follow through.

He moved everything to the Goat—the drugs, the packages, the checks—and tossed them in the trunk. Then he broke the steering column of the Merc, started the engine, and let the air conditioner do its thing. He kept an eye out for her. It took her twenty-five minutes to hit all the stores again and make the returns. When he saw her exit the mall, he shut off the Merc, slid out the passenger seat, and weaved among the parked cars so he could come up behind her.

"Hello again," Chase said, stepping up and snatching her purse from her.

She spun, recognized him, and put her fists up. She had good form, a proper boxer's stance. Somebody had taught her the basics. A glimmer of anxiety lit her eyes for an instant, but she controlled it well and eased her lips into a smile.

She dropped her hands, going waifish again. "Mr. Gentleman, who's always willing to help a lady in distress."

No weapons in the purse either. He found a wedge of cash. Fourteen hundred dollars. He pocketed it and watched the amusement in her expression shift to anger.

"Sucks to be boosted, doesn't it?" he asked.

"Look," she said, "you seem like a nice enough guy. So why don't you return that to me, blow now, and I won't have to scream rape?"

"You do that and the cops might look in the trunk and discover the merchandise you tried to double up on. Or they'll find the pot or the coke. Or they might check the registration."

"I can walk away from this car right now and there'll be no one who can connect me to it."

Chase figured that would be her next move, but he still thought she was small-time enough that losing the car, the drugs, and the merchandise would hurt her crew. "Yeah, but would your boys be happy about your losses for the day? The X? The coke? The checks? The DVDs? Some nice two-disc sets there. Your string's going to be upset about having to watch sitcoms tonight. They going to be able to work their usual scores with one less car on the road? Seems to me they demonstrated a lot of faith letting you drive the club car around. I wonder how miffed they'll be that you let it go?"

This time he saw a touch of genuine fear in her pretty face. "Listen—"

"They the kind who might smack you around a little? Somebody knows boxing. He better than you?"

Her brows knit together and the distress stiffened her features. Unconsciously, she flattened a hand over her belly. Whoever the slugger was, he'd worked her stomach over.

"What kind of shakedown is this?" she asked.

"It's not."

"Feels like it to me. You've been on to me from the beginning, even back at the motel. I should've known it. You acted too much like a mark. You went out of your way to show me your back pocket."

"You're clever but not all that quick with your hands," he told her. "You need to clip your nails before you dip for a wallet."

"Thanks for the lesson. What's it going to cost me?"

A family of four walked past, heading down the lot to their car. Mother, father, and two little girls eating ice-cream cones. A swelling sorrow rose in his chest and he had to look away. He asked, "They pull real scores, your crew?"

"You don't act like a cop, but you sound like one. You come on strong with my friends and they'll hurt you."

"Answer my question. They into anything larger than short grifts like this?"

"Yes."

"You use a wheelman?"

"A what?"

"A getaway driver."

"We don't knock over banks, if that's what you mean, but there are times when things have gotten hinky for us." Her hands drifted toward him, rubbing his forearm, like they were on a first date and moving slowly toward something of great value or something that might break their hearts. He bet a lot of boys and middle-aged men were still tossing in the deep night thinking of her. "So, come on, what's this going to cost me."

Chase told her, "I want you to introduce me to your crew."

She didn't have the most nimble fingers maybe, but she was a quick thinker. He could see it in her eyes, that she thought she'd buy time to figure out a way out of the problem, somehow set him up.

The grin crossed her face again and she unlocked the trunk. She nodded when she saw he'd taken everything in there.

"They won't like you."

"And I won't like them, but that doesn't mean we can't string together."

"That's a bad attitude when you're running up against my friends. Really, you should just give everything back and take off."

"If they were as tough as you think they are, then they wouldn't need you out here running the return merchandise swindle."

"It's a pretty good one, and it's side money for me."

"What's your name?" he asked.

"You're not listening to me."

"I'm bearing it all in mind." He led her to the GTO, opened the passenger door for her. "Please, get in."

"You still haven't told me what you want."

"I did tell you. I want to meet your crew."

"Yeah, but why?"

"To hook up and make some cash."

"No," she said, tightening her face, her chin dimpling. "No, that's not the reason."

He really had to work on his straight face, at least in front of women. Sherry Langan, Cessy, now this one, none of them had any trouble seeing right through him. "Let's put it this way. I'm not out to heist you and I'm not out to get anybody in trouble with the cops."

"What kind of con is this? You think you can just roust your way in?"

"Maybe," he said. "I'm either right or wrong. Let's go find out which."

She kept her distance while he moved to her, took her wrist gently, and tugged her forward, helped her into the car the way he used to help Lila.

In his head, Lila said, You're handling it wrong. You've offended this little white-trash vixen already. She'll never forgive you. If it takes a lifetime, she'll make sure she spits in your blood.

The girl said, "I'll get the hell beat out of me if I tell them how you boosted me."

"So don't tell them. I won't either. And nobody is going to hurt you."

"You sound damn sure of yourself."

He got behind the wheel and looked at the girl again, who was still trying to distract him by showing more thigh than she needed to. She'd plucked another button loose on her blouse so that he could see the curve to her nearly bare breast.

He looked in her eyes and said, "What's your name?"

"You can call me Hildy. What's yours?"

Chase gave her the fake one and she turned it over, repeating it aloud. "Sounds fake."

"It is. Which way we headed?"

"South." She sat in the passenger seat, gnawing her lip, her discerning eyes alive with shrewd thoughts. She let her ponytail loose and the wind tossed her hair around. "Watch out for Mackie," she told him. "He's a sneaky little shit."

The guys in Hildy's crew were sitting around drinking beer and playing poker in a shitty apartment, trying to take down two rubes.

They looked up and nodded to Chase, believing that Hildy had brought another fish by to get reamed in the game. There were three on the string. The two rubes would be strangers even to each other. They had pained expressions and only a handful of chips and a small amount of cash showing. The string wouldn't quit until they were sure the rubes had been taken for all their money, even the emergency stash squirreled away at the bottom of their shoes. Then the fish would get the blowoff. Chase had seen it a hundred times.

The crew was going to lose the next couple hands in order to keep the marks in the game and sucker Chase in.

One of them asked, "Hey, you want to sit and join in?"

"I'm just going to watch for a while, if you don't mind."

"Sure, relax, get a beer."

It went off in a classic pattern. They'd been taught old-school grift sense, same as Chase. It brought back a lot of memories, most of them bad but a few of them good. He started to smile. It's what would be expected of him. They wanted him to think he could walk in and clean them all out. The betting increased and the marks won four pots in a row.

Everybody in the crew was a little younger than Chase, early twenties, but with a lot of the same wear. They'd lived out of places like this most of their lives, with their fathers or grandfathers or on their own.

They were good but not as good as the guys Chase had played against when he was a kid. He spotted the shill immediately because the string had a lot of cross-fire chatter going, too much talk between the outside men and the inside man. The shill was pretending to be a bad player, forcing the two rubes to kick into the pot hoping to take him down and win back their losses in one grand play.

Both marks were pale and sweating despite the

air conditioner being turned full blast. It was another grift. You keep the room cold and you can get away with putting on a sweatshirt or jacket already loaded with cards. The crew members kept rotating the aces and face cards, then dropping the extra clothing back on the couch where one of the others could pick it up in turn.

The crew member who'd invited Chase to join in turned to him now, handed him a beer, and said, "Hey there, I'm Mackie, you ready to play?"

"Sure," Chase said.

Hildy went to the kitchen and returned with a bottle of water. She sat on the couch behind and to the left of Chase, giving him a sly look, a little hopeful but tinged with tamped-down panic.

He had to give it to her, she had guts. Chase figured the guys sat around the apartment most days, drinking even when they weren't filleting fish, and she was getting a little tired of the lifestyle and looking to trade up. He felt an odd gratification that she was willing to tamp down her fear and put some faith in him.

He also knew she had gone for a gun hidden in the kitchen and, if he flopped or sold her out, she'd probably put one in his head and tell the crew he'd forced his way in.

Chase removed five hundred of Hildy's fourteen hundred bucks from his pocket and traded it in for chips.

* * *

Twenty minutes into the game, Chase said, "Man, it's freezing in here," and snapped up one of the loaded jackets. Hildy watched him carefully. A magazine lay open and facedown on the couch cushion beside her. If things got too tight in here, he'd go for the piece hidden beneath it.

Chase let another fifteen minutes pass before he carefully slid the extra cards into his hand. He won with a full house, kings over aces. Then he traded out the cards and reloaded the pockets.

It took Chase three hours to win half the cash on hand, about two grand. He wasn't sure he could get the rest. The crew had a nice grift going, playing off each other. Chase was good but he wasn't a pro card handler, and one of the string especially was giving him a hard time. The kid's name was Boze and he had exceptional skill in misdirection, dealing off the bottom, false cuts, top-card peeks, and doing a three-card, sometimes four-card lift. Boze had put hundreds of hours into the moves. Grabbing four cards at a time and making it look like he was holding one. The best magicians in the world could only handle a five- or six-card lift.

The two other marks had long since been wiped out. They left despondent and very drunk. Mackie kept up a lot of talk, trying to get Chase to reveal details about his life, but Chase staved him off with the usual bullshit.

Mackie had taken a piss break and talked briefly with Hildy, no doubt asking where she'd hooked Chase. Boze said almost nothing but kept watching

Chase's hands. Chase knew the kid saw at least every other sleight Chase made, but when you had two con men in the same game, you didn't call one another on it, you just upped your play. Boze had gotten sharper as the game went on, and seemed to enjoy the competition. He had ratty teeth that he showed more and more, smiling whenever Chase raked in a pot.

The third guy on the crew was called Tony Tons, and he was the strongarm. Didn't say much, not even during the cross chatter. Looked a little dopey. Muscular but fat, he tipped the scales at around two-seventy and was maybe five-foot-ten. Not all that imposing for a strongarm despite the ham-hock hands. His smile was a little too wide and his laugh was a couple seconds off, like he had to wait until he heard others laughing first, making sure something was funny before he joined in.

The cross fire died out. There was no point to it anymore. The fish were gone and the crew knew that Chase wasn't a rube.

Mackie finally got up and dragged Hildy into the bedroom. The guy had held out for a pretty long time. He'd been cool but not that cool. Chase sat in his seat for another few seconds, pocketed his cash, and then followed.

Tony Tons reached out to stop him and said, "Hey you, stay here. That's none of your—"

Chase kicked out the back leg of Tons's chair and watched the tubby thug fall over and hit the ground hard enough to rattle a painting on the wall. Boze was still smiling.

No big surprise about anything happening so far. Chase stepped into the bedroom. Mackie had a tight grip on Hildy's upper arm, his fingers pressing in deeply, the edges of her mouth tilted in pain.

Chase said, "That's enough."

Mackie immediately released the girl and held up his fists. He was the boxer who liked to teach girls how to fight and then work them over a little. Chase wasn't sure if he should throw down with this guy or try to smooth things out. The situation wasn't too far gone yet.

The five-finger impressions on Hildy's arm were a bright red. They were going to bruise pretty badly. Chase had promised to protect her and he enjoyed the rising anger making its way up his back, settling between his shoulders like his grandfather's powerful hand giving him a shove forward.

Whatever the fuck.

Chase moved in and Mackie feinted with a looping left, then spun and set Chase up for a right cross. Chase saw it coming and tried to counter but Mackie had excellent footwork and eased in through Chase's defenses, suddenly right there a couple inches away having covered half the length of the room in two quick, fluid steps. Chase had enough time to angle his head back before Mackie's fist collided with his jaw.

Molten colors quivered and flared at the edges of Chase's vision. He centered himself, dodged left, and swung his hips and brought an arching shot up from his knees that landed in Mackie's ribs. An animal grunt of pain erupted. It made Hildy grin.

Something about her smile triggered Chase's memories. In the garage, shadowboxing and working out on the mats while Lila cleaned her gun collection, the stink of gun oil so heavy that he'd start coughing, and Lila asking him if he wanted to learn how to shoot. He'd remind her that the night they met he shot three guys in the leg, and she'd remind him that that wasn't really shooting, standing two feet away from three arguing assholes and just blasting them in the calves. He'd say, "It worked, didn't it?" and slide up behind her while she shined the barrels of her pistols. He'd pull her backward off her stool and down onto the mat and they'd make love right there. In the garage, in their house, and he'd be reminded he was a married man, a man of property, a regular joe, and he'd somehow made it through the fire and come out the other side.

Now he was back again where he'd started. Not even a fall from grace so much as a fucking swan dive. It was the draw in his blood.

Without warning, the rage was alive inside him, wanting out. He twisted hard to the left as Mackie hurled a crushing right cross toward his temple. If it had hit, it might've fractured his skull. Chase let loose with a bitter laugh and moved in tighter, cutting loose, full-on rock 'em, pummeling Mackie in the belly before wheeling to club the guy in the chest with an elbow.

It was a nice move but not nice enough. Mackie was incredibly fast and had already pivoted and danced away. He connected with a halfway-hard shot to Chase's throat that rattled him pretty well and got his bile grooving. Chase's mouth filled with sourness and his breathing hitched. He let out a sickly cough and went after Mackie, threw two hard jabs into his gut and another into those battered ribs.

With a groan, Mackie fell across the bed on his belly and had to grip the ornate wooden footboard to heave himself up. Chase followed once more and saw that Mackie was bent to one side, protecting his ribs.

But no, that wasn't it at all, Chase realized a second too late. Mackie had pulled a popgun .22 from where it had been jammed in the space between the mattress and the footboard.

Sneaky shit, all right.

Everybody in the life sleeping with their weapons of choice.

Mackie made a show of brandishing the .22, except it wasn't the kind of gun you could really brandish. A snub .22 wasn't worth shit beyond a couple feet. Crappy aim, hardly any kick. It wasn't any good at all unless you held it right up to a man's temple when you pulled the trigger, the way Jonah did it.

Chase stepped back, not all that worried, still coughing and having a hard time swallowing.

"Well?" Mackie said. "What's your con? You're good enough to figure out our grift, but you don't mind us knowing you're trying to beat us with a lot of the same moves. Using my own planted cards against me, you prick? You've even managed to hold your own against Boze. Almost nobody can do that. If you were just after the money, you would've tried to walk out by now."

"I'm new in town," Chase said, his voice gruff and weak. "I'm looking to hook up with a new string, pull in a couple of scores."

"Why should we believe that?"

Asking about Dex wouldn't get him anywhere at the moment. If they did know him, they'd deny it until they got Chase into focus. It was going to take time and at least a modicum of trust. Chase stood there, trying to keep himself from thinking about a dead boy in a lagoon.

"I'm a driver."

"You're giving us back our two grand."

"Like hell."

"Like hell you will, you—"

Then, staring over Chase's shoulder, Mackie's expression shifted to one of surprise and he shook his head hard.

Too late, Chase heard Tons rushing up behind him. Had it really taken the guy this long to get to his feet? Jesus Christ, the dude really was slow. No time to do anything now except begin to turn, try to roll the fat guy over his hip, but no, it wasn't going to work. Tons behind him, a punk with a gun out front, a hot chick playing all the angles and waiting for the fallout, he'd lost control pretty damn quick.

Jonah told him to get out the switchblade.

Tony Tons didn't even try to throw a punch, just hurled himself across Chase's back, driving him forward. It hurt like a son of a bitch and Chase tried to let out a shout, but the sound was tight and hardly a squeak.

Covering up as best he could, Chase fell into Mackie and the two of them smashed into a nightstand, destroying it. The popgun went off.

Chase didn't feel any pain, but a hot splash jetted across his hands. He hoped it wasn't his own blood.

Howling like a wounded water buffalo, Tons rolled around on the floor, only half a pinkie now on his left hand. Chase and Mackie wrestled for the gun, and Jonah said it again, louder than if he'd been behind Chase and saying it directly into his ear, The knife, forget the goddamn popper, use the knife.

Chase chopped at Mackie's throat and enjoyed the abbreviated squawk of pain that it brought up from the guy. Good, see how you like it, fucker. Mackie's grip loosened and Chase snagged the pistol and rolled to his feet.

If Hildy had wanted to, she could've shot him in the back, but he hoped she was swinging to his side now. He turned to look at her and she smirked at him. The sudden thought struck him, There it is, that smirk is what's going to get me in to see Dex.

Still wailing, Tons clambered off the floor and came straight at him once more.

Chase said, "Hey, quit it," but didn't point the .22

at the guy for fear it might go off again and do more damage this time. Tons didn't notice one way or the other. He spun in circles, lifting his knees pretty high for a tubby guy, doing a rain dance in place, blood squirting all over.

Chase had been wrong. Tony Tons wasn't the muscle. He was just the stupid younger brother, the stupid-ass boyhood buddy that the others dragged around. The loyal dumb dog. Tons kept hiking his knees, his heart hammering, the blood pumping worse because of it.

"Cool it," Chase said. He looked at Hildy and Mackie, who remained motionless, and thought, Well, they sure don't give a fuck about the guy. Chase let out a small groan thinking he was going to have to tie off the chopped-sausage pinkie before Tons bled out. "Quit moving around. Settle down."

Boze had been in the doorway for the last minute or two, just watching. Now he entered the room, walked to Tony Tons, and said, "Stop jumping around, you're painting the room!" Tons quit hopping about and Boze sighed, tied the finger stump off with a sock he got from the dresser drawer, and glanced around the place. "Everybody check around, we have to find the fucking finger, see if they can stitch it back on."

Tons found it himself, hanging from the broken lampshade on the floor. Boze told Tons to stick it in a bag and then stick the bag in ice. He said it twice, and took the time to explain himself. "If you just stick it in ice, you'll freeze the nerve endings and they won't be able to do anything with it."

Mackie said, "If we take him to the hospital, the gunshot wound will be reported."

"A .22 in the pinkie isn't going to look like a gunshot wound. We'll tell them he was messing around with firecrackers and blew it off with an M-80."

Chase thought, This is definitely not going the way I expected.

He pocketed the .22 and, once the pistol was out of sight, Mackie started to puff his chest out again. "That's mine. I want it back."

"Quit it," Boze said. "Enough with the roughnecking. He's bent like us. First we'll talk. Who knows, maybe we can use him."

"What? Why? We don't know anything about this character. And shit, you could've helped me out in here, you know. Where the hell were you?"

"You're the one set him off by laying hands on the girl."

"So what!"

"We're out of ice!" Tons shouted.

"So, we know plenty," Boze said. "He's smart. He's tough but not too nasty a character. While you had your thumb up your ass he was actually trying to help Tons. He's got something else going on and needs us in order to get into position. Until then, we own him. If he's any good, we can use him." He turned to Chase. "You want in with us, you start by kicking back the money."

"That's just not done," Chase said.

"You weren't here to score cash anyway. You were here to take a look at us and see if we can give you what you want, right? Since you're still here, we obviously can. You want to try to run a play on us, that's fine. It's the world we live in."

Chase was impressed with the little speech, and found himself a little worried by how sharp Boze was. The four-card lift had already alerted him that Boze was a very focused, patient man.

"We're out of ice!" Tons shouted.

Boze said to Hildy, "You brought him here. He caught you fleecing him?"

"Yeah, he caught me but let it ride. He followed me to the mall, boosted everything in the Mercury, then grabbed my purse."

"How much did you take off him?"

"Fifty."

"What'd he get off you?"

"Thirteen, fourteen hundred. And like I said, what was in the car."

It got Boze smiling again, made him wag his chin at Chase. "All of that you return. You keep your fifty. We start square or we don't start at all."

Chase said, "The clock never resets to zero." He emptied the .22 onto the floor, kicked the bullets aside, and tossed the gun on the bed. He took out the thirty-four hundred and peeled off half the cash and tossed it next to the .22. "You can take back half the paper and everything that was in the Merc."

"For a guy who's new in town, looking to make friends, you sure like to push buttons."

"We're the same breed. I'm a thief. I worked my play against three of you tonight and I won. Respect the experience."

"You still at the hotel where she put the touch on you?"

"Yeah."

"We're out of ice!" Tons shouted.

"Stay there, we'll contact you. But first, let me get this guy's fucking finger reattached."

Chase called Georgie Murphy, gave him the names of Hildy's crew, and asked for them to be checked out. Georgie was distracted by a lady trying to return a Mazda Miata that she said rattled whenever her daughter drove it over 40 mph. The daughter was there in the office, speaking very little despite her mother's constant attempts to get her to explain the situation. It was clear to both Georgie and Chase that the girl had fucked up the Mazda and couldn't manage to tell her mother the truth.

Georgie, who was usually a little remote, kept putting the phone down to try to talk sense to the woman, who was becoming more and more shrill. Chase heard stuff hitting the floor. The lady was getting wild. Her daughter started to cry. Georgie spoke gently to the girl trying to make her 'fess up. Mom banged her fist on the desk or the wall or something.

Chase hung up and called the Deuce. Deuce jotted down the names but said very little. Chase asked

about Deuce's wife and felt his scalp prickle when
Deucie let go with a small hiccup of a sob. He
thought the wife must have died until Deuce let
loose with a giggle and Chase realized the guy was a
little drunk.

The Deuce said, "She had to go back into the hospital a couple days ago, but they finally fixed whatever was wrong. She's like an ox, that woman. Looks
like one too. She rototilled the whole goddamn
backyard, wants to start raising her own vegetables.
To be healthy, right? We can't take vitamins, gotta
eat asparagus and string beans. Can't buy them from
the store, she's gotta go be Mrs. Farmer Brown, and
you know what that makes me. She's just like her
mother. At death's door for six minutes, then she's
ready to run a marathon."

"I'm glad she's doing better."

"She's doing great, and I'm going to be puking
asparagus for the next six months. Still it's a miracle.
We're a blessed breed."

Chase waited a five beat and said, "Who?"

"Us. Thieves. You know why?"

Another fiver. "Why, Deuce?"

"Because the last kind words spoken to Christ
were by a thief, up there on their crosses."

Chase thought, He's really been pouring it down.

"Any news about the Langans?"

"They buried Lenny, now everybody's in mourn-
ing. Their pie's already being divvied up. The other
families are working deals left and right with the
Koreans, the Russians, the Thais. You know they got

Thai gangs now? Who the fuck ever heard of such a thing? Anyway, last I heard, they're mostly packed up for their move to Chi, but they're keeping a couple of local places, bought a mansion out on Long Island. And they're fighting back here and there, got some good hitters. A lot of blood is running, but it's mostly contained."

"Jackie still alive?"

"Why wouldn't he be?"

"His sister's going to cap him."

"Yeah? Well, probably not the worst thing that can happen to the Langans or the world at large."

"Just keep sharp."

"Me?" He broke with a burping sob, chuckled low and a bit wildly. "Hell, I'm a razor."

Deuce called back the next afternoon. As Chase suspected, there was nothing on Hildy's crew. They were too low-class, off the map. Deuce told him that neither Dex nor Jonah had resurfaced yet. They were either working a score or they were on the run because of the fallout from the murder.

Chase said, "Jonah doesn't run."

A half hour later Georgie phoned. He told Chase that he'd heard back from a few folks that somebody was making inquiries into Chase's and Jonah's whereabouts.

"Who is it?"

"I don't know yet. I can't track it back. Guys I know pass it on to me, but they get it from friends of friends, pick up word in a bar, hear something when they're dragged in by the cops for a few hours, and it meanders back to people I have no idea about."

Chase took a shot. "Feebs?"

"No, I don't think so. Seems to me this guy's in the life. Just runs with a different string. I've been trying to lock it down but these people, they don't act like they should. They don't do things the old way."

"Nobody does."

"Except us and the people who taught us."

Chase asked, "Whatever happened with that lady and her daughter from yesterday?"

Talking about the dealership, they didn't need a code. Georgie could let it all out. "Goddamn nasty witch started to pull out the wires on my computer. The daughter was terrified of the bitch, and I can't blame her. I was scared too, almost called in Dunkirk from the garage, guy's six-foot-four, can bench press three-fifty. But I was worried she might hurt him and send him out on workman's comp. I finally just let her trade the Miata in. The daughter must've been letting her boyfriend plow her down at the beach. The undercarriage was dinged to shit and there was sand and salt trails covering the crankshaft. If that lady shows up again then I don't give a shit, I'm sending Dunkirk after her. With a sap. From behind."

Hildy showed up at Chase's door two days later.

She came in, sat on his bed, and said, "Man, I've

never seen a flash entrance like yours before. I've seen a lot of different kinds, but nothing like that one. You just bulled your way right into our lives, toughing it out." She looked in his face, saw the slight bruises around his eyes. "You don't seem too worse for wear either. Mackie usually does more damage."

Chase didn't know what to say to that, so he let it pass.

Sunlight poured across her knees. "Well, despite all the shit you started, Boze still likes you. It's your brazen attitude, he says. Slick, but gutsy, and you're good at cards. That works in your favor so far as he's concerned. He respects anybody who can steal a pot from him."

Chase leaned against the dresser and crossed his arms. "One-on-one he would've crushed me. The others actually held him back during the game. He'd be better off without them."

"They're foster brothers. All three of them were orphaned early and taken in by an elderly couple of Bible-beaters. They ran some kind of boys' home, did charity work at a halfway house for ex-cons. That's where the three of them picked up a lot of grift sense. Well, Boze and Mackie did. Tons just does whatever they tell him to do."

"He's not even good for muscle."

"No, not much. He's stupid. But Boze is loyal to him. He's like that. He latches on to people. He thought it was funny how you picked up on the loaded jacket and started using his own planted aces against him. He waited and watched but you still managed to pull them when he wasn't expecting it. You've got good hands, he says. Mackie and Tons wanted to break in here and kick the shit out of you, but Boze talked them out of it."

"Mackie gave nearly as well as he got, and it was his fault that the other guy lost his pinkie anyway."

"They don't see it that way," Hildy said, shrugging, her breasts giving a little bounce, "and they're still pissed about the money, but it doesn't really matter. We've got a job, and we need a driver. You interested?"

"Sure."

"Good."

She lay back on the bed and went through a rapid variety of provocative poses. Lifting her knees so he could see the tanned muscular thighs, the powerful contours of her legs, dipping her toes out in the air as if it was a cool lake. She flapped the hem of her blouse so her midriff was exposed. Pierced belly button with two blue stones on show.

For a moment Hildy studied him, then shook her head. "Aren't you going to ask me?"

"Ask you what?"

"If I'm sleeping with Mackie. Or any of them."

Chase said, "No."

"There's something about you—"

"It's my lonely eyes."

"They're not lonely. They're mean."

"I was told they were lonely."

"Whoever told you that was lying."

Now she'd get to the real reason why she was here. To dig up whatever she could on him. He had no doubt that they'd already riffled his car, but unless they took it apart, they weren't going to find the cash and there was nothing else worthwhile in the Goat. The gym bag with his burglar tools and the extra ID and cash was hidden in the air vent. It was a good spot, hardly anybody ever checked there even though all you needed was to take out two screws. She'd try to seduce him and when he fell asleep or took a shower she'd go through the room. Until then, she'd keep him talking and try to get him to give something away.

"Why us?" she asked. "Why'd you home in on me?"

"I didn't. You homed in on me."

"Only because you had a bull's-eye on your back."

"Yeah, and you just happened to be the first one to give it a go."

"What kind of talk is that, give it a go? That the real reason?"

"Yes," he admitted.

"So you haven't been in town long."

Shit, she'd played him on that one. "Have you?" he asked.

"Born and raised."

"So what are you doing on the grift? You could do a lot better for yourself. You've got the looks and the sharpness to keep out of the life. Shouldn't you be a beach bunny, sitting on the sand in a bikini, out dating surfer dudes?"

"Is that what you think I want?" she asked.

"I suppose the answer is no."

"You almost sound sad."

It did bother him a touch. She was just a kid, and running lowball scams was only going to get her picked up by the cops or run down by the bigger crews. The bruises on her arm looked painful. He did wonder if she was shacked with Mackie or one of the others, or all three. It worried him imagining her picking the wrong guy's pocket and getting beaten or raped or worse for it. She was smart and sexy and already on borrowed time. Looking at her he thought about Kylie. In sixteen years this would be Kylie if she stayed with Jonah. Living in shit motels, on the run, hip but uneducated, sophisticated but cultured only in the bent life. He thought, This is really why I'm here, to save Kylie from this.

"Do you have anything to drink around here?" Hildy asked.

"Sorry, no."

It made her smile and twist her hair aside, showing off the throat again, the hint of freckles. "You're a different one, all right."

"Because I don't drink?"

"Because you're after something and you won't let yourself be distracted from it, not by anything."

He had a good poker face for the boys but not for the girls. He had to work on that. He cocked his head at her, started to ask something, but she shifted her legs again, showing off the dimpled knees.

"So tell me," Hildy whispered. "Why are you here? What do you really want?"

It was a good ploy. A pretty young woman's whisper was a hell of an enticement. You didn't have to be weak to go with it, to shut your eyes and fall for it. You could be at your best and still slip up. She'd clipped her nails. He watched her fingers stroke her taut belly, more pink than tan, he thought. The piercing caught the light and flashed it back at him, the blue stones twinkling.

What else did he want?

Answers. To find out if Jonah really had killed Chase's mother. To figure out how the old man had been able to murder a four-year-old boy. Sloane had said, *You were his rudder, kid. When he lost you, he lost his way.* Maybe, in the end, all he wanted was to apologize to everyone Jonah had hurt since Chase had gone his own way.

"What's the score?" Chase asked.

"I'll let them explain it. They'll want you to take a dry run, to see if you're any good. You are good though, aren't you? Otherwise you wouldn't have called yourself a driver. It's what you do."

"Mostly."

He could feel the need to talk rising up in him. It had been a long time since he'd opened up, and he'd still never really talked about Lila and Earl Raymond and Angie and Jonah and what had happened in the Newark parking lot. Her voice was getting to him. The vibrancy, the constant assault of questions and apparently sincere interest. He looked down at his wedding band and wondered how much longer he was going to be able to ride out his silence.

"Mostly," he repeated.

"Along with cards and fighting and pickpocketing and breaking into cars and knowing about the check scam." It seemed to impress her. "How long have you been at this? You don't seem to be much older than the others, but you've put your time in."

"I started early."

"Me too," Hildy said, casually patting the bedspread.

She seemed to have run through her list of tricks, rejecting one after the other. She started to speak once or twice and thought better of it. He felt a little worried for her. Boze was going to be irked that she hadn't gotten much off him, but then again, Boze would like that Chase had held his own. It would earn him a bit of respect, the same as the card game had. It didn't really matter much. They would either get him to Dex soon or Chase would move on.

Stymied, she let out a soft sigh, and stood to leave.

Chase asked, "So did they ever reattach the chubby guy's finger?"

"No," she said, "nobody had any ice. We took it to the hospital wrapped in tinfoil, but it was too late. Tons was mad until Boze told him chicks like guys with scars. Now he wiggles it at me all the time. Looks like a cocktail wiener with little black stitches in it. Makes me goddamn sick to my stomach."

Georgie called and said, "I got a name for you. Kel Clarke."

Clarke had run with Earl and Ellie Raymond. He'd been one of the crew that had boosted the diamond wholesaler where Lila had been murdered.

"He's on my tail?" Chase said. "Why?"

"Why do you think? You took out most of his string."

"I didn't want anybody but Earl. The others got in the way. I've got nothing against Clarke."

"I guess he doesn't realize that."

Chase thought of the carefully sliced-open crime-scene tape on the front door of the Dash household. Had Clarke somehow managed to track Jonah? He might've heard that Jonah and Chase were together when they met the rest of his crew in a Newark motel.

Clarke had already taken a portion of his cut and split for another job. Maybe Clarke knew where Jonah was.

"How did he get on to me?"

"I don't know. Maybe you'll get a chance to ask him before he double taps you in the head."

"You're not worried about the feebs anymore?" Chase asked.

"Nah, you were right. I'm sick of sounding like a nitwit. I have the place swept every other day. If they bust me, I'll just pay them off. They're bigger thieves than we are."

"If anybody else on the circuit asks, let them know where I'm staying down here."

"You want this guy to know where you are?" Georgie asked.

"Yeah. I've got questions."

"You think you'll get a chance to ask them?"

Boze and the others spent twenty minutes talking over each other, arguing, going through the score, Tony Tons waving his half pinkie around at Hildy. When they were done Chase said, "Wait a minute. Let me see if I have this straight. You mean to tell me that you guys heist *dresses*?"

"Don't laugh," Mackie said, leaning in a little too far, invading space, still acting pissy. "We steal forty top names, going three grand each on the market. Even with the fence's cut, we can clear thirty or forty g's."

Chase thought about it. Dresses. He'd stolen a lot of shit in his time, but this was something new.

"Go through it again," Chase said, pointing to

Boze. "Just you. You're the brains, don't let others chatter when you're laying the action out. It undermines your authority and muddles the plan."

It was obvious that Boze agreed, and he was a little annoyed at the others for talking while he was, but it also bothered him that Chase had called him on it in front of everybody. Chase realized his mistake a moment too late. He wasn't used to working with amateurs, it was a whole different set of dynamics. Being pushy the other day had worked in his favor. Now it wasn't going to. He had to rein it in or risk bad blood with the last guy on the string who might help him get where he needed to go.

He backpedaled, put a hint of compliance in his voice. "Please, explain it to me once more."

That mollified Boze. "All right, from the top. The entire fifth floor of the building is taken up by a fashion wholesaler and designer warehouse. We rented an office on the seventh floor so we have a key to the building. We pop the lock on the warehouse, go in smooth. It's wired, and response time for the cops is under five minutes, but it doesn't matter. We don't make a mess. We never take more than one or two dresses per rack, so to appearance's sake nothing is missing. We lock the door on the way out. Then we take the service elevator up to our floor and wait in the office. The cops show up and check out the place. Nothing's broken. Nothing appears to be touched. So they think it's a false alarm."

"Why do you need a driver then? You're already situated in the building."

"Purely as a backup. If something goes wrong, we want out of there fast." He glanced at Tons and said, "It only takes one small mistake and you're burned forever."

Chase wanted to ask him why he was crewed up this way. There was something to be said about loyalty to your foster brothers, but he should've been higher up on the chain of the pro career circuit. Or working solo scams taking down major poker players. He could grift the big games and make more money with less hassle.

Dresses. Chase kept thinking about it. He tried to imagine Mackie up on C-Block, telling the hard cons he was inside for ripping off backless gowns.

Maybe it was a smart heist, maybe a goofy one, but it didn't have the feeling of a true score. Maybe he was being a snob. If they actually cleared what they said they would, then it was a smart heist.

But it worried Chase that he wasn't doing enough. That this job was so low-key that nobody else up the chain would be getting a taste, and so it wouldn't get him to the next level.

"When do we go in?" he asked.

"Friday night. Everyone in the building leaves early, and the cops are usually busy on the other side of town dealing with brawls in the bars. But before that, we have another small job to take care of first."

"Sure," Chase said, thinking, This is where things might go bad, which is exactly what he needed.

* * *

Time coasted by. The small job was in Tampa, an hour north. Supposedly a nice city, but Chase couldn't tell. It was night and they were in the shitty part of town. Every shitty part of town looked like every other town's shitty part of town.

The crew was ready to sell their drugs and merchandise, all of it in the trunk. They didn't give Chase any specifics and he was glad. It was nickel-and-dime crap but Mackie seemed tense and hyped and still worried about Chase a little. Chase figured if he didn't show too much interest, Mackie would calm down and he could start taking advantage of Boze's good graces.

All he had to do was find Dex, then get from Dex to Jonah, and from the old man to Kylie.

They left Hildy at home. She had a line on some new joe who was eyeing her at a different motel than the one Chase was in. She would pull the whore-with-standards act. Get the fish on the hook, have a few drinks with him, but before the action went down she'd tell him to take a shower. While he was in the bathroom she'd rip off his wallet and make a run for it. Chase thought it was a low-class and dangerous grift, even for someone as sharp as Hildy. You never knew what the mark might do in a position like that. He might refuse the shower and just rape her. Chase let Hildy know his reservations but kept them to himself around everybody else.

"Are you packed?" Mackie asked from the back-seat.

Chase thought of luggage. "What?"

"Are you strapped, do you have a gun?"

"No."

"Why not?"

"I'm a driver."

"So?"

"So drivers don't carry guns."

Mackie held a .32, tapped Chase's shoulder with it, and Boze said, "Put it away."

"He should be carrying."

"Not if he doesn't want to. And you shouldn't be waving the damn thing around while we're on the road."

When they got to Tampa, Boze gave Chase directions and they turned into a block lined with bars and third-rate clubs. People milled out onto the street. There were a couple scuffles going on, lots of noise. Bouncers bookended most of the doorways. High-pitched laughter slit the night. Drunk twentysomething women walked arm in arm, trying to hold each other up.

There was way too much action on the scene. It went against Chase's grain. You didn't fence stolen property with so many eyes around. He turned to Boze and said, "You do this out in the open?"

"Hiding in plain sight. Everybody's loud and drunk and there's pussy all over the place. Nobody's going to notice us. Pull over up here."

Chase looked around one more time and tugged the Goat to the curb in front of a club called the Curse of Nature. "You expecting trouble?"

"Not really. This fence is something of a prick.

Name's Arno. He manages the place and does his own business out the back office. Sometimes he deals with the syndicates, old fat Italians on the down slide who come here to go out on his boat and get blowjobs and go fishing. Arno pushes his deal as hard as he can, we push back, it ends up in the middle. You'd think we could just start there and walk away with no hard feelings, but it's not the way this guy does it. He's surrounded by his entourage, usually has one or two toughs on hand and a couple of girls and prettyboy fags who laugh at all his jokes. He's only in this to feel like a hot shit."

Tony Tons murmured, "I don't like Arno. He's got a wise mouth, and he can't say a word without being insulting."

"You're right, Tons."

"He's said some shitty things about me."

"But you're strong, Tony Tons, you're rugged and staunch, and you don't let him rattle you."

"Hell no."

Chase asked, "How much do you expect to net off this guy?"

"Worried about your cut?" Mackie said. "You didn't do anything a cabbie couldn't have."

"Not much," Boze said. "Four, maybe five grand. But you know how it is. Not all the scores can be big ones. You do minor grifts from time to time to keep yourself in beer and hamburgers." He turned and grinned, reading Chase's face. "You've done it plenty yourself, haven't you?"

Not for more than ten years, Chase thought, but

he remembered the times well. When Jonah would be planning a big take and he'd send Chase out to pick up seed money. A little burgling, a quick three-card monte setup for the afternoon. As a kid he'd loved the life.

"How long will this take?" he asked.

"No more than five minutes."

Twenty minutes after the crew had carried the merchandise through to the office of the Curse of Nature, Chase shook his head and thought, Well, here we go.

Inside him, Jonah said, Leave them and hit it. A wheelman never gets out from behind the wheel.

Lila told him the same thing.

Sometimes you could cut and run and sometimes you just had to see the thing through for no reason you could name. He didn't owe this string anything. The longer he stayed with them, the better the chance that the sneaky shit Mackie would slip Boze's leash and ambush Chase. The setup had been precarious from the beginning.

But he was their wheelman. Boze had shown trust, and Chase couldn't just leave the guy inside without knowing if something was wrong. You gave your word, you followed your course.

The moment he hit the sidewalk he felt the music pounding. Lots of steel kettledrums, the kind of noise that made your fillings hurt. If you wanted to listen to that sort of thing, you might as well climb into a garbage can and roll down a hill.

Moonlight engulfed him and he let it hold him for a moment.

College kids out on the street danced arm in arm and drank from huge liquor bottles, guys making moves, girls half-out on their feet. Neon flamingos and cockatiels buzzed and flashed on both sides of the road, casting baby blue and pink colors that nobody used except in Florida.

Chase walked into the club and the sultry heat and music hit him like a fist in the chest.

The place was packed, and from a quick scan he saw that a lot of the patrons were underage. Arno didn't much care for running a respectable establishment, and having kids around him all the time probably just enhanced his self-image. Surrounding himself with an extended teen entourage, it was one way to play king shit of the castle.

Jonah telling him, Turn back now, or I'll have to kill you. Don't come after me.

Chase checked the corners, found what he thought might be an office, and moved to it through a gauntlet of gorgeous girls gyrating across his path. But it was just some kind of cordoned-off private alcove where VIPs were supposed to sit. A handful of well-dressed people were hunkered in each other's laps trying their best to appear indifferent and superior.

He made his way along the nearest wall past braless waitresses wearing T-shirts two sizes too small. One smiled at him and he smiled back, slipped in close and said in her ear, "Arno's office?"

She pointed to the opposite end of the club and he saw a door guarded by a huge, bald bouncer who stood with his hands open at his sides. Chase suspected this mook might actually be trouble. Other bouncers crossed their arms or carried drinks, compromising their hands. But this guy was waiting, revved.

Chase thought about it and tried to make a decision—go in easy or go in hard.

What the hell. He put his hands in his pockets, stepped up to the strongarm, and said, "Heya, how are you tonight? I'm here to see Arno."

Sometimes the world whipped against you and sometimes it went your way. The bouncer grinned, reached for the doorknob, opened the door, and politely ushered Chase inside.

The office looked like the newlywed suite in a really tawdry motel. Lots of chintz and maroon and teal and shag. A large desk took up nearly one-half of the room and a massive round sofa took up the other. On the wall hung a flat-screen TV with porn running on it. Chase looked at it for a minute, cocked his head one way, then the other, and still couldn't quite figure out what he was watching.

On the floor, leaning back against the desk, was the crew. Mackie's nose bled freely and he was holding his left arm like it might be broken. Tons's pinkie had been torn open again and he was gripping it tightly with his other hand but it was still spritzing against his chest. Boze's features were contorted into a disgusted expression as if he couldn't quite believe that a guy as smart as he was had found himself in the middle of this situation.

Boze nodded to the sofa and said, "Meet Arno."

Arno was a serious fatcat. He tipped at about three-fifty, all of it soft pink and stretched, moist flesh. He lay back on an enormous sofa, surrounded by his attendants. Three not-so-beautiful chicks covered in glitter and wearing shiny clothes drooped in various states of drug-induced repose. A couple prettyboys stood behind him, massaging his back and stroking his greasy black hair. It all made Chase think of some of the really twisted Roman emperors right before the big fall.

Something happened on the screen and the entourage oohed. Chase looked and still couldn't make out what was going on. He was starting to think that maybe he wasn't as cosmopolitan as he'd previously believed.

Chase said, "Hello, Arno. What's the problem?"

Arno wasn't eating peeled grapes but he was sipping some kind of fruity frosted drink, holding it lightly in one hand and clutching some serious hardware in the other. Looked like a .44. He took his time, swallowing with such verve that his jowls jiggled and shook. When he finally lowered his glass he focused on Chase and said, "Who are you?"

"Just someone stopping by to say Hi."

"You with these dinks?"

"Sort of, for the moment."

"I see." Arno examined the bottom of his glass. "Voorman, grab him."

Chase had never been a weapons man, really. But he had to admit he was liking the switchblade.

He snapped it from his pocket, just as fast now as he had been before the recent wounds and setbacks. He held the point of the knife to the inside seam of Voorman's thigh. Pushed just hard enough to tag flesh, going maybe an eighth of an inch into the muscle. A small circular stain of blood appeared through the bouncer's pants. Voorman let out a cute little puppy yelp. The noise made one of the stoned girls giggle.

Chase said, "Voorman, you know what a femoral artery is?"

The bouncer's bald head had such a nice shine to it that the action on the TV was reflected in it. He whimpered, "Yes."

"Okay then, how about you just stand there and not move an inch and I won't have to bleed you out all over this tacky French-bordello decor?"

"Okay."

"Thanks for being so accommodating, I appreciate it."

"No problem."

Tony Tons said, "I don't feel so good."

Arno lifted the .44 and pointed it at Chase. "Do you see this in my hand?"

"I do," Chase told him.

"Then what's your problem?"

"My very question to you. What's the beef, Arno?"

As it happened on occasion, a player liked to talk to somebody in the know. Who ran up against him and kept his cool and didn't feed into the ill will of the moment. Arno, who was already one of the most relaxed pricks Chase had ever seen, visibly relaxed even more, sinking farther into the cushions and damn near melting like a scoop of ice cream left out too long. The prettyboys lost their hold on him and just stood there, staring.

"They ripped me off."

"They did? How?"

"I think I'm gonna be sick!" Tons said.

"The X they were trying to sell to me was originally stolen from me."

"I see."

It was the kind of scam that worked when you were dealing with major insured items. Steal some rich lady's jewelry, then peddle it back to the insurance company for half of what it was worth. No need to deal with fences and you avoided a lot of hassles, including the cops. The companies just wanted their merchandise back and they saved at least half their bread.

But you couldn't do the same thing with drug dealers or pink fatcats waving .44s around. Especially if they were egomaniacs, which damn near everybody was. They didn't like having to buy their own product back from the rip-off artists who took it in the first place. Boze should've known that.

Looking into his eyes, Boze certainly seemed to have picked up on it by now. Chase got the feeling this was Mackie's stupid score.

"Okay, so what's the damage?" Chase asked.

"The potential damage is to my reputation," Arno said. It was the kind of thing that someone without much of a reputation would say. "I can't let it out on the street that I'll pay top dollar for my own drugs. That invites further piracy."

Chase couldn't really argue the point. "You're right. How about the other shit?"

"The other shit doesn't mean much to me. I'll pay fourteen hundred for it."

"There was about a thousand in coke. Was that your product too?"

"No."

They'd expected four or five grand on the deal. "Make it twenty-five hundred for everything."

"Why should I deal at all?"

"Because you're not going to dump four guys in the ocean over this."

"What makes you so sure?"

"Because you're a businessman with some weird fetishes, not a maniac."

"Twenty-two hundred."

"Done," Chase said.

Mackie started to protest. "It's worth more than twice that! We—" The blood from his leaking nose was thickening across his lips and turning his teeth red. He jumped to his feet and took a step. Arno's gun hand swung over and Mackie stopped moving. Surprisingly, it looked like he could make a smart move when the moment called for it.

Boze helped Tons to stand. He looked for something to tie a tourniquet. Tore a piece of Tons's shirt off and tried to knot it in place but it wouldn't stick well. Tony Tons's finger continued to bleed against his chest. He said, "I'm getting sleepy."

"Stay awake, Tons."

Voorman tapped Chase on the shoulder and said, "Could you take the knife out of me now?"

"No." Chase tugged the blade a little and the bouncer gurgled in the back of his throat. "Shut up."

He nodded to Boze and said, "Go pick up your money."

Smiling, Boze ambled across the room and met Arno, who was also smiling. He nodded, got his jowls moving again, and one of the prettyboys took the bills from his own pocket and handed them to Boze. The girls giggled. The boys giggled. Everybody happy now that the storm had passed.

Except that Boze turned to Chase, still showing that grin, and offered an honest flash of humiliation in his eyes as he passed. It was the kind of small and meaningless shame that you couldn't live down. Chase shouldn't have taken the money without deferring to Boze, and he shouldn't have ordered him around.

Another foolish move. They were piling up. Chase tugged the switchblade out of Voorman and the bouncer went "Ahhh," and put a hand out onto Chase's shoulder, steadying himself. Chase waited to see if the strongarm was going to throw down now. He didn't. He patted Chase's shoulder twice the way a thankful buddy might.

So, he'd made friends with the troublemakers and

stirred more shit with the crew he was working with. The Jonah in his head had been right. He should've just run.

Chase followed the others out of the office and gave a last backward glance to Arno, who was starting to use the .44 in an unholy manner on one of the girls.

Crazed music and crushing body heat swarmed Chase as he made his way along. Tons yawned and staggered from the loss of blood. When they hit the street he said, "He insulted us again. He called us dinks. He had Voorman break your nose, Mackie. Does it hurt?"

"I'm going to kill that piggy son of a bitch," Mackie said.

Moonlight and a soft breeze dipped across the back of Chase's sweaty neck. Boze turned to him and said, "Man, you've got the touch, all right. You're cool, you're cold, and you've got the heat, all at the same time."

Not a thank-you, and Chase hadn't been expecting one. He read the subtle anger in those words and realized that Mackie wasn't going to be the problem after all. Boze, with his hands as fast and dangerous as Chase's, faster even. Who knew what he could do when he held a knife or a gun? Chase was going to have to pull up stakes very soon.

But he hated to leave without managing to swing any info on Dex. It was the wrong time to ask, but it couldn't be helped. He couldn't work it naturally into the conversation, especially since there was no conversation. But he had to give it a whirl.

"You think this will get back to Dex?" he asked.

No one answered him. Mackie was tearing another section of Tons's shirt off to use as a tourniquet. He tied it very tightly and Tony Tons wavered and almost passed out. Chase got behind the wheel of the Goat and as soon as everyone was in he threw it into drive.

"We have to get Tons to the hospital again," Boze said.

Chase thought, Florida, what the fuck am I doing down here with these idiots?

After Tons had gotten stitched back up, Chase dropped the string off and returned to his motel. The spot between his shoulders grew tight and hot as he crossed the lot. He hoped there was a shooter nearby. His ears quivered as he fought to hear beyond the warm breeze whispering in the darkness. He got to the front door and held back a moment, giving Kel Clarke or Bishop or his grandfather another chance to break from some shadows and come after him. He stared at the dim reflection of himself in the glass, searching behind him, hopeful, waiting. Then he stepped inside.

He checked his watch for the third time in ten minutes. He was wasting time. Mistakes were heaping around him, the weight of them slowing him down. He decided he'd give himself another twenty-four hours to push the others and see if anything would rattle free. If he couldn't get any useful information on Dex from the crew, he'd go back to Arno and see if the fatcat could get him in touch. If noth-

ing there, he'd have to start over and find himself a
new thief working some grift on the dark end of the
street in another part of town.

Shirtless, he stood in the window of his room and
willed someone to make a move on him. The rage
built in him, rising from its great depths until his
skin felt on fire. Chase was suddenly furious with
himself that he hadn't checked the Dash house more
thoroughly. Maybe he could've found a photo of
Kylie. Her face, he thought, could possibly stir the
things inside him that needed to be awakened, perhaps could cool the overheated parts of his mind
and warm what remained on ice.

He kept seeing the little girl he used to imagine
would one day be his own, back before he and Lila
had started visiting the specialists and they still had a
little hope left. He flashed on the daughter that
wasn't his. The threefold hook tugged. At this instant, he was as close to tears as he could possibly
come. He hadn't cried since he was ten and his
mother had been shot to death in their kitchen.
Hadn't sobbed even once for his suicided old man,
or for Lila.

But now the image of a daughter he didn't have
filled his head. It was a revelation of sorts, thinking
of her again and remembering what wholesome
pain he used to feel, holding Lila in the sweaty
nights of Mississippi and dreaming of family. And
now, still holding on to some bizarre hope that saving Kylie would somehow be saving himself.

He lay on the bed and watched a movie. The picture unfolded before him and he watched and listened, and when it was over he didn't have any idea what the movie had been. He turned the TV off. Within seconds he was asleep and had started to dream of his old man under the icy water, his father's eyes black and frozen. Chase was reaching out to take his father's hand and pull him to the surface when a knock on the door woke him.

Switchblade ready, he answered. Hildy stood there wearing only a bikini top and some kind of wrap knotted at her hip.

Lila said to him, This one, if she don't sink her claws in soon, she's likely to give up and put on a habit.

Chase stood without his shirt on, all the mottled scars and bruises on display. Hildy gently placed a hand to his shoulder and let the backs of her fingers trail down across his chest, flicking against the thatch of hair. He noticed she had on orange nail polish today, an awful color in its own right but somehow looking appropriate on her. She touched his collarbone where the stitch marks were still red and ugly, the skin puckered badly.

"You have a nice body," she said, and he put his shirt back on.

On the bed again, moonlight coursed across Hildy's knees. This time she only hit one provocative pose and held it, her eyes on him. She'd been on the beach and was even more tan than the other day, the twinkling blue stones of her pierced belly button flashing across his face whenever she took a deep enough breath, the rays of moonlight slashing.

"I've heard there are shakers who move right in on a crew and take it over," she said. "Is that what you're after?"

"No."

"Then I don't get it. You're not after the money, or the juice. You'd get plenty more on your own. And you don't want me. When that bullshit went down with Arno you could've bailed. I mean, Jesus, did you really go in there with nothing but a switchblade? Anybody else would've run, but not you, and you've got nothing invested."

She angled her chin aside, the veins of her throat and light array of freckles presented to him. An animal gesture of acquiescence, meant to agitate and excite a dominating red-blooded American mook. Lila said, She's been thinking on you, trying to get inside your head, practicing in a mirror and putting on cold cream. All this sun, by the time she's thirty she'll look like a worn-out saddle.

Chase said, "Not everybody would've run."

"Everybody I know."

"You know a lot of third-raters."

Nodding, she took another deep breath and held it, her stomach muscles fluttering and the moon splashing into his eyes. "You're a different one, all right."

"You said that before."

"And it's still true. They're not sure what they want to do with you. Boze isn't as happy with you as he was before. A brazen attitude will only carry you so far. You've been stepping on him."

"I know. I didn't mean to. I just wanted to keep everybody alive and keep the situation from going nuclear."

"But you also saved their asses, and they understand that. Mackie still wants to kick the hell out of you, but it's different now. I think that's more his way of saying that he respects you. Throwing down on you."

"Some guys are mixed up like that."

"Isn't that the truth." She slid higher onto the bed, relaxing across the pillows, and Chase knew she was really going to turn on the heat now. "Why haven't you tried to make me?" she asked.

"You mean besides the statutory-rape charge?"

It got her smiling. "Yeah, besides that. None of the other guys ever cared about that."

"That's why they've all done time."

"That's not why, and you're avoiding my question."

"It's the kind of question anybody who's smart avoids."

"I am eighteen, you know, if that kind of thing really bothers you. And I see the wedding band. But she's not here. Something tells me she's gone for good. Maybe you're divorced, maybe she split, maybe she's dead. But you're alone. I was wrong before about your eyes."

"Jesus Christ," he said. The eyes again.

"They're not mean. They are lonely. And sad. Can I stay here with you?"

"No," he said.

"Why not? I want to know."

Like you had to explain such a thing. Like it would make sense to a kid like her. "It's not something I can tell you."

"Of course it is. Why do you think not? Because your heart was broken?"

"Yes."

"I like to hear about love," Hildy said. "Nobody ever talks about it. My parents sure as hell never did." Her eyes took on a faraway look. "My mother was a diabetic. She used to go into sugar shock. It was like she was drunk. She wouldn't know me, wouldn't know what day of the week it was, who the president was. She'd talk to me like I was a stranger and ask me to take her home. She'd cry like a lost little girl and I'd force-feed her candy bars and orange juice, then sing to her to calm her down until the sugar kicked in. It was the only time we ever got along. My father, he lost an arm in Desert Storm but it didn't slow him down from fucking around all the time. One of those guys who was always flirting, always on the make like his life depended on it. Maybe it did. Maybe it had something to do with the war, maybe he was just an asshole. I once caught him with a Mary Kay saleslady who was going door to door around the neighborhood. He was working the nub of his amputated arm all up inside—"

"Jesus Christ, kid, I don't want to hear this!"

"—her and she was screaming. I wonder how big a check he cut her. He brought back all these cosmetics, a rainbow of fingernail polish. My mother wore green eye shadow for months after that. Come lay down and talk to me. Tell me about your wife and what gave you your sad eyes."

Any other time and he wouldn't have said a word, but he'd fallen into a strange, heavy mood and his thoughts were moving from past to future without halting on the present. He sat on the bed, propped against the headboard, thinking about Kylie out there with Jonah again, and forcing himself not to obsess on Little Walt's last ride. With Lila's voice echoing his own inside his head he talked about her to Hildy. It felt as if the sob that had been building in him might threaten to break at any moment, but it held back and back until he almost wanted it to leave him once and for all. Hildy shut off the light.

His voice seeped from him in a way that made it almost impossible for him to hear. He seemed to be talking about the specialists. Broadway shows. The day he'd rushed to the hospital and forced his way into the morgue. Lila's voice took on a strength his own lacked, the Southern twang just a little stronger than usual, the way it happened when she was a little upset.

Words slid from his lips full of significance but no context, already edited of most names and places. He was surprised he had the presence of mind to do that considering his state, but maybe it was Lila lending a hand. He ran through the high points of the last several weeks, painting a vivid and accurate picture. He spoke of Kylie, his fears for the little girl, then talked about the lagoon. Hildy perked and let out a little sound like she'd stabbed herself with a needle. Maybe she'd heard about it, maybe it was just that awful a story that it could affect anybody, no matter how hard they were, so long as they weren't Jonah. Hildy murmured beside him with sorrowful, sometimes nearly sexual whispers.

"What do you want now?" she asked.

She placed a hand on his inner thigh, but didn't move it. No patting or massaging or groping toward his groin. Just the touch of a lovely young woman. She looked into his mean or sad or lonely eyes and moved away from him.

He wanted to save his two-year-old aunt Kylie even though he couldn't offer her anything truly stable. What the hell was he going to do with a little girl? He didn't have a job, he'd reentered the bent life. It didn't matter, he thought, he hoped. But he couldn't leave the girl with Jonah.

It was nearly three in the morning. His chest pained him as if a steel band were tightening around it. The moon washed across Hildy's face and lit her in silver. She stared at him, eyes black in the dark, her lips shining.

"You didn't burgle houses with those three," Chase said.

"No," Hildy admitted.

"Who then?"

"Why do you want to know?"

Whatever Jonah's score was, it was most certainly already in play. He was close to the old man and didn't want to have to start over again.

The smirk. The smirk was what he'd focused on before.

He turned to Hildy, the pillow hot against the side of his face, and said, "I want to meet Dex."

"Oh. You trying to get in on that big job?"

Turned out she was one of those chicks who floated through crews, latching on to guys here and there and then breaking off again, always in motion. A familiar face who got her action, brought friends around, served drinks, picked up a few tricks of the trade, and usually heard more than she should've. Chase had seen a lot of women like that growing up, but never when a major score was cooking.

Georgie had said that Dex didn't usually work on the same circuit with the likes of Jonah, and Chase could see why. Letting girls get in close enough to overhear your setups was worse than sloppy, it was sometimes lethal. Chase realized that if Jonah had known Hildy knew anything about this latest heist they were planning, she'd be dead.

She spilled what she knew about Dex, which wasn't much despite the fact that she drifted in and out among his boys, the way she did Boze's crew. She was one of several girls who revolved around the Sarasota circuit. They called her a greeter. She made the pros coming in from out of town comfortable. She'd been on hand when Lamberson came in. She called him the prostate guy.

"That's all he talked about. How he had to go in once a week for radiation. He thought his dick was being burned off. Said his father died from cancer and he figured it was his turn now."

"Can you get me in to see Dex?"

"He always moves the meets. I haven't heard a word from anybody on his string for a couple of weeks. They hardly ever need a girl around. When they do, I show up and sometimes there's other chicks too, sometimes not. It's not quite as sleazy as it sounds. Those guys, they don't like whores much because a streetwalker doesn't know the rules. She's not really part of the bent life, and she's likely to give up what little she knows about somebody if she gets dragged in on a vice rap or a drug charge. The strings like girls in the life who know about grifting and scores and won't ever open their mouths unless they're told to. They like a little company just so they can talk about their jail time and their biggest heists. Most of them don't even want to screw around. They want someone to ooh and ahh, make them a sandwich."

"You don't have a number for him?"

"No, not Dex. But one of his string. Guy named Russ Declan."

"Call him and find out what you can."

Hildy shook her head. "That's not how it's done. If I call him, he'll suspect a setup right from go. It's easy to disappear forever in a state that has almost twelve hundred miles of coast."

All that coastline but Milly and Little Walt had been dropped in a lagoon. What did that say?

"Give me his number," Chase told her. "I'll call. I'll say I got it from Lamberson and I want in on the job."

"Lamberson wouldn't know it."

"That doesn't matter. He'll have to tell Dex that I know about the job. Dex will have to reel me in and check me out anyway. I just need to get inside."

"Once you're in they might just cap you."

"Not until they talk to me to find out what I know."

"Then you'll give me up."

He looked at her and said, "No."

She stared into his face for a while. She brought her lips to his, pressing and urging, but he was stone, as he thought he'd always be from now on, and eventually she gave up. "Your wife's dead."

"What's the number?" he asked.

They slept late, lying there on top of the sheets with their clothes on, her hand on top of his chest. Hildy showered first and used most of the towels. Then he went in. The sexual tension had vanished. It was gone because she'd finally turned it off. She was smart enough not to keep wasting energy.

He called and tried to break into Dex's string. Chase spun his story about getting the number from

Lamberson and hearing about a big score cooking. For added credibility he threw in Sloane's name. Russ Declan was friendly and talkative and eager to meet. He mentioned a bar that Chase had passed a few times.

They'd have to check him out now to see if they had a leak and if the score was blown. Chase figured he'd immediately be ushered to where Dex's crew was holed up because everybody involved would want to get a look at him and see if he was wired. They'd make nice for a while, play some cards, drink some beers, try to squirrel info, and if he wasn't forthcoming enough they'd shatter his kneecaps.

Chase took Hildy out for breakfast. Over French toast and hash browns he said, "Tell me about Russ."

"He's like me kinda, on the edge of the circle. A little jittery sometimes because he used to be a trucker and he picked up a taste for speed. He used to live on it during the long hauls. He likes to be behind a wheel. Not getaway stuff, but just long drives, up and down the Intracoastal, to the Keys and back again."

"But he's in on the heists?"

"He's muscle. Preferred weapon is a twelve-gauge. Covers crowds, keeps anybody from being a hero during bank jobs." She drank her milk and said, "This is sour. Is your milk sour?"

"No."

"Try it."

"I have tried it."

"And it's not sour?"

"No."

"You hardly sipped yours."

"Order another."

"I don't want another if it's going to be sour."

"Get orange juice then!"

She did, and more hash browns, toast, and another side of bacon. He liked watching her pack it
away. Lila had loved to eat too.

"Any idea what the score is?"

"A circus," she said.

Chase took an extra second to see if he'd heard
her right. "What?"

"This traveling carnival-circus comes through.
Calloway & Dark's Traveling Fair and Sideshow of
Wonders. They're still popular around here, the
old-fashioned carnivals. Touring all through the
South."

Chase remembered just how fucked up names
could get down here. He'd met Lila while on a string
with three guys who planned on robbing Bookatee's
Antiques & Rustic Curio Emporium. Later on, he'd
bought Lila's wedding ring from Bookatee himself.

The rage wanted to crawl up his spine again. He
thought of armed men running into a circus tent
filled with kids holding balloons and cotton candy.
One shot and the horses and elephants stampede,
stomping folks underfoot and knocking over the
bandstands, crushing dozens. He saw Jonah drawing a bead on midgets and dancing poodles.

But it would be a cash-only venue. Probably no real security. Tickets and cash boxes, bored teenagers and carny hawkers working the crowd. It seemed a little stupid and not all that big a score to call in so many pros, but maybe there was more to it than Chase was thinking. Compared to knocking over a traveling fair, the dress heist sounded a lot smarter.

"I don't suppose you're going to drive for Boze anymore now, are you?" Hildy said.

"They don't need a driver."

"They think they do."

"That's part of their problem. They think too much and not enough."

She nodded at that, turning it over. He wondered if she was in love with Mackie or Boze or anybody else. The fact that she wandered through the crews didn't mean she didn't have her heart set on some-one.

Like most women in the life she had a hard-line worldliness fused with a kind of naive romanticism. Cynical but fanciful, the two never balancing out, always working against each other. No one would ever be able to earn her love. She wouldn't want it that way. In the bent life you only took what you could steal.

They finished their meal and Chase paid. Hildy moved to him again, leaning forward on her toes, as if she might try to kiss him, and he found himself edging toward her, as if to receive her in his arms, except his arms were tight at his sides.

She twirled aside and said, "Can you drop me off?"

"You didn't drive to the motel?"

"No, I took a cab."

It went against all the rules, taking taxis and leaving a record of your movements. "Where's the Merc?"

"We had to ditch it."

Chase led her outside and they climbed into the GTO. She said, "You don't have a gun."

"I don't like guns."

She pulled a Smith & Wesson .38 out of her hand-bag. "Here."

"What are you doing with that?"

"What do you think?"

"You didn't have it the other day when I checked your purse."

"If I had, maybe you wouldn't have been able to check my purse."

"But last night I told you—"

"You don't have to like it, just use it. You think too much and not enough too."

"You keep it. Your friend Russ will just snatch it from me when I show up. Or it'll spook him and he'll be edgy enough to draw down on me before I've had a chance to meet Dex. I don't need it."

She shook her head and said, "Are you for real or what? How have you lived so long?"

He was almost back in the groove. When he saw Jonah again, the old man would be palming a .22 down against his leg for a quick draw and pop.

Chase would snatch it away and stick it in his grandfather's eye and say, How could you do it, you prick?
How could you snuff a kid? Where's Kylie? The old
man would stare at him, as inured and implacable
as an ancient altar where hundreds had been split
open by stone knives. Chase was eager to find out
what would happen next.

PART

III

His cell rang before he even started the car. The Deuce told him, "Jackie Langan just got aced in Vegas. One between the eyes while he was sleeping in bed."

Chase snapped his phone shut and knew Bishop would be coming.

Looking at his face, Hildy said, "Jeez, even more bad news?"

"Nothing I didn't already know about."

"Most people, they know about trouble, they step out of the way. You walk in front of it."

"Yeah, you might be right about that, but I have my reasons for doing what I do, same as you."

She gave a practiced titter, the kind of thing drunk businessmen might like to hear. "Sometimes you sound as stupid as Tons."

"Oh man, that's just low."

Halfway across town they picked up a tail. A Ford

Taurus, hanging back about fifty yards but being fairly aggressive, jockeying to stay in position. The roads were packed with surfer dudes hanging out of Jeeps, boards and coolers on show everywhere. The Taurus almost clipped some shaggy-headed golden boys in a crosswalk. Worried that Chase would notice, the driver fell back for a while. Chase made a sharp left.

"Where are you going?" Hildy asked. "You were supposed to take a right there."

He glanced at her again and thought about his promise to her. "I know. Hold on."

"Hold on? What kind of talk is that, hold on? Keep your eyes on the road, would you? Are you going to explain the 'hold on,' or what?"

The Taurus kept with them as Chase took occasional turns, running plans through his head and discarding them one after the other until his mind was made up for him. An old Dodge pickup burning a lot of oil crossed lanes in front of him, got directly ahead and started leading the Goat along, blowing clouds of blue smoke. Behind, the Taurus closed in doing its best to stick tight without really tailgating him. They started to box him in.

For a minute Chase thought it might be the Langan crew having caught up much faster than he'd expected. But he decided Sherry and Bishop just wouldn't play it this way. They wouldn't hire out to hit him twice in a row. The next time the Langans came at Chase, Bishop would come on his own and

Sherry would be in the room, trying to get a look into Chase's dying eyes.

It could just be another cheap scam. Guy in front hits his brakes, you crack into him, and then the guy in back speeds up to smash into your car. First guy takes off leaving you to pay out of pocket to avoid the cops or insurance hassles. It happened on American highways a hundred times a day.

Hildy perked in her seat, checking the side mirror. "So this is hold on, huh? You got clowns behind you."

"And in front. Either of them Russ or Dex?"

She looked ahead, saw the Dodge braking for no reason. "I don't think so. How would they know you? It's an insurance scam."

"I thought so too at first, but they're boxing me in too tight."

"But we're barely doing forty. Maybe they're just really bad at the swindle."

"Nah, they definitely want to pin us."

"They want to pin you. I'm not the one who goes around looking for trouble. You ready for the .38 now?"

"Buckle up," he told her.

"Oh shit. Jesus Christ, you could've had me if you'd wanted me, there's no need to show off now. What are you going to do?"

Chase said, "Put out his lights."

"Isn't that like crashing?"

"A little."

The wide street was empty. He sped up and nosed

the Dodge in the rear. He could push the GTO and put some real muscle into this race, do a lot of body damage, maybe crack the others up, but he wasn't in the mood to run these assholes around for a while. Chase had things he had to do.

The driver in the pickup was talking on his cell. Chase checked the rearview and saw the driver of the Taurus talking animatedly too. Jesus Christ, they were actually on the phone to each other, probably doing a countdown.

Pulling a gamble like this meant they wanted him out of the car. So he'd get out.

He slammed the brakes and the Taurus plowed into him from behind. The Goat rocked hard, but you had to love classic Detroit steel. Serious grillwork, solid as all-hell bumpers. Hildy barely bounced in her seat.

But a little tap like that and the Taurus's headlights exploded and its front end crumpled. The hood lock detached and the hood sprang open. The driver slammed on the brakes and the car slewed over the curb and tapped a fire hydrant.

The Dodge pickup slowed but didn't stop. It roared off as Chase watched it, the blue smoke dwindling in the sunshine.

Chase said, "Stay here."

"Where else am I gonna go?"

He threw the Goat into park, leaped out, and ran to the Taurus. He got the driver's door open while the guy behind the wheel wrestled with the inflated air bag. They fill hard and fast and explode into your face so that it's like a punch in the nose. The driver was dazed. Chase grabbed the guy by the collar and yanked him out of the car, threw him down in the street and kicked him twice in the stomach.

Okay, so it wasn't an insurance scam, wasn't Russ, wasn't Bishop, wasn't Mackie or Tons, and it wasn't Jonah. That left only one person Chase could think of.

*Y*ou *Kel Clarke?" he asked.*

Chase got his first good look at the guy. He was young, even younger than Chase. Maybe twenty-one, still had crummy skin. Skinny, only needed to shave once a month tops, almost effeminate, with a lot of wild James Dean hair that smelled of fruity shampoo and spray. His nose was bleeding from the air bag.

He tried to roll to his feet and Chase slugged him in the chest. The kid's sternum rang like a bell and he let out a squawk of pain. Chase frisked him. The mook wore a deep concealment Kel-Tec P32 clipped to his belt and he kept trying to reach for it. As small as a dollar bill, the frame clip made it look like nothing more than a folding knife. Another sneaky fucker. Chase slapped the kid's hands aside and snatched the tiny gun away.

You had to love Sarasota for one thing besides the bikinis. Broad daylight, buildings all over the place, traffic at the cross street ahead, but everybody minded their business. When you lived on the beach and always picnicked with your kids, you had even less cause to get in someone else's face.

"I asked you a question. Who are you?" Chase said.

"Like you don't know?"

"Like I don't know. Are you Clarke?"

"Yeah."

"You ran with Earl and Ellie Raymond."

"That's right."

Clarke tried to stand and Chase put his foot on the guy's chest. "Just sit there."

"Come on, man, in the street? The cops might show up."

"Then talk fast. Who was in the pickup?"

"Nobody."

Chase pulled one other name that he remembered from the guys who had crewed up with the Raymonds. "Jason . . . Fleischer?"

"No, someone else I work with on occasion."

"Okay. So what do you want?"

It seemed to confuse him. "What do I want?"

"My very words. What do you want?"

"What you mean what do I want? What do you think I want? You wiped out my whole crew. I want you dead."

It took Chase back a little. "Why?"

"You're asking me why?"

"Were you that close with them?"

"No. We only pulled a couple of scores together. Come on, let me get up."

"Stay there. Did you get your cut from that diamond heist?"

"Some of it anyway."

"So why come looking for trouble?"

"I thought you were after me too. I wasn't about to sit around and wait for you to come find me. Not after what happened in Newark. Not after what you did to them. That motel looked like fucking Beirut. You drove a car through a wall and ran over Slip in his goddamn bed!"

"That's not what happened."

Chase did drive through a wall, but Slip and the others hadn't been crushed. The room was small but large enough for two double beds, with a nightstand between them. Earl Raymond had been behind the bed farthest away, his sister Ellie between the two, Slip Jenson closest to Chase so he was the one Chase popped first even though he didn't have anything against the guy.

"However it went down," Clarke said, "you racked them up pretty good. Bodies in there, bodies next door in the other room. I did some checking. The old man killed his own woman. She was what? Twenty? Twenty-two?"

Not even. "How do you know that?"

"Like I said, I asked around. I called in favors on the circuit. I found out about you and the old man. You're vicious. You don't stop. You're maniacs."

Clarke was one of those guys who couldn't keep anything bottled inside him. He liked to talk, let you know what was on his mind. He'd worry about the consequences later, maybe have to go out and find somebody who had listened to him too closely and plug the leak. But he liked getting it all out of his system in a rush.

"I barely remembered your name. Earl pulled the trigger on my wife. You were there in the diamond merchant's shop that day. You saw what happened. All I ever wanted was him."

"You still killed Ellie and Slip too."

"I told them what would happen," Chase said. "I gave them a chance to give up the driver. They didn't take it."

"Why should I believe you?" Clarke asked.

"Why shouldn't you? I never made a move against you."

"Maybe you were just working your way up to it."

"You've got an inflated sense of your self-worth, kid. If I wanted you dead, I wouldn't be standing around trying to convince you otherwise."

"Maybe you just—"

"Shut up."

He stared at Kel Clarke and thought that it only would've been a matter of time before Ellie Raymond had taken him out of the game. She had a knack for finding young stupid guys, and Chase could tell this kid hadn't been in the bent life for too long. He was dumb as hell and paranoid on top of it. He overreacted. No cool, no calm.

"So how did you find me?" Chase asked.

"I've been asking around."

"Yeah, but nobody knows I'm here."

Clarke's eyes started to shift. He wanted to come up with a story quickly but didn't have the imagination for it. No wonder he needed to partner up with people smarter than he was.

Chase smacked him in the nose and got a little blood flowing again. "Don't lie, just tell me."

"I tracked the old man."

"What?" No way did this idiot catch on to Jonah. "You? Impossible."

"His girlfriend used to run with some people I know. I followed the story after Newark, started asking around, found out who she crewed up with, what scores she pulled, where her family lived."

"And you found him?"

"No," Clark admitted. "But it got me down here to Sarasota."

"Be glad you didn't get any closer on his trail. If you had, you'd be dead."

Chase glanced back at the Taurus again and something snatched at his attention but didn't hold. He couldn't figure out what it might be. Lila shouted something in his head so loud that it resounded painfully and made him frown. He turned as if she was standing beside him, shot her a look and wanted to say, What is it, honey?

He tried to piece it all together. "You've been following me since when? Since I checked out the Dash place?" Chase thought of the cleanly sliced police tape. Someone had tried to break into the house after the family had been murdered. Could this mook have been parked up the street, just waiting for

Chase or Jonah to come traipsing by? "You've been onto me that long?"

Smiling, Clarke said, "You're sloppy. Or crazy. You act like you want somebody to come after you. You don't take precautions. You're a suicide waiting to happen."

"So why didn't you make your move sooner?"

"I was worried about the old man."

"You should be."

"I wanted to get you both. But I can't find him. And neither can you. So I figured I'd take you on today."

"That was your big plan? Drive me off the road? You insulting prick." Chase kicked him hard in the chest again. "Take my advice. Don't run with any more hot dogs like Earl. Don't rile the old man. And stay the fuck away from me."

He got back into the Goat beside Hildy and drove on.

She said, "You're letting him go?"

"Yeah."

"Well that was stupid. I always thought you guys, the pros, you wouldn't ever let someone who crossed you just up and leave."

"Where'd you hear that from?" he asked.

"From everybody. It just makes sense." She frowned and gave him the look again. "You sure you know what the hell you're doing? When he comes back to waste you I hope I'm nowhere nearby."

"You won't be." He handed her the Kel-Tec. "Here, this suits you better."

"It looks like a knife."

"That's the idea."

"You should keep it. Like I said, Russ, he's a little jittery sometimes, depending on how much speed he's taken and how much he's slept in the past few days. Tiny gun like this, he'd miss it. Dex won't, but Russ will."

She spun the P32 around in her hand, looked in his face. "So what is it now?"

"What?"

"Something's on your mind. You were nice and cool before, even while you were kicking that guy around, but now your eyes are burning."

The girl beside him, radiating heat and intent, muttering her wiseass humor like his wife used to do. That firm resolve always a solid weight pressing against him, like her warm hands as they rode, wherever, whenever they rode. He stared at the girl and kept flashing on Lila, straining to make sense of what she'd shouted at him back at the scene. If only she hadn't yelled, but the Lila in his head had been anxious in a way his wife had never been during her life. He sat there hoping she'd repeat herself. He kept asking, demanding, thinking, What? What, damn it. Honey? You there?

"I don't know," he said.

You sure you don't want me to come with you?" Hildy asked. She put a hand to his wrist. Not sexing him up this time, just going in for contact, being real and human and kind.

"No, you've done enough. I don't want you around in case anything goes wrong. I appreciate you getting me this far. Thanks for your help."

"I really hope you know what you're doing."

"We'll see."

Chase dropped her off at Boze's place and then drove over to the bar to meet Dex's contact man, Russ.

Russ was a fidgety bastard all right. Looked like he hadn't slept in three or four days, pepped on uppers. Pretty much nondescript otherwise. Muddy eyes pressed into a muddy face. Greasy-dishwater blond hair. His left arm was so suntanned it was almost black. They called it trucker's arm. It came from all the miles of hanging it out the driver's window.

They got a booth in the back and made small talk

for a while. Chase didn't spot any other players in the bar. Mostly barflies and some early-duty whores waiting for happy hour. Russ commented on most of the ladies, intimately familiar with them.

Chase could sense the need to drive within the guy, the compulsion that would take over some wheelmen he knew when he was a kid. It wasn't about the getaway or the money or the action or the juice, it was about living behind the wheel. Some of those guys used to try to outrun roadblocks. They wouldn't hole up even after a big job. They'd get on the road and just break out on a highway and get nabbed crossing state lines doing triple digits. He figured Russ had tried to be a wheelman but nobody trusted him enough to include him on their scores.

The guy talked incessantly, saying nothing but rambling on, unable to sit in his seat without bouncing his knee or rat-a-tat-tatting his knuckles on the tabletop, all lit fuse and burning flare.

They drank beer and did a few shots. The plan would be to keep Chase drinking to loosen him up so he made a mistake. He drank the watery beer but sprinkled out the shots under the table into the inch-deep grime on the floor.

Russ was so hyped he didn't notice anything. The speed ruled him but he wasn't entirely gone yet. He kept asking questions, most of them meaningless but with a few sharp ones tossed in to dig deep for real info. Chase answered them all truthfully. It was his honesty that would keep him alive, at least until he was inside Dex's door.

Two hours passed. After another four shots of Wild Turkey, Russ became a lot more mellow. Chase didn't try to act drunk. Nobody ever did a good job at it. They always overplayed and everyone saw through it anyway. Chase excused himself and went to the bathroom. Either Russ would attack him in the john or he'd use the time to phone Dex and tell him to get ready.

Russ didn't make a play. Chase returned to the table and said, "How about it?"

Smiling and nodding, Russ hopped to his feet and nearly fell over. He wasn't just mellow, the speed was wearing off and the liquor and lack of sleep were taking their toll. Chase watched the guy steadying himself against one of the ladies, who made a crack and got the whole bar laughing.

Russ was so fucked up he couldn't drive. Chase got the guy situated in the GTO and asked how to get to Dex's place. Russ couldn't seem to remember. He soon passed out and looked very peaceful in the passenger seat, snoring lightly. Chase reached over and found Russ's cell, hit the redial.

A voice went, "Yeah?"

Chase said, "Your man's asleep. I need directions."

He got the address, left Russ asleep in the Goat, and found the right apartment. He knocked and the door snapped open. He looked around at four guys eating salami sandwiches and playing poker. Maybe Dex's string, maybe just a few others like Russ and Hildy, on the outskirts of the crew, put to use from time to time. Chase was hoping Dex might have pulled in someone else that he knew but they were all strangers.

The place was a one-bedroom shit hole, rented on a weekly basis. It was just a meeting ground, nobody stayed here. Chase figured they'd already packed up and had a new shithole ready to call home base until the big circus heist went down.

Quick introductions were made. All the names would be phony. Dex wouldn't be here, he'd be off somewhere safe waiting to get a report. They'd continue to size Chase up and try to wheedle bits of information from him. They needed to know if he was a cop. They'd keep feeding him liquor and wait for him to drop his guard.

One guy had already set up station near the front door to keep Chase from making a run for it. Someone went to the window, saw Russ with his head against the passenger window, and said, "It's the Wild Turkey that gets to him. He can stay hopped on reds for a week straight, but the minute you give him a shot of cheap whiskey it hits him like an ax handle."

They poured Chase three fingers of bourbon. He bought three hundred in chips and they dealt him in. They'd be cool another twenty minutes, and then the anxiety would stretch and widen until they cracked him in the head, threw him across the table, and frisked him.

Twenty minutes max to make his move.

If only he could figure out what it should be.

Two of the guys were cheating and making a game

out of it, trying to one-up each other. In some circles, you pulled something like that, it would leave at least a couple of people dead, but this bunch was playful, showing one another their tricks. Chase lost four pots in a row and then they fed him a big one back to keep him in good spirits, prove to him that they weren't out to cheat him. It was a smart thing to do but they shouldn't have pushed four pots. They didn't know him well enough. He could've been an edgy type who didn't dig their merry ways. But then, they would know that much about him.

Nobody mentioned Dex's name or talked about any scores or jobs they'd pulled. He might be wired. If he asked any questions, they'd think he was a cop or a snitch, so he let them lead the conversation and once again answered everything honestly. Where he was from, where he'd been, who he knew, some of the old scores he'd been involved with. All the info he relayed was ten years old.

He kept an eye on his watch. He figured someone would stand up to get a beer, walk behind his chair, and throw an elbow into the back of his head. It was all right, he could take an asskicking. The idea of four guys yanking his pants off to make sure he didn't have a wire under his nuts was a little more bothersome, but he could handle that too. He just hoped he wouldn't have to try to stare down his grandfather with his crank hanging out.

They fed him good hands trying to get him to bet large, then at the last second pulled out flushes and full houses to beat him. It was all a matter of trying to get him a little riled. Chase started cheating too, and won back what he lost but no more than that. They didn't know what to make of somebody who worked the pots to stay perfectly even.

One of them asked, "You want another beer?"

"Sure," Chase said, thinking, Here it comes, here it is.

The guy passed behind his chair. He didn't throw an elbow. He pulled a blackjack. Chase decided that was excessive. You miss the sweet spot and you can shatter a man's skull. He turned in time to take the blow on his good shoulder. It still hurt and the guy came in for another pass, brushing Chase's ear with the leather-covered lead weight.

Four on one and they had to try to sap him? Going with the flow was one thing, but rolling over to die like a dog?

No guns on show yet. Chase wanted to drop and let them frisk him, but everybody's cool was gone. It didn't really matter anymore because now Chase was pissed. Like he hadn't taken enough shit down here.

He picked up a beer bottle, spun, clocked the guy with the sap, and watched him go down. It was a nice move, he had to admit, and he hadn't even given the mook a concussion. Somebody threw a jab into Chase's face and his field of vision blazed red and black. He fell back to the wall and the three guys still standing moved in. That was fine. Nobody knew how to fight as a team, they all just waded in and got in each other's way.

Taking a deep breath, he fired off a couple solid

jabs, slugging ribs and chins, holding back a fair amount but too angry to completely give in. A little nonconducive to what he was trying to accomplish here, but to hell with it. Let them work for it now.

Chase danced around the table, trying not to laugh as the three came around together, nobody thinking to head him off on the other side. That's what happened when you had no chain of command, just a group of thugs who all listened to one guy. Without Dex to give orders, they barreled ahead. Still no guns, which was a touch surprising. Chase held his ground, threw a few jabs, a few uppercuts, watching the blood squirt. He chopped at a throat and the guy gagged and went to his knees.

Someone else picked up the fallen sap and swung wildly. Chase backed off and found himself cornered, stuck beside a ratty couch and an unplugged refrigerator that smelled like a lot of shit had died in there. He got his arms up and pulled his elbows in, ducked his face, and took a lot of hammering before he went down.

The fourth guy finally got to his feet again and stumbled around some. Then he jumped into the fray too. They started to work Chase over pretty good, everyone joining in. He rolled onto his belly, balled up, and tried to ride it out. He'd let them get their shots in. He'd taken worse.

They started kicking him, which he also thought was excessive. Sons of bitches, was he going to have to get back up and fight some more? No, he tightened up further. Not too much damage going on until someone caught him in the groin. The rotten pricks.

Finally, huffing and weaving, they lifted him up, threw him down on the couch, got his clothes off, and gave him a solid frisking. You couldn't tell nowadays with microtransmitters and bugs. They looked between his ass cheeks. They looked under his nuts. They combed through his hair with their fingers.

Someone eventually went away and got Dex.

Middle-aged but honed, everything about him lean and tight and sharp, Dex was another hard-ass with too much strength and not enough mercy.

You only had to take one look at him to know he'd left a lot of blood in his wake. Good references, Georgie had said. Been around a while, does good work. The man's eyes were dark and they glistened with judgment and deliberation. Chase figured Dex always made off with the score no matter who he had to leave behind. Chase wondered why he'd never heard of him before.

He must've been up river for a while. Or maybe he really did heists so seldom that he never got known wide on the circuit. At least not when Chase was a kid.

Dex spoke to his man at the door, his lips hardly moving, puffing his words under his breath the way a lot of ex-cons did. Dex had a .32 in his back left pocket. He stepped over, tossed Chase his clothes, and said, "Get dressed."

Chase wasn't even bleeding badly, a couple threads

from his nose and his mouth. His nuts still hurt though, and he hissed through his teeth as he got back into his clothes. Dex wet a hand towel in the sink and threw it to him. Chase wiped the blood off, sat back, and waited. Everyone else did too.

"Who are you, kid?"

Chase gave his real name.

"So what the hell's your problem?"

"Me? I don't have one."

"You didn't get my number from Lamberson."

"No," Chase said.

"And you're not here for any job."

Chase could barely say it with a straight face. "The circus score? No."

"So what's it all about?"

Ready to double-tap him if he didn't immediately follow up with the truth.

So here it was. "I want to see Jonah."

Five minutes later the door opened, and there was his grandfather.

Jonah, the murderer of his own woman, the murderer of children, perhaps even the murderer of Chase's own mother. Cold, abiding, impenetrable, looking down at him, lips tilted into the thinnest smile in the history of the world, a grin barely there but as much as a man of stone could muster.

That's all it took.

The rage ignited inside Chase. Lila said, Don't be foolish, love. You've come this far.

Jonah in his head said, You're dead.

Chase started to reach out and snatch the old man's .22, except Jonah didn't have it in his hand. That startled Chase enough to make him hesitate for an instant—where was the lethal .22 that Jonah always had cupped against his leg so he could jab it against a man's temple when the guy least expected it?—and then he went for the .32 Dex had in his back pocket.

His hands, as fast as ever. Chase snaked his fingers out, grabbed the gun butt, and yanked it free before Dex realized anything was going on.

The gun, like holding on to ice.

Chase aimed the pistol at his grandfather's face.

He knew exactly why Jonah had entered the room. It wasn't because anybody suspected Chase was his grandson. It wasn't because Jonah was in charge of the circus score and had come around to check out last-minute details. It wasn't because he was about to play cards and have a few beers with these mooks. It was because Dex was using the old man too, keeping him on hand in case it turned out there was a snitch or a cop in their midst. Jonah was there to remove the problem.

But there was something different about the old man.

Chase frowned, even while all the hardware came out around the room, pointed at his head. Nobody saying a word. He realized with sudden clarity that he'd been planning it this way from the beginning. Take out the old man and suicide right alongside him. What a stupid move. After all this, who would be left to save Kylie? She'd wind up in the system, nearly as fucked up as if she'd been raised by Jonah. He should've listened to Lila. He should always listen to Lila.

So what was it about the old man now?

At sixty-five Jonah remained hard and powerful. The two bullets in the back hadn't slowed him at the Newark motel, and even now didn't hitch up the man's step at all. His back straight, arms corded, every ridge and muscle cut to perfect definition. Same steely eyes.

The seamed face, the white hair, the prison tats on display. An angel on the left forearm and a devil on the right, both in midflight with drawn flaming swords.

Under the angel: *Sandra, Mary,* and *Michael.*

Jonah's mother, his wife and his son, Chase's father.

Under the devil, peering through a pitchfork: *Joshua*. Jonah's father.

And beneath that, not a tattoo exactly but a scar, a homemade scratching that had gotten infected and would forever remain mottled. *Chase*.

Something different about him, but what?

It took a moment.

Jesus Christ.

The old man's face.

The old man's face with a hint of human expression. Something like worry.

Chase couldn't believe it. He lowered the gun an inch. Jonah said, This is a trap, you're going to die.

Jonah said, "I'm glad you're here."

Dex gave orders and the others cleared out. That told Chase that they hadn't been Dex's circus score crew but the hangers-on, the ones he put to use when he needed them to do the minor jobs and rough stuff. A crew wouldn't split without seeing the outcome.

Jonah held a place of certain respect. Dex moved across the room and sat at the table, lit a cigarette, and said to Chase, "Think I can have my gun back?"

Chase ignored him, staring at his grandfather, trying to figure out his next move. He'd thought that maybe he'd wanted the old man dead. Did he still? He might never get another chance. He could feel himself wanting to say to Jonah, Seriously, are you totally cracked? The fucking circus?

"Where's the girl?" Chase asked.

The worry, if it had ever actually been there in the old man, was gone. Jonah gave him a long, steady look, emotionless as always. No hate, anger, or surprise. Jonah studied him, his gaze moving almost imperceptibly. Flicking over Chase's face, his hands, noting body language, lining up the angles. "What kid?"

"Your daughter. Angie's daughter. Kylie."

Jonah, immovable stone. Giving nothing, showing nothing, incapable of even pretense.

"Why did you have to ace them all?"

"Who?"

Chase brought the gun up again and pressed it against the hollow of Jonah's throat. His rage, more alive than he was, clawed at his back, scrambling to get a better toehold. It crawled down his arm and ignited his trigger finger.

Sweat trickled down his forehead, easing into the furrows and wrinkles between his eyes. He let out a sound that was part laugh, part snarl, the kind of thing he might've done in bed with Lila. He thought that two in the chest wouldn't be enough for Jonah. Maybe not even the whole clip. He still had the switchblade. The point of the switchblade driven through the old man's left eye and sinking it to the hilt in his brain. Maybe. Maybe that would do it. But first he had to find out about the girl. All that mattered now was making sure the girl was safe.

He tried to speak but nothing came loose. Little Walt in the lagoon. Chase's mother in the kitchen. Angie in the Newark motel. All of them crowding his head.

Who. The old man had actually asked who. Like he couldn't remember. Like maybe the list of victims was too long for him to remember.

"Dash," Chase said. "Milly. Walt. A four-year-old

kid. He played with your daughter. You dumped him in the water."

A new kind of sheen appeared in Jonah's granite eyes, like rain on rock. "You think I did that?"

"Where's the girl?"

"Why do you care?"

Chase wet his lips but nothing would come for a minute. "Where is she?"

"I don't know," Jonah said.

"What the hell does that mean?"

"I'm looking for her. You've got it all wrong. She was taken. The family was already dead when I got down here." Then the old man spoke in a voice that was almost graced with a hint of love. "I could use your help."

Chase dropped back a step. It was a show of weakness and he fully expected Jonah to take advantage of it. Rush forward and cripple Chase with a vicious hook to the sternum.

But the old man did nothing, just stood there staring, waiting.

It took a few seconds to put it all together. Chase had everything backward. He'd imagined Jonah had gone in and murdered Dash and then hunted after Milly and Walt and iced them after he'd gotten Kylie back. He recalled being shocked that Jonah had been able to recover from his wounds so fast and get down to Florida so much quicker than Chase had been able to.

But no, Jonah had been running behind too. He was the one who'd slit the crime-scene tape.

"Oh Christ," Chase breathed. He finally understood what Lila had been trying to tell him today, what he'd seen but hadn't understood.

Kel Clarke on the ground, the Taurus laid up against the hydrant with the hood open. Chase had glanced into the back of the car and seen the seat belt angled downward, the hint of gray plastic.

There'd been a baby seat in back. He'd seen the top of it and the fact had registered deep within him. If he'd only taken a step closer, he would've seen Kylie there.

The only other family blood he still had. She'd been within arm's length.

Little Walt in the lagoon, put there by Kel Clarke.

Chase backed up until his legs touched a chair. He sat heavily, sick to his guts. Part of him couldn't stick to the idea, the guilt was too strong. In the backseat of the car, just sitting there, but quiet, so quiet after Chase had slammed on the brakes and the Taurus had cracked into him. Not a sound out of her. Maybe she was dead already. Maybe her neck had snapped in the accident. It might be his fault.

A baby's blood on his hands.

Dex and his grandfather sat at the table too. Dex, sure of himself and caring little about the personal shit going on around him, kept his eyes on Chase and didn't go for another piece. There was no need.

He knew this had nothing to do with him. He'd spent a lifetime sizing men up. Those dark eyes had judged Chase and found him an incapable enemy. Still, he listened intently.

Jonah reached out, took the gun gently from Chase's hands.

"Tell me what happened," Chase said.

It was a short story. Jonah came for Kylie and found the house taped up. He got inside and saw what had happened. He held out a little hope that Milly and the kids had gotten away. Dex had a couple good snitches tied in to the cops, but the police had no leads. Then, the other day, Jonah saw the same news broadcast Chase did when he learned Milly and Walt were found in the lagoon.

"Somebody was sniffing around. I spotted him hounding my tail while we were setting up the score at a motel."

"That the guy by the ice machine?"

"Sloane told you."

"Yeah. What'd you get out of him?"

"Nothing but the name on his license. There wasn't time. He pulled a piece on me."

Dex let out a chuckle. "Now that was a hell of a day. We were just getting ready to talk business with some boys when your grandpa here, he gets up and leaves the room saying he's going to get some ice to cool down the beer. He walks down the hall, shoots this guy standing in the alcove. The bullet ricochets, sounds like a tommy gun going off. There's candy machines, soda machines, all this exploding glass.

You got low-class tourists right next door, a couple of fat kids in flip-flops and hip waders, their fat parents right behind them wanting to get some chocolate bars. Jonah comes back in says we have to move the meeting, so we move, except half the guys we want to bring in on the score all vanish."

Dex talking just to make sure that nobody forgot he was there, that he knew secrets, that this was his pad, and everything that occurred here was under his banner. And if there was money involved, he wanted his piece.

Jonah knew it too and said, "We shouldn't talk here."

Chase said, "So who was he?"

"The name on his license was Fleischer. Jason Fleischer."

Kel Clarke's partner, another one from Earl and Ellie Raymond's string. Another stupid kid too dumb to even get some fake ID. So they'd been in it together. Grabbing Kylie.

A little shaky now, the adrenaline easing back, the rage dissipating. Chase was starting to feel the ass-kicking. He said to his grandfather, "Let's go."

*R*uss *was still asleep in the GTO. Jonah looked at* him and said, "What's this?"

"This is Russ."

"He was your first meet."

"Yeah, but he has a drinking problem, a drug problem, and a driving problem too."

Jonah opened the passenger door and Russ flopped out onto the sidewalk. "Dex needs to clear out the third-stringers and find himself one real solid crew."

"This way he keeps his finger in every pie. And there's a lot of bodies between him and the cops." Chase moved around the front of the Goat. Russ gurgled and snorted but didn't wake up. Jonah climbed in over him and Chase gunned it.

The wheel in his hands steadied him. Held him firmly in his seat, in his space, despite the fact that the presence of the old man was a storm sweeping down on him, even now growing in strength.

He threw the car into drive and the engine's

power moved into him. He checked the rearview thinking what it would be like for the girl to be back there, strapped into her seat, playing with a doll. The unfairness of it heated Chase, got the sweat prickling his scalp again. The dead owned him. The old man owned him.

"The guy who has Kylie, his name is Kel Clarke," Chase said.

Jonah showed nothing. He didn't even turn in his seat to look at Chase. The old man just listened, already formulating some kind of plan that would vary and shift and adjust as Chase spoke. You had to wonder if Jonah started off every new minute with the idea of killing you, and that you were still alive now only because you proved yourself useful enough to keep breathing.

"Is she still alive?"

"I think so."

"But you don't know for sure."

"No."

"Clarke. I don't know the name."

"He ran with Earl and Ellie Raymond. So did Jason Fleischer. That's why the two of them were down here."

"Because of what happened in Newark."

"Yeah."

"They were that close a crew?"

"No. Clarke thought we would come after him."

"Why?"

"He rattled."

"Another moron that Ellie Raymond had wrapped around her finger. How'd they find Kylie?"

Chase took his time before allowing himself to say her name. "Angie. They knew some of the people she strung with before she hooked up with you. Somebody pointed them to Dash's house."

"How do you know that?"

Chase didn't want to explain that he'd run into Clarke and let him go. It would only increase tension. But he didn't have a lie ready and the old man would only smell it on him anyway. So he told the truth. Jonah listened impassively, the way he listened to everything, even when it was about his missing daughter. He said, "You should've killed him."

"I didn't know what was going on."

"You still should've killed him." Jonah shook his head. "It still doesn't explain how Fleischer found me."

"Maybe luck. He could've connected with any of the third-stringers and picked up on your name. Maybe he figured you'd eventually make contact with Dex and just kept watching some of the crew. The grifters on this circuit, they don't have many rules. They don't act like pros. They talk easy. They're sloppy."

"I knew Dex had too many people around. I should have pulled out."

"Why didn't you?"

The old man said nothing but Chase thought he could figure it. Jonah really had been hurting after

Newark. He didn't want to have to do a lot of work. He allowed someone else to run the score and maybe, as he recovered, he got a little lazy.

"After you aced Fleischer and the meet got moved to a new place, Clarke lost sight of you."

"I got more careful then. How did he get onto your tail?"

"He's paranoid, a little nuts. Maybe he was in love with Ellie Raymond and wanted to ice us for her. He had the Dash house staked out. He's working with at least one other person. When I checked on Kylie, they followed me."

"And you didn't catch them?"

What else could he say. He'd been hurting too. His shoulder still infected, popping tranqs, bennies, the dreams making him even sicker. "I was sloppy too."

"Okay."

"Why didn't you check in with Georgie Murphy?" Chase asked. "He could've told you some of this. Could've warned you."

"Murphy's dead. His kid Georgie is a worrier who cares more about selling cars than acting as a drop. He's been getting more and more nervous. He thinks the feebs are onto him. I don't trust him anymore." Inclining his head the slightest bit in Chase's direction. "What are you doing down here?"

"I came looking for you."

"I told you not to."

"Yeah."

Leaving it at that. With everything between them

still right there, growing by the second. The static charge picking up serious wattage. Jonah not even bothering to say, You thought I could ace a little kid? How could you possibly believe that? Not even annoyed by it. Not denying it. Not caring in the least. Saying nothing more about Kylie, never actually asking for help.

When Chase had needed the old man to hunt down the crew that killed Lila, he'd been forced to cough up a hundred grand to buy his grandfather's talents. In the end, Jonah hadn't done much of anything at all, but there the prick sat satisfied that Chase was in his pocket.

The wheel in his hands steadied him. You had to hold out hope. "We need to find someone who ran with Angie before you hooked up with her. Clarke might've stayed in touch with them. Maybe we can work backward and find him. The guy he was working with drove a Dodge pickup. Give me the names of who she worked with."

"It's a big list," Jonah said.

"Good. More chance we'll get a hit."

"So what if we do? People know people, especially down here on this circuit. It's smaller. The big money here is in drugs and illegal Cubans."

"Not carnivals and circuses? Stealing balloons? Holding up the lion tamers and the guy who shovels the elephant shit?"

"It was a solid score."

It was the first time in days that Chase felt like

laughing, but he swallowed it down and held it close inside his chest.

"We have to start someplace. This is it. We might get lucky."

Even for Jonah this was hitting a little close to home. The idea that he had to start asking around for Angie's friends. The woman he'd killed, following the murders of her sister and her family. All these people dead because Jonah had wanted a teenage lover.

He found an old pen in the glove box, grabbed the map, and began writing in the borders. He scribbled name after name without hesitation. The man on the slide to seventy but his memory as sharp as ever.

He threw the pen in the backseat and tossed the map on the dashboard.

"Add Clarke's and Fleischer's names to it," Chase said.

"I did."

"Good. You can ask Dex for contact info."

"No, that's over. He knows we're trouble now."

"He didn't figure that out when you waxed the guy at the ice machine?"

"The score is blown and it's my fault. He'll be looking for a way to burn us and make some cash off it."

"Since when is that something new?"

The wheel in his hands steadied him, but his thoughts twisted backward to Newark, the look in Ellie Raymond's eyes when he shot her twice in the heart. He eased down on the gas, started flying up the road, with no real idea of where he was going, and liking it. The old man, always a shitty driver, even a shitty passenger, never wearing his belt, stared through the windshield and said nothing.

Earl and Ellie Raymond had been first-rate pros, but they'd put together strings using fall guys and assholes, whoever they needed at the time, nitwits they could use and abandon, set up and decimate.

"I've got some people I can ask." Thinking of Hildy and the others. And if not them, then Arno and his oily play pals.

*C*hase didn't bother to knock, just walked in and found the crew sitting back watching a DVD. The three foster brothers and Hildy there with popcorn—no, cheese curls, their fingers and faces orange and flaked with crumbs—everybody taking it easy after the bad night with Arno.

Mackie's left wrist had a cast on it. Tons's decapitated pinkie had been splinted and retaped. Boze looked like he'd spent the day wondering how he could get out from under the other two, scowling at the screen, orange lips pursed in thought.

Her ponytail bobbing as she turned to him, Hildy said, "Jeez, who knocked you around this time? Dex? Your grandfather? It couldn't have been Russ."

"No."

"Did you find the old man?"

"Yeah, he's out in the car, and now I need to find somebody else."

She licked her fingers, not even trying to be sexy

about it, but somehow she still was. "How's the little girl?"

"We don't know yet, she's missing."

"Missing? I thought he had her."

"He doesn't. We're trying to find her."

"God, let me guess. Now you're after the guys who ran us off the road?"

"Yeah."

"I told you it was stupid letting them go."

"You did tell me," Chase said. "I do recall that."

"And I told you that I didn't want to be near you when they came back to cap you."

"And I said you wouldn't be." He handed her the map with the names written along the edge. "Here, look at this list and tell me if you recognize anyone who works the area or who recently came into town."

Boze got to his feet and checked over her shoulder. No surprise in his expression at all. That meant she'd told her boys everything. You had to figure that. Boze's eyes flitted back and forth from the map to Chase, trying to see how much of this might be trouble that might work back to him. Chase thought Boze was the only smart guy he'd run into since he left Jersey.

Mackie, sitting there and taking the time to pause the DVD, wasn't so pissy-faced this time around. Maybe he'd finally decided he should be a little thankful that Chase had saved his life. Maybe he was just working up a new mad-on, getting ready to take another poke. You just couldn't tell. Chase was sore,

but the action was still inside him, his fists still aching
to flash out.

Hildy said, "No. Nobody sounds familiar to me."

Boze grabbed the map and studied the list carefully, his mouth moving, breathing names, trying to
see if any of them might be fake but maybe sounding
like another name he might've heard.

Now here came Tons. Chase didn't get any nega-
tive vibe off the tubby guy, who seemed to feel some
obligation to Chase and actually looked eager to
help. Smiling, wagging his half pinkie all over, first
at Hildy and then at Chase. He started forward with
a slack smile, but Mackie jumped to his feet and
blocked him. Tons running into him and saying,
"Hey."

You'd think, if you were going to sit around eating cheese curls, maybe you could dial down the
attitude at least a little, but Mackie had to keep his
front up.

"Why should we help you?" he asked.

"Because I saved your lives last night?"

"Oh bullshit, you did not. Arno wasn't about to do
anything. Not serious anyway."

"Looked serious enough to me."

Tons was still trying to move forward, and Mackie
giving him a soft elbow in the guts every time he
tried to step around him. The bag of cheese curls hit
the floor and Tons backed up onto them, orange
dust gusting up in the air. He held his belly. "Ow!"

"You don't think a lot of guys would've lammed
it?" Chase asked.

"You were part of the crew!"

"Then I still am. So help me out here."

"Oh fuck that."

"Ow!"

Trying once more, knowing it was going to flop, Chase said, "You don't think Tons would've been any worse for wear if I hadn't come in when I did and driven him to the hospital?"

Still trying to get past his foster brother, still getting elbowed in the stomach, Tony Tons was starting to look a little pissed. Puffs of cheese poofs rising around his ankles, turning his socks orange.

"Tons can take care of himself."

"And you?"

"I can take care of myself too."

"Ow! Quit it! My stomach!" Tons fell back onto the couch and went a little green, dry heaving, working his way up to tossing up all the munchies.

Hildy went, "Oh brother, do you two really have to get into it again? Don't—"

"Yes!" Mackie shouted.

You could put up with a lot. You could handle arrogance and ignorance on their own, but together they could really crawl up your ass. Mackie stomped forward, leading with his chin. Chase grabbed the mook's bad arm and twisted it hard. Mackie dropped onto his knees, let out a squeal, and looked up in agony. Chase jabbed him twice in the face, flattening what was left of Mackie's already mashed nose. He spun to the left to avoid the spurting blood and let go. The guy folded up on the floor and started rolling around. Tons heaved on top of him, a fountain of bright orange splashing down.

"Aw goddamn it, Tons!"

Chase turned his head. Boze glanced down and got that faraway look again, like he was finally making a decision to go solo.

"I didn't leave you boys out to dry," Chase said, "don't do it to me."

"He's right," Hildy said. "He helped out when he didn't have to. If you know anything, tell him." She glanced at Mackie and said, "Oh jeez, I can't look."

Boze looked at the list. "Only one. Phil Revereson. They call him Reverend. Part of his grift is working the holy rollers. When he needs a little cash he checks out a church in one of the rich parishes, hangs around the parking lot Sunday mornings, then follows some blue-haired biddy in her Rolls Royce back to her house and knocks on her door pretending to be a missionary. Spends a couple of hours drinking tea and tweaking a few grand out of her, says he's going to bring God to the heathen pygmy tribes in South America. Sometimes he hires black midgets and says they're converts."

"How do I get in touch with him?"

"I don't have any idea. He drifts around the Intracoastal."

"Dex will know," Hildy said.

"I can't talk to Dex."

She looked deep into him, gave him that smirk again. Knowing what the trouble was already, without him having to say anything more. "You were only there a couple of hours. He pissed at you too?"

"Yeah. So this Reverend. Would Arno know him?"

"Not his crowd, he's all about X and whoring and jewelry, buddying up to the wiseguys, playing king of the hill for his little friends. Nobody else I've ever worked scores with would know."

"Except for Dex," Hildy said. "Shit, I'm going to have to go mop the goddamn floor, aren't I?"

Mackie still rolling. Tons about ready to cry, ashamed of barfing, hiding his face in his hands. Hildy, young but already settling in with second-raters, walked into the bathroom and started hunting up some rags and foaming cleaners.

Catching Boze's eye, Chase said, "You and she would be a lot better off on your own."

"Yeah, but what the hell can I do? These other assholes, they're my family."

*F*amily. *The word held an almost mythical meaning.* Blood was important. Everybody dead so loud in his dreams, always talking, whispering, going out of their way to wrestle his attention. And yet as Chase got in the Goat, chirped away from the curb and sped through a yellow light, accelerating as the sun poured into him through the open window, his grandfather remained beside him silent and intractable.

They passed a poster in a bank window. *Calloway & Dark's Traveling Fair and Sideshow of Wonders.*

Chase told Jonah about the Reverend still being around. Jonah said, "It doesn't mean anything. We don't know if Clarke is hooked up with him."

"You're right, but who gives a shit. Let's move on it anyway. Call Dex."

"No. We open ourselves up like that and he'll try to make a deal with Clarke first, sell us out for an ambush."

"Only if Clarke has cash."

"Maybe he does."

"The clock is ticking here," Chase said. "Kylie's been gone for what? Two, three weeks now? You think Clarke is feeding her regularly, changing her diapers?"

"She's potty-trained."

The old man actually using the word, potty. It made Chase turn away, the kind of thing you do when you're not sure if you want to laugh or cry or hurl a fucking chair through a plate-glass window.

"He made a run at me with your daughter in the backseat."

"But you're not sure about that."

No, he wasn't. He hadn't seen the girl, just the top of what could have been a car seat. And if it was, it might not have even been hers.

"He aced a little boy," Chase said.

"He won't hurt her. It's all he has over me."

"What makes you think he needs anything over you at all?"

"Fleischer flopped the hit. Clarke never made contact with me. He botched the contact with you. That means he's waiting to take another run at our backs. If he's as scared as you say he is, he'll be hunting us down. He might get to us before we get to him. And that would save us time."

Even now, when other fathers would've been breaking down, doubled over, on their knees, praying for the safety of their children, Jonah was still only thinking of himself. Chase couldn't even find the energy to hate the bastard anymore because he realized with a great understanding that Jonah was incapable of giving or being anything else.

"Call Dex."

And again, with a greater resolution than Chase had probably ever felt about anything in his life, the old man said, "No."

"Okay."

What the fuck.

Jonah, always iron, adamant, and invulnerable, but still capable of making mistakes.

Chase stomped the gas pedal, loving the immediate response of the engine, the steel around him bending to his will. The hum in his head as they went from forty to eighty in four seconds. He slammed the brakes and jerked the wheel left.

Jonah put his arms out, but it did no good as he shot forward and cracked his forehead first against the dashboard and then against the passenger window. The bloodstained glass cracked into a colorless kaleidoscope and the old man fell back in the seat semiconscious, pawing at the door handle.

Ruthless, fearsome, merciless, and unyielding, the prick still should've put his seat belt on.

Gunning it again, Chase made a quick turn into a movie-theater parking lot. He watched as Jonah managed to get the door open and flopped outside onto his belly. This might be it, the point of no return. You had to roll with it.

The old man was on his knees now, spitting gobs

of blood from a split lip and reaching for his back pocket. That's where it would be, the .22.

Chase rushed over to make sure his grandfather hadn't broken anything and wasn't concussed. Jonah, still so strong, took a swipe at him, dizzy and hurting but already on the comeback. God damn it. Chase was going to have to do it. He tensed up, moved into the cold spot where his fear and anger left him, and kicked his grandfather in the face. Jonah grunted and spun aside. Chase reached into his grandfather's back pocket and took out the gun. Then he searched until he found the old man's cell.

Saying sorry would be pointless. But even here, iced down where nothing could touch him, he still felt the need to say it. "Sorry."

It would have to be contact by phone now. Chase was sure that Dex had cleared out of the room. The phone number would change soon too. It might be too late already.

He scanned the numbers. No names, not even initials. He recognized Dex's number from Russell's phone.

Chase should've remembered it, shouldn't have needed the old man's phone at all, but he had to admit he had a lot on his mind.

Up on the lamppost, another sign was stuck there for *Calloway & Dark's Traveling Fair and Sideshow of Wonders*. They sure knew how to publicize. Get the whole town out there on the calliope, the merry-go-round, go play in the house of mirrors, buy cotton candy. Maybe it did bring in a ton of cash. Maybe it was a solid score, knocking over the barker, snapping his cane, punching out his straw hat.

Dex answered and Chase said, "I want you to find somebody for me. Guy called the Reverend. You know him?"

Playing it close and cagey, as expected. There was always something comforting about the predictability of a thief. "Why?"

"Just do it."

"Give me a few hours to see if I can find him. He'll want to be paid."

Meaning, Dex wanted money. "He will be."

"How much?"

He had to come up with a round number, but not too large. Something that sounded like it would make it worth the time for both of them. "Eight."

"He might want more."

"He can tell me that himself."

A few shoppers walked by, staring, but nobody approached. Someone yelled, "You guys okay?" and Chase nodded. Others around, on the street and walking through the lot, were watching but minding their own business. Jonah had managed to sit up now, a black knot in the center of his eyebrows, gray hair at his temple turning black with blood. Drawing the back of his huge hand across his mouth he looked over at Chase and tried to decide his next move.

Chase wondered if his grandfather would've tried to wrestle the gun away and pop him if there hadn't been a crowd around. The old man, rudderless for so long, hesitating again just as he did when it came to his own baby girl. Chase felt a sudden immense sense of pity for Jonah, but it was gone before he even had to deal with it.

"It might take a day or two," Dex told him.

"You just said a few hours."

"Just saying it might take longer."

"Make sure it doesn't. And you can go through with the carnival score. How goddamn hard can it be to take down that you have to fret about it so much?"

"Your grandfather and I set it up together. If I take it, he'll ace me."

"I get the feeling it was more your idea than his. Besides, he just talks tough. He's really a softie, likes to crochet, drink cocoa, sit in a rocking chair."

"You've got worse troubles than me, kid."

The old man got to his feet and took a step. He stumbled, went down to one knee again. Looking up, blood in his eyes, raw murder in his eyes, all power and hate once again. In a way, it was good to see. Chase grinned and held out his hand to help Jonah up. Inside him, Lila told him to duck. Inside him, Jonah told him to duck, I'm going to shatter your rib cage and drive the shards into your heart.

Jonah, taking Chase's hand, said, "This had better work."

Both of them checked out of their motels and took a room together in an even shittier one. No matter how beautiful a town there was always a skid row where the transients, junkies, and alcoholics on the downslide of dementia lay waiting while the pimps and whores plied their trade. Paying out by the hour, the afternoon, the last week of your life. The failures, the head cases, the hesitant suicides waiting for the final tap off the ledge. This is where they came and readied themselves to die, and prepared themselves to kill.

The air was different. The despair palpable. The curtains always shut. The heat unbearable, the air conditioner gutless. Somebody murmured and hissed his love in Spanish.

Chase set up on one side of the room and Jonah on the other, secure in the intimate understanding of each other, returning to a familiar form. This was the way things used to be, the life they'd led together when Chase was a kid. He had a sense of déjà vu that wouldn't quit.

There were rituals your body would remember even if you could not. He took the bed closest to the window. Jonah needed to be near the door.

You'd think it was the safer place, being by the window. In case of a fire you jump out. Some hitter breaks in, you dive behind the bed, you're better protected. But the fact was, anybody trying to get in would try the windows first. Anybody looking for an easy kill might just pump a few shotgun shells inside. Jonah had always put himself first, and Chase, early on not understanding, and later only responding to his grandfather's will, learned he was always the one in front of the first bullet.

Jonah unscrewed a ventilation grate up near the ceiling and hid guns and a wedge of cash. Before he sealed it back up he glanced at Chase, expecting him to have something that needed to be cached. Chase shook his head and the old man nearly pulled a face.

Well, that was something.

They were both bruised and smeared with their own dried blood. Jonah took a shower first, leaving Chase lying on the bed listening to the sounds around him, focusing on anything to avoid listening to the sounds inside him.

Doors slammed. Televisions were loud and static-filled. Some surfer dudes sounded like they were starting early with a whore at their bachelor party. Maybe it wasn't a bachelor party. Maybe it wasn't a prostitute.

The walls were little more than Sheetrock.
Someone was vomiting a room or two away. Someone
else screaming, maybe sex, maybe the D.T.'s, maybe
murder. Most of the time you couldn't tell the difference. A hooker was arguing with her trick. He was
taking too long. The guy started crying. He wanted to
kiss. She made him pay double. One of them started
smacking the other. A bottle clanked around on an
uncarpeted floor but didn't break. The sounds of his
youth.

White sand and ocean only a mile away, paradise
right there in your arms waiting, and these people
were as far from it as the other side of the grave. So
was he.

He split the curtains and checked out front. No
one on the prowl.

Jonah had been in the shower for five minutes.
Chase figured the old man hadn't even taken his
clothes off yet. He was in there waiting to see if
Chase was about to sneak in to try and ice him.

Another five minutes went by. Jonah finished
and walked out naked. Nearly sixty-six now and still
carved from rock. The bruise on his forehead looked
like a Catholic daub on Ash Wednesday. The bullet
scars in his back were still raw and awful. The tattoos
stood out sharply in contrast to his scrubbed and
flushed skin. Jonah had been in Florida for a few
weeks, but had no tan. Always moving in shadow,
hardly ever catching the sun.

Chase thought about the toys around the Dash
house. Kylie out there on the beach with little Walt,

the two of them playing together with the salty breeze rolling in off the ocean.

Going from that to living like this with Jonah. Hearing the whores robbing the johns, the curtains always drawn, the walls always thin. The girl sleeping by the window so she could take the first bullet.

Without turning, Jonah said, "What is it?"

"What do you mean?"

"You're sitting there ready to jump out of your skin."

The man forever aware and onto you.

"Nothing," Chase said, wondering if his grandfather was going to throw a punch now, payback for that move in the parking lot. He stood and cautiously walked past, realizing the old man knew he was being wary, and why, and so right there he'd managed to retaliate.

Chase took a shower. There was no hot water. It didn't matter to him. He stayed beneath the freezing jets for a long time, and still he was burning.

The rest of the afternoon stumbled past. Night came on fervent and thick. The motel filled and emptied by the hour. The drunks started to sing and fight and die a little more. Noise on all four sides. Moaning that sounded more like getting knifed in the kidneys than sex.

"Why did you come after me?" Jonah asked.

"How about if we let it slide until we get Kylie back?"

"She's nothing to you."

"She's my blood."

"Is that important to you?"

"You know it is."

"Even now?"

"Especially now."

So, was it finally time to come out with it and ask Jonah, Did you murder my mother? Did you drive your own son to suicide?

Other men, even the hardest jailbirds, the guys who'd spent half their lives in solitary, would answer human questions. You ask them what it was like pulling the trigger, strangling the woman, boosting the bank, kidnapping the mayor's kid, blasting into the crowd, and you'd get a serious response, some kind of answer. It might be the truth and it might be a lie, but they'd talk, they'd tell you.

Jonah wouldn't. Chase wanted to know about Angie, ask about Kylie, find out what the old man planned to do now that the Dash family was gone and there was nowhere else for Kylie to go. The questions built up inside him and he knew his grandfather could feel them charging the air.

"You don't know what you want, do you?" the old man said. "You've got no idea who you are anymore. You managed to stay straight a long time, but in Newark you cut all the way loose, and now you think there's no coming back from that."

Maybe it was true. Chase tried to respond but nothing sounded real or true enough to waste his breath on.

"Go on home to New York," Jonah said. "You don't need to be here."

"You could use my help. You said so yourself. Besides, I don't have a home anymore."

"You made one for yourself once, you can do it again."

Jesus, listen to this, his grandfather almost sounding protective, with four guns in the air vent.

"I'll stick around for a while longer," Chase said.

"Where'd you pick up the forty g's?"

While Chase had been inside talking to Boze and his crew, Jonah had taken off the car door panel and found the cash. Chase wondered how much the old man had grabbed. Not all of it, but some anyway. Maybe ten, maybe fifteen. He wouldn't have been able to stop himself.

"What do you think. I stole it."

"That much I figured. Where? And why?"

He didn't want to get into the story about the Langans and the tie and white gloves, Sherry insane because he wouldn't fuck her, Jackie dead in Vegas. "Because I'm a thief."

"You're an auto-shop teacher."

Chase turned to the old man and said, "Do you love Kylie?"

"We weren't talking about that."

"I was. I am. Do you love her more than you did Angie?"

"You're still stewing about that?"

"You killed your own woman."

"Only because she shot me. In the back. Twice."

"Yeah, but do you know why?"

"For the same reason anybody shoots you twice in the back. Because they want you in the ground when they steal what you've got."

Nearly sixty-six years old, been in the joint and spent a long time dodging it, partnered with Chase and a lot of others along the way, enough blood on his hands to fill a city gutter, and the man still just didn't get it.

In a voice he knew was weak and full of sighs Chase said, "Or because they're afraid you'll steal what they've got."

"We already talked about this. After Newark."

"You said you expected her to make a play. You said you always do."

"That's right."

It was back then after Newark, with the old man driving to Chase's empty house, while Chase lay in the back still fighting fever and infection, one lung collapsed, that Jonah had said, *It happened once before. And for the same reason. Over a kid. Another foolish woman.*

And Chase couldn't get it out of his head that the old man had been talking about Chase's mother.

"You remember what else I said?" Jonah asked.

"You asked if I was going to try you."

"And are you?"

"You sound like you want me to."

Jonah said nothing more, letting it go just like he let everything go that had any worth, while he lay in the dark and made sure he was always one step ahead.

* * *

Two in the morning, the moonlight drenching him, Chase sat at the window while Jonah slept the way he always slept. Lightly. Without dreams.

Clap your hands and the old man would roll off the covers and go for the hidden gun clipped under the bed that he'd put there while Chase was in the shower.

Something was happening out in the world, Chase could feel it.

Moves being made.

Eight in the morning, Jonah went out and brought back a greasy, bagged breakfast. The stink of it filled Chase's head with more memories. His grandfather had fed him this same meal a thousand times before, while they were planning scores, sometimes on the run. Tossing it underhand across the room, the way he did now, and Chase catching it, opening the bag and eating without knowing or caring what the food was, without even tasting it.

"Dex is setting us up," Jonah said.

"Maybe."

"No maybes, he is."

"Nothing we can do about it now," Chase said. "Unless you know where Dex has moved on to and we can get close to him."

"No."

"Then we wait."

*   *   *

At noon Jonah's cell buzzed. He drew the phone, handed it to Chase, and said, "Dex. You talk. This is your agenda."

Agenda—it wasn't a word he expected Jonah to ever use. Chase nearly said, I'm trying to save your daughter.

Chase answered and Dex said, "One-thirty this afternoon."

"Why'd it take so long?"

"I had to find him. Bring the money."

"You'll be there?"

"No, but the Reverend will give me my cut."

Dex was a perfect liar, and the perfect lie rang like crystal.

Chase said, "I told you the circus score was yours. If you've fucked us on this, tell me now. It might save your life."

"I'm way down on your list of worries."

Chase thought, Jonah is going to turn your switch off, all because in a town full of money, you two couldn't find your own scores.

"Where's the meet?"

"At a club called the Curse of Nature. It's in Tampa. Don't be late. You need directions?"

"No," Chase said, and hung up, knowing there was going to be a lot of blood, and almost glad for it.

Jonah unscrewed a ventilation grate and pulled out his weapons, kept two Browning 9mm automatics and handed Chase a S&W .38. "Here." Then Jonah reached beneath the bed and pulled his popgun .22, stuck it in his back pocket.

In the Goat on the way to Tampa, Chase told his grandfather about Arno and the club and what had happened there the other night.

"There are no coincidences. Dex is out to burn us. So why'd this place get picked for the meet?"

"I don't know."

"He must've made a lot of calls last night. He's heard about you. What you've been doing here in Florida. Someone's been talking about you." Jonah chewed on that for a while. "We're supposed to meet the Reverend, who ran with Angie and might give us a line on where Clarke is. Your connection said the Reverend wouldn't know Arno."

"That's what he said."

"So this Reverend wouldn't call the meet here."

There are no coincidences. "Doesn't seem likely."

"And if Dex set something up with Clarke to take us down, Clarke wouldn't call the meet here either."

"I don't see why he would."

"So maybe this Arno wants to settle a score."

"It wasn't that big a thing," Chase said. "But even if he did want me dead, and was willing to pay for it, why bring us to his front door, where things could get messy?"

"He wouldn't."

"I don't see why."

Dex and Clarke and Arno all working together? Had he really pissed so many people off?

Silent in the car now, Chase and Jonah both worked the angles, thinking of who might get paid, and how, and from whom, and who was selling them out. What the connections were, who might stab who in the back to get to them.

Chase kept hitting walls. He felt stupid and blinded by his need to save the girl. He wanted Lila to tell him what would be coming around the next corner. He was a little light-headed, but still drove perfectly, slick and fast, as they entered sun-glazed Tampa.

"Nice city," Jonah said. His voice was loud as a rifle shot in the car.

"Not where we're going."

They hit the block lined with bars and dance clubs. In the day it looked even worse than it had the last time Chase had been here. Abandoned, stagnant, like the place was a hair away from planned demolitions and urban renewal. Metal shutters were locked over a lot of the windows. The streets were empty. They'd looked a lot better with the drunk girls wandering from bar to bar, holding each other up.

"There it is," Chase said, pointing out the Curse of Nature.

"Doesn't look like much."

"It's not."

"There's no real cover," Jonah said. "I'd like to get a look at the back parking lot, but we might get pinned."

Chase turned around, eased up and down the area until he found an alley two blocks away that still gave them a line of sight to the front door of the Curse of Nature.

Jonah asked, "The hell does the name mean?"

"I have no idea." Chase checked his watch. It was 1:10.

Claustrophobia set in as they sat, Chase feeling like his skin was on fire. His grandfather's strength of presence was pushing him right out of the fucking car. He looked at the old man's tattoos and wondered why Kylie wasn't among the other names.

His thoughts raced along. He had no control. He couldn't stop thinking about all the specialists he and Lila had visited while trying for a baby. The docs had said it wasn't impossible, but the odds were worse for Lila than the "average young female" to become pregnant and carry a child full term.

He remembered how she'd said, "Well, I was raised to believe in miracles."

"Tell me about Kylie," Chase said.

"What do you want to know?"

"Tell me about her."

The old man looked at him, having no idea what to say. Other men, they talked to you about their kids until you were shitless. The little girls all angelic, the boys smart and great athletes. They sometimes put on adorable voices to sound like their children, and you wanted to cover your ears and howl because you couldn't take listening to that cutie-pie crap. And those same guys had felt the same way too until they'd had kids. It was just the way things went.

But Jonah had nothing to say.

"It's one-thirty," Chase told him.

"What time do clubs like that open?"

"Maybe six o'clock? Seven?"

"You don't know."

"No."

"Then say that."

"I just did."

The old man stared through the windshield, sighting the front door. The only apparent hint of tension in his body was that the veins in his thick wrists were sticking out and throbbing. Chase knew exactly what his grandfather would say next.

"Never follow someone else's rules."

Chase nodded and said, "We wait."

Fifteen minutes later Jonah's cell went off. He ignored it.

The temperature in the car had to be topping one-ten, but Chase didn't feel it. He was bathed in cold sweat, trails running down his throat and chest. He didn't know where the willpower was coming from for him to stay in his seat. Thinking of the little girl out there someplace, surrounded by enemies, maybe hungry, crying, wearing dirty diapers. No, Jonah had said she was potty-trained. Chase held the steering wheel tightly in his hands and gained no comfort.

At 2:20, someone came to the front door of the club, opened it a few inches, peered out.

"Trying to get us to jump," Jonah said. "Any idea what this Reverend looks like?"

"Like a reverend I guess."

"Could it be Arno?"

"Can't tell."

"They're getting edgy."

Chase wanted to say, So am I.

"Another half hour or so and we go."

Touching the keys, trying to draw strength from the Detroit line of forty years ago, when they cared about their craft and the roads were full of cars with style and attitude and cool, but Chase still couldn't calm himself. He was freezing.

It was almost three when a figure came to the door with Kylie in his arms.

"Oh Christ," Chase said.

Jonah never rattled. "So we know she's still alive."

The door opening wider.

Molten sunlight flooding inside.

Shadow becoming color and form.

A lot of muscle stood around in back, filling the entranceway. Not Voorman and not the prettyboys.

Chase finally understood the setup. How Arno fit into it. Boze had said, *Sometimes he deals with the syndicates, old fat Italians on the down slide who come here to go out on his boat and get blowjobs and go fishing.*

All these years thinking he'd been fast, and yet now he saw that he was so very goddamn slow. Chase had been too close to the situation, hadn't been able to focus. As usual, he'd been worrying about the wrong things. He'd known it was happening and still hadn't been able to help himself.

Dex had been busy on the phone all right, making a lot of calls, gathering info, swinging deals. But the scheme couldn't have come together so quickly if it hadn't already been in motion.

Jonah swept his arm out, holding Chase in his seat. He hadn't realized that he'd started to lean forward and begun to turn the key.

The little girl, Chase had never seen her before. He thought, My God, she's a golden beauty.

"That Clarke?" Jonah asked.

"What?"

"Is that Clarke holding Kylie?"

"No."

"The Reverend? He doesn't look like someone who'd be chasing down the Ladies Christian Coalition."

"He's not. His name is Bishop."

He looks hard," the old man said. "He's wearing a black suit and tie in Florida. His jacket is cut to hide his shoulder holster. A torpedo?"

"What?"

Jonah thumped Chase in the chest once, trying to get him to concentrate. "You know him?"

"Yeah."

"Is he a shooter?"

"Yeah. He works for the Langans."

"The New Jersey Langans? Lenny Langan's dead. What are they doing here in Florida? They've got no real muscle anymore."

"They've got him," Chase said, "and he's good. The daughter, Sherry Langan, took over. I bet she's inside. When we go in, she'll have Kylie sitting on her lap."

Jonah looked at him, gave him the empty, lethal stare. "So this isn't only about what happened at the motel in Newark anymore."

"No."

"What did you get into?"

"I stole some money from them."

"From the Langan syndicate?"

"Yeah, I was a driver for them."

"They don't use drivers."

"I was a chauffeur."

"How much did you heist?"

"One forty."

The old man almost imperceptibly shaking his head. "That's not enough for a mob princess to get personally involved. If she's here, why's she here?"

"She's mad at me too," Chase said.

"What else did you do?"

"I wouldn't fuck her doggie style."

"Did you fuck her some other way?"

"No."

"Maybe you should've."

Chase wiped sweat from his eyes. "The situation probably could've been resolved a bit more tactfully."

"That's one way of putting it. A woman scorned is bad enough. A syndicate princess you scored and left high and dry, no wonder she's chased you down here."

Jonah turned his attention back to the front door, and they saw that Bishop had pulled the girl back inside.

Chase said, "Dex found the Reverend. The Reverend led him to Clarke and Kylie. Clarke had been following me around. He must've followed me to the club."

"Followed you for over an hour on the road?"

"I told you I'd been sloppy."

"Sloppy is one thing. You've been something else."

"Yeah," Chase admitted. He'd been disconnected even worse than he'd thought.

"Why this place though?"

"Clarke must've talked to Arno. He mentions what happened in Newark, tells him we're pros from the East Coast. Asks him for help in tracking you down and in popping me." He thought, That's who was in the Dodge pickup. Voorman or one of the prettyboys helping Clarke out. "Arno has some dealings with the weaker mob families. He must've put his ear to the wire and eventually heard some buzz about what I pulled at the Langans."

"Contacted them and told them to come on down, he's got my baby and he knows where you are. They tell him there's a big payday if he grabs and holds you." Jonah turned, looked into Chase's face. "This broad really hates your guts."

"Yeah."

Jonah said, "While we were making calls trying to find Kylie, they were making calls to the same people and using her to find us."

It was true. Right from the day Chase hit Florida he'd thought he was so slick and in control, but he'd had everything backward, and everyone else had been using his blind stupidity against him. "It's my fault. I wasn't watching. I wasn't thinking."

"So this has nothing to do with me anymore."

"No," Chase said. "It never really did."

"You should've told me," Jonah said, and swung in his seat, bringing his fist up from the wheel well and smashing Chase in the mouth.

The old man climbed out of the car, gave Chase a final once-over, showing nothing, walked out the alley, and headed for the front door of the club.

Hell of a turn, Chase thought, spitting ribbons of blood and half a molar out the window.

It took him ten minutes until the bleeding stopped enough for him to speak clearly. Then he made one last phone call, spoke calmly but sharply, hung up and threw the cell against the alley wall. The phone splintered into pieces.

He drove out of the mouth of the alley, turned the corner, went around the block and parked down the street from the Curse of Nature. He took the S&W .38 out of his gym bag and had no idea what to do with it. He had no holster, and all he was wearing was a T-shirt. He got out of the car, untucked his shirt and stuck the gun in his waistband but it wouldn't fit. Tried it at the small of his back and it didn't fit there either. He decided to just carry the damn thing. He felt like an idiot. Decided fuck it. Threw it back in the gym bag and left it in the passenger foot well.

His mouth filled again and he spit more blood.

The tooth hurt. He embraced the pain. He walked down the block, opened the front door of the club, and walked in.

Sherry Langan sat at a table with Kylie on her lap, a glass of what was probably Glenlivet in front of her, the little girl playing with one of Sherry's diamond earrings.

The Langans didn't kill kids.

They sold them.

Jonah was having a beer with Bishop.

Bishop was laughing, holding his .44 loosely in one hand. The wrist where Chase had stabbed him had healed up with hardly a trace of a scar. Two knee breakers were nearby, flanking the old man. Jonah was grinning, doing a bad job of acting normal but much better than Chase had been expecting. He held the beer to his chest with his right hand, not drinking. His left was cupped to his leg, hiding the pop .22. They hadn't frisked him. Jonah wouldn't have allowed that, which was why Bishop was right on top of him.

Arno and his entourage weren't around. Moe Irvine wasn't around either. Chase wondered if that meant Moe was dead too. That once Sherry Langan and Bishop started down their road together, they couldn't stop punching tickets.

Chase recognized Elkins, the thug he'd fought in Jackie's office. The one who'd paid the hitters on the street. So he was number two under Bishop. Chase had worked grease into the guy's eyes and yanked his .357. Good. When things went bad, he'd stick close to Elkins. The goon carried heavy hardware.

Bishop looked over at Chase and called, "Hey there!"

No need to be rude. Chase waved. Bishop was having a good time, trying to have a little fun with the old man before pulling the trigger.

As Chase stood there, Elkins came over and searched him for guns.

The other knee breaker doing nothing but wearing mirror shades and trying to look suave in a newly bought Hawaiian shirt.

"Miss Langan would like to talk to you," Elkins said.

"Did she ice Moe?" Chase asked, curious for some reason.

"Moe saw the writing on the wall and split for Israel."

"You should've too."

Chase moved to the table and sat across from Sherry. Elkins and the other thug covered both him and Jonah. Kylie was enraptured by Sherry's earring and didn't look up at Chase. He wanted her attention, wanted her to smile at him, but he had to fight to hold steady, to keep focused on Sherry Langan, who was watching him with her cruel, hot, amused eyes, one hand stroking Kylie's hair.

"You're not surprised to see me," Sherry said.

"No."

"Not even interested in knowing why I'm sitting here with your . . . aunt . . . isn't it?"

Still brushing through Kylie's hair, the thin wisps of veins in Sherry's hands hidden now beneath sunburn. She'd been here a day or two already, out on the beach.

"I already know why."

"It's not the money you stole," she said.

"I never thought it would be."

"It's not even because of the disrespectful way you treated me."

Yes, it was, assuming she meant the fact that he hadn't fucked her.

Chase waited.

"It's because you chose to warn my brother."

No, it wasn't, but let her tell her lies, it was all she had to live with. "Jackie was a moron. You ought to be ashamed of yourself for acing him. He was no challenge to you."

"He was becoming a liability. Even my mother knew that. *She* didn't warn him. She understood. We've lost enough respect over the years. I can't afford to waste any more. I already have to deal with many of my father's former business associates, so many of them stealing from our pockets and playing golf during working hours, the ones you mentioned back in Jersey, who were causing so much more trouble. It's now time for the Langan name to regain its esteem."

Jesus Christ, she said it like she meant it. Chase caught a glimpse of his watch. He figured, maybe three or four minutes left. Maybe not that many.

"So you're through wowing the politicians' wives with your insights on Ibsen?"

"Your grandfather gave you up," Sherry said. "He's turning his back on you."

"I know."

"All he wants is his daughter."

"I know."

"And I believe him. I don't think he's simply fooling us in order to save you at the last minute."

"No, that wouldn't be his style. But if you hurt her, he'll kill everyone in this place."

"He said we wouldn't have to come looking for you. He said you wouldn't run, that you'd walk right inside even though we had nothing over you."

"You do," Chase told her.

"Because you care about children. And poor innocent women new to our shores. That's why you involved yourself with my merchandise. I found Ivanka working with a competitor and persuaded her to tell me the truth."

Chase nodded. Not much else to do.

She lifted her chin and gestured at his pulped mouth. "Did your grandfather do that to you?"

"Yeah."

"He offered to kill you for us. He doesn't like you much."

"He doesn't like anybody. Did you offer him a job?"

"Yes, as a matter of fact."

"And he turned you down. He only works for himself."

Lila in his head telling him, Oh sweetness, she's so precious, this Kylie girl.

"Did you change her?" Chase asked.

Sherry bounced Kylie a touch. "She's not wearing a diaper."

"Right, I forgot, she's toilet trained. Looks like Clarke did a pretty good job of babysitting."

"He's a foolish boy. I offered him money for helping to set you up, but he refused. He seemed to think he was getting revenge for a lost love."

So Ellie Raymond had wrapped Clarke around her finger and promised him the world, the same way she'd promised a couple other guys in her crew. Clarke, kidnapping a kid and murdering Little Walt, all for a woman who would've eventually gotten him killed.

Sherry reached for her Glenlivet, took a sip, and held the glass against her bottom lip, the same way she had in the back of the limo. She was furious but also entertained. The heavily electrified atmosphere between them nearly crackled with blue flame. She wanted to stretch this out as far as she could. He was the safest guy in the room because she hated him the most.

"So what should I do with you?" Sherry asked.

"You want my opinion? You should give the girl back to the old man. You should let me leave, and you should go take over the Chicago rackets."

"You think I can't?"

"I think you can, if you keep your eye on the prize. Taking the time out to snuff Jackie and come all the way down here just so you could toy with me shows me that you're pretty easily distracted. But I can understand it. I've been distracted lately too."

A laugh started low in Sherry's throat and kind of just hung there, never really leaving. Sophisticated, but with a slight taint of debauchery. He wondered if she could hear it.

She drew away from the table and crossed her legs. Still giving him a show of her best feature, still hoping for a reaction. What, he was going to flop on the floor, crawl to her ankle, kiss her calf? Maybe he should give it a go.

"When I say the word these gentlemen are going to beat you to death."

"Bringing back the old-school charm to the Langan outfit, huh? Figured you might want to do me yourself. Take Bishop's .44 and put my lights out."

"Slower and more amusing the other way."

"Like I said, you're too distracted, Sherry."

Elkins slapped Chase in the back of the head. Just a little eye-opener, nothing too mean. Sort of ridiculous, really, when you considered the situation, but these people were all about the drama.

"Still got your pistol on you?" he asked.

Sherry Langan, almost sweet in her own strange way, gave a lovely smile. Seeing her again, he felt the same way he had the first time. You couldn't call her beautiful, or even pretty really, but there was something about her that made you look twice. "Always."

"Good," he said. "You ever find yourself a real driver?"

"No, but Elkins makes for a passable chauffeur."

Chase turned to the mook. "Yeah? You wear the hat and gloves?"

Elkins, abashed.

"You poor bastard." The edges of Chase's ears started to twitch, hearing what he'd been listening for. He looked back at Sherry Langan and told her, "He's probably not good enough behind the wheel to get you out of here unless you leave now." Sirens broke in the distance. "See, I called the cops."

His grandfather looked over at him like he was insane. Bishop quit grinning. Everyone spooked because they hadn't gotten a chance to say their big speeches yet, run out their plans, get all that they wanted. Chase shrugged. His mouth was still leaking and he spit on the floor. "Never follow someone else's rules."

Elkins went, "Fuck." The other strongarm immediately panicked and moved out of position. He locked the front door.

Jonah, not exactly trigger-happy but still always the first on the trigger, raised the .22 toward Bishop's face. Just covering himself, making sure nobody got the drop on him in a time of frenzy. But Bishop hurled his beer glass at the old man and whipped his .44 around to fire. Both of them moved away from each other on the run, ducking behind empty tables, aiming but neither one shooting. Jonah crouched, dipped and came up holding a 9mm in each hand.

Elkins flexed his knees like a kid doing a gotta-piss dance, looking at Sherry for orders. Kylie finally glanced up at the sound of the sirens and stared directly into Chase's face. She held her hand out to him, offering the diamond earring. He felt something inside himself shatter. He couldn't help himself and reached for her.

Sherry tugged the girl back, the black-hearted bitch.

She said to Chase, "What did you tell the police?"

"That someone was being murdered."

The diamond earring caught enough light that sparkles moved across Kylie's face and glittered in her eyes. She held it out to him again and cooed and spoke baby jabber.

Elkins and the other leg breaker wanted to cheese it. They sighted down on Jonah and Chase half-heartedly, but nobody wanted to pull a trigger with two cruisers pulling up out front. It was kind of ludicrous, but then again everything felt that way lately.

Sherry nodded to Elkins and said, "Go start the limo. Be smart and stay relaxed. If you run, you know there's nowhere on earth you can hide from me."

Elkins rushed out the back door, probably wondering if he could crew up with Moe in Israel.

"This has nothing to do with me," Jonah said. "Give me my girl."

Bishop, eyeing Chase with some real disgust for calling in the police instead of handling things on his own, said, "Let's go, Sherry."

"No, not yet."

"He's a snuff case, he doesn't care if he lives or dies. It's time."

"Not just yet."

Jonah slid forward as the cops started moving up the sidewalk. The police started hammering at the door. They paused and then banged some more. Maybe they thought it was a put-on, some teenager making a fake 911 call. Chase thought maybe he should've phoned the fire department instead. Better response time, more sirens and vehicles, and they would've just smashed the door in with an ax.

Sherry pointed the .38 at Chase and he almost burst out laughing, suddenly filled with the need for action, as far away from the cold spot as he could get.

He rose and dodged into Bishop's arms, like they were about to do some serious ballroom dancing. They whirled around, Chase getting a tight hold on the slippery bastard, knowing Sherry and the other thug weren't going to be able to get a bead on him now. Hoping that Jonah wouldn't cut loose for the hell of it despite his baby being here. Hoping Sherry wasn't going to hurt the girl either.

His voice almost agitated now, Jonah said, "My

kid. Give her to me." He sighted both 9mms on Sherry's face, maybe two inches above Kylie's head.

The knee breaker sighted on Jonah and figured he had to earn his pay somehow, took some initiative in a tense situation and let loose with a shot. Sherry shouted something, but she was way too late as Jonah spun, didn't even seem to aim with his left hand, and blew out the guy's throat.

The gunshot got the cops cranking. They'd be going around back now for sure.

Jonah looked over at Kylie once, saw that Sherry Langan had her .38 trained on the girl, and the old man ran for the back door, leaving his daughter and his grandson to fend for themselves. Then there was plenty of gunfire out in the sun.

Chase figured, two cruisers, four cops, a couple probably already wounded or dead, the others hunkered down, calling for backup. Response time was shit, but it would perk up now. Bishop had to know it too. He looked into Chase's eyes as they struggled and said, "You've got no class."

This from a torpedo who walked around with a blood-speckled shirt.

"Tell me," Chase said, burning time, squeezing Bishop's wrist hard and willing it to break, "when you're parked on Broadway, her face pressed to the window, you ever worry the tinted glass might not be dark enough and you'll scare the tourists?"

"I should've taken you out in Jersey."

"You tried and couldn't."

Chase glanced over to make sure Kylie was okay. It opened him up and Bishop shrugged loose and started to raise the .44. Chase dug into his pocket, fast, he had to be faster. They got in tight again, both of them with their lips moving as if they were trying out some cute witty repartee in their heads first, but nothing was good enough to actually speak aloud.

The barrel was almost level with Chase's chest. Bishop was going for a center shot, put a nice cannonball-sized hole right through the middle. Chase had the switchblade opened already in his right first, swept his left hand out to almost daintily push the .44 aside, like he was being proffered flowers he refused to accept, the speed back again so that Bishop could only stare in and grunt, knowing what was about to happen as Chase drove the point of the knife into Bishop's left eye.

He dug it in deep, trying to sink it to the hilt in Bishop's brain. Sherry gasped. It was a sexy sound full of appetite. Bishop didn't shriek, just gave a short, gruff groan, his free hand already up and grabbing Chase's fingers, fighting to hold him in place. The gun angled toward Chase's groin this time.

Chase snapped his left arm down and batted the gun aside a couple inches. Bishop's eye oozed across the blade, along his hand and down the handle and into Chase's fist. The gun went off and Chase felt an insane burning along his hip. His blood leaped from him.

   Bishop's legs gave out and he tumbled backward off the knife to land at Sherry's feet.

   "I told you that you wouldn't always be so strong and gritty," Sherry Langan said, holding on to Kylie, almost nuzzling her like a new mother. The little girl silent, watching. The terror eating Chase now as he realized he'd failed again. He hadn't saved her. Hadn't gotten her away from the old man. He'd only delivered her into the hands of his own enemies. "That there'd be a time when your guts were gone. When you were dying and feeling every inch of it. You remember what else I told you?"

   "Yeah. That you wanted to be there to see it."

   She smiled. "And I am."

   "So, do you remember what I—" Chase said, but didn't get to finish before she shot him in the head.

He dreamed.

He dreamed he was alive and dreamed he was dead.

Someone called his name and he moved toward it through the house he'd lived in as a child.

You'd think with Lila dead, with Angie dead, with Ellie and Earl Raymond murdered by his hand, he might not always be drawn here. He might be in the Newark motel. The homes he'd shared with Lila in Mississippi and on Long Island.

But always here, back with his dead parents, the unborn sibling.

He opened his mouth to speak and heard his voice. He flinched at the sound of it, the harsh inflection that was barely more than a hiss.

"This is it, my last time."

The dead were packed tightly together in the garage. They milled in front of his father's sedan.

He thought, They ought to be in the car. That's a better symbol. I get in the car and back it out and I nudge the gas, the car lifts off, we go flying into the sky.

But no, they're all just here in the garage. Nobody moving anywhere. No speed or horsepower.

The garage door shut, the sedan running. If he was going to suicide he wouldn't do it this way. Or were they telling him to get a move on, book out of there?

No one spoke. He said nothing, even though now he finally could.

I'm still alive, he thought, knowing he was lying.

Here it is, he thought. Here I am.

His unborn sibling wasn't among the others.

He broke through their ranks and searched inside the car. He shut it down, grabbed the keys, and opened the trunk.

The kid in there. The kid unfurled, got up close, put its arms around his neck and kissed him.

He asked, What's it all mean? and the kid said with an even greater need, You're not done yet.

*C*hase came out of it with his head wrapped in bandages and a nun sitting beside him. She was young and pretty and didn't have the whole big penguin with the huge hat deal going. But still, you see a nun in a hospital room and it's bound to be a bad sign.

She asked if he was thirsty and fed him some ice chips. Doctors and nurses came in and out throughout the day, asking him a lot of questions to check his memory, telling him to do tests like touching his nose, following a penlight, tossing a tennis ball back and forth. He got the feeling they were just screwing with him.

Turned out he had a fracture and a severe concussion, what they called a mild traumatic brain injury. The bullet had grazed his temple, taken out a thick furrow of hair and skin, and given him a hairline crack in his skull. He'd been out for almost a week with a subdural hematoma of the brain. The wound to the hip was stapled shut and baby pink.

He lay in the hospital bed semizoned on painkillers, trying to figure out how much they had on him. His own name was still clean, even if he had been off the map for a few months. He'd never been in prison, never been arrested. He had no job or house anymore, but they still didn't have anything on him, except maybe vagrancy.

The Tampa cops questioned him about what happened at the Curse of Nature. He said he'd just been fuckin' shot in the head and didn't remember anything. They didn't believe him and by turns became tough, smooth, friendly, childish, talkative, and vicious. The talkative feint interested him because they spilled more than they intended.

Two cops had been killed along with the thug Jonah had aced. Elkins had been a solid enough driver to get the Langans the hell out of there, and Bishop's body hadn't turned up so he'd probably made it. Of course the old man hadn't been nabbed. And Arno appeared to be missing.

Chase was weak and drugged and in a hell of a lot of pain, but he never had to ride out the questioning for more than ten minutes before the nurses came in and shut the heat down.

Hildy visited him. She wore a bright orange wrap and an even skimpier bikini top than before. She smelled of the ocean, and the scent moved across him tickling him in places he didn't want to be touched. His brain was still a little cloudy and he knew he was staring. The twinkling blue stones on her flat belly jabbed light in his face. He swallowed and his throat was dry.

She found a bottle of water beside the bed and without asking poured him a cup and helped him to drink. Her hand was tender on the back of his head, and when he'd finished she ran the ball of her thumb along his bottom lip. She said, "Some girls think scars are sexy. This might improve your sex life dramatically."

"Highly doubtful."

"Me, I think they can add a certain amount of character. Of course, you'll probably have a big bald spot on the side of your head, and that's sort of yucky."

He checked the hall to make sure no cops were hanging around. "What's the word?"

"I knew there must've been big trouble when I found out Dex was dead."

Jonah, cleaning up loose ends. He should've gone on to Chicago and tried to get Kylie back before losing any more time. But the old man couldn't move forward without making sure everything behind him was finished. Chase thought Arno was a reach and probably didn't deserve to go down just because his place had been used, but Chase wasn't going to sweat the loss.

"I thought you didn't like guns," Hildy said.

"I don't."

"You didn't pull the trigger on that guy in the club?"

"No."

"How's the little girl?"

"They took her."

"Who are they?"

He didn't want to think about it, much less say anything aloud, but just as he was about to tell her that he didn't want to talk, he was talking. From somewhere nearby, he listened to himself explaining the rest of his story. He wondered why that kept happening, why he was so comfortable with his chatter around her.

"So you're not finished," she said.

"No, not yet."

She nodded, the ponytail bobbing. "Tons is upstairs in ICU. They don't think he's going to make it."

"Don't tell me that the dress heist went bad?"

"No. All the damage to his pinkie, he got a staph infection. Mackie and Boze are up there crying their eyes out. I told you they were loyal to each other. They've got a nun in there saying prayers."

"So that's where she went."

A look of real grief washed over Hildy's face. "I'm splitting."

"You're better off without them."

"Probably, but I'm not like you, I hate to be alone."

"Then you are like me."

She relaxed against the bed, threw her shoulders back, hitting another really sweet pose. He shifted beneath the sheet. She moved over him and into his arms, pressed her lips to his, and murmured against his mouth while he too allowed odd whispers to escape him. They held each other for a while. The tranqs swept up like a low tide on the beach and drew him forward. When he opened his eyes again it was night and she was gone.

The cops came around again.

He stuck to his amnesia story. They'd finished his background check and knew about Lila and what had followed. They wanted to know why his wallet had fake ID in it. He said it wasn't his wallet. They had the driver's license with his photo. It was a bad picture and he claimed it wasn't him.

There was talk he was connected in some way to what had gone down in Newark, but all they really knew was he'd taught high-school auto shop. They started another round of questioning, saying they were certain he was in on the motel murders.

But their hearts weren't in it anymore. Lila had been one of their own. The blue wall had finally worked to his advantage.

They told him to get the fuck out of Florida and never come back.

For the first time he told them the truth and said, "Count on it."

He'd always heard they made you leave a hospital in a wheelchair, but after he signed the paperwork and had them send the bill to the house he no longer owned on Long Island, they went about their duties and left him standing there for three or four minutes before he realized he could go.

He hadn't even made it to the curb before Jonah pulled up in the Goat. It had been repainted and had new tags.

Chase walked to the driver's side and said, "Move over, I'm driving."

His grandfather got out and stepped around the back of the car to the passenger side and climbed in. Chase noticed that the old man had gotten some sun too. He was tan and looked rested and well fed. He also had a new tattoo. Kylie's name was listed among the others beneath the angel on his left forearm. *Sandra, Mary, Michael, Kylie.*

Chase got behind the wheel and took it in his hands, but he didn't feel the strength, the cool or the muscle at all. He was just a guy holding on to a steering wheel.

First things first.

"I heard you took care of Dex and Arno."

"Dex, yes. Arno must've gone into hiding. He can wait."

"Clarke?"

"Yes."

"How?"

"How what?"

"How'd you do it?"

"What's it matter?"

"I want to know."

Jonah said nothing.

"Did you drown him?"

"No."

"You should've."

Two more dead, and the old man looking younger and healthier for it.

"Did you murder my mother?" Chase asked.

Jonah said, "Yeah."

The flat, unbearable, insignificant truth of it hit him like a fist under the heart. Chase, drifting inside the hurricane of his own head as the cold shock hit his belly and his limbs began to buzz, heard the voice of his unborn sibling telling him again that he wasn't done yet.

"She was pregnant."

"The kid was mine."

Chase let out a small cough of agony. His lips twisted trying to frame words, but nothing would come. He reached out and touched the dash hoping for horsepower, for the thrum to work inside of him. He waited. He gave up.

"No."

"Yeah."

"You're lying."

"I'm not lying."

He turned in his seat and said, "I'm going to kill you, old man."

His grandfather, showing nothing. "Wait until after we get Kylie back to take a run at me."

Jonah in his head said, Do it now, you'll never get another chance.

Chase hung his head out the window and vomited. He couldn't catch his breath and thought he might black out. The lung felt like it had gone bad again. His vision turned red at the edges and yellow streamers whirled and fluttered in front of his eyes. But finally the hitch in his chest lessened and his head cleared. He threw the car in gear. It would take three days to get to Chicago without pushing it. They'd hole up for a while and decide on a play, maybe put together a crew, call it a score. He eased down on the gas pedal to make the engine first growl and then moan and then scream. But nothing else was louder than the inside of his skull. Lila said to him, Never let your heart dim, love. He wanted to throw up again. The last kind words spoken to Christ were by a thief. He was protected. His gaze met his grandfather's, and the chains of blood grew stronger as the threat of impending murder filled the hopeless space between them, and the world continued to grow wider and more deranged and distant on the other side of the windshield.

ABOUT THE AUTHOR

TOM PICCIRILLI lives in Colorado, where, besides writing, he spends an inordinate amount of time watching trash cult films and reading Gold Medal classic noir and hardboiled novels. He's a fan of Asian cinema, especially horror movies, bullet ballet, pinky violence, and samurai flicks. He also likes walking his dogs around the neighborhood. Are you starting to get the hint that he doesn't have a particularly active social life? Well, to heck with you, buddy, yours isn't much better. Give him any static and he'll smack you in the mush, dig? Tom also enjoys making new friends. He's the author of more than twenty novels, including *The Cold Spot, The Midnight Road, The Dead Letters, Headstone City, November Mourns,* and *A Choir of Ill Children.* He's a recipient of the International Thriller Writers Award and a four-time winner of the Bram Stoker Award. He's also been nominated for the World Fantasy Award and Le Grand Prix de L'Imaginaire. To learn more, check out his official website, Epitaphs, at www.tompiccirilli.com.

A blind ex-cop.
A blizzard that's isolated a small,
private school in upstate New York.
Two killers whose hunt for blood will
expose the secrets of his past.

Look for

SHADOW SEASON

by Tom Piccirilli

Coming soon from Bantam Books.